Tomorrow at Daybreak

Eden Monroe

Print ISBNs
Amazon print 9780228638100
Ingram Spark 9780228638117
Barnes & Noble 9780228638124
BWL Print 9780228638131

Dedication

To: Linda T

Acknowledgements

BWL Publishing acknowledges the Government of Canada and the Canada Book Fund for its financial support in creating the Canadian Historical Mysteries collection.

BWL Publishing acknowledges the Province of Alberta for their ongoing support through the Alberta Publisher's Cultural Industry Operating Grant.

Table of Contents

Chapter 1

Pate Kavenagh – 1879

Pate steeled himself as he glared at the woman who had broken his heart. And now he had her in his crosshairs. He could not miss. His finger trembled on the trigger. If he lived to be a hundred, he would not forget the day he met Dinah Gladstone...

* * *

It was a balmy July afternoon, ideal for the community picnic underway to celebrate the creation of the Dominion of Canada on July 1st, 1867. Dominion Day had now become a public holiday to commemorate Confederation, albeit twelve years after the fact, and all were in a festive mood. Women wore their best full-length white muslin dresses, many in the fashionable princess line. Their elegant straw hats were elaborately festooned with artificial flowers and ribbons of every colour, and of course, there were plenty of parasols. The men were attired in their Sunday best, with several wearing top hats. Pate wasn't much for stiff and staid apparel. Even if he could afford to be appropriately tailored, he would still prefer a clean shirt and sturdy trousers. However, in salute to the occasion, he had polished his boots. And if his hat looked a bit too battered, well, so be it. He truly didn't care about such things. At twenty-four, he was his own man and prepared to defend that to anyone who might suggest otherwise.

He smiled at the woman by his side. He and Colleen Sullivan had been a couple for just over two years. He knew everyone expected them to marry, including Colleen, but he wasn't of a mind to set down roots yet. He figured there was plenty of time for that.

He was aware that Colleen was speaking to him, but he wasn't paying close attention. He was more interested in the food tables, which were in the process of being set up. Truth to tell, Colleen had talked him into attending this event, and he was counting the minutes until the refreshments were laid out and they could eat. Then they'd be on their way home to the country. Gatherings like this weren't something he relished, he much preferred being back on the farm tending to his horses.

"Pate, are you listening?" Colleen asked patiently. Soft-spoken and lovely, she smiled up at him with lively blue eyes that crinkled merrily at the corners. "I have to go now because I've agreed to volunteer at the cake table. You can come along and help too if you like. We could always use another pair of hands. Maud Sansom said we have quite a few cakes."

The last thing he wanted to do was cut and serve cake, he didn't even particularly care for the stuff. All that sticky, sweet frosting, not to mention spending the rest of the afternoon with a bunch of gossipy old crows. He'd seen them gawking in his direction, talking behind their white gloves about him. Likely disapproving of Colleen keeping company with one of the Kavenaghs. He clearly didn't have the right pedigree, and for that reason alone, he almost maliciously agreed to make his presence felt at the cake display. Rub their noses in it, so to speak. But no, leave them to it. He'd stand over here where the air was better.

"No thanks, Colleen. You go on ahead," he told his fair-haired girlfriend. "I think they're waiting for you. I'll get myself something to eat when everything's ready."

One thing he liked about Colleen, among her many positive qualities, was that she usually wasn't one to argue. If he said no, she knew he meant no and accepted it. He afforded her the same courtesy. So off she went, glancing back with a shy smile he'd always found endearing.

He felt new eyes on him. Funny how a person could do that, and he turned in that direction, a shock of awareness racing through him. He supposed it was akin to being struck by a bolt of lightning when he locked gazes with that pair of sparkling emerald eyes. Her hair was the colour of open flame. She beamed at him, and he involuntarily did the same as he felt his face lighting up. She was mesmerizing, the most stunning creature he had ever seen in his life. But where on earth had she come from?

The only thing he could think of that was as radiant as her smile was the sun cresting the horizon on a summer morning. Breathtaking, and oh so welcome. She was dressed all in white, except for the vibrant blossoms and matching silk ribbons that adorned her substantial straw bonnet. And now she was covering the short distance between them.

He glanced around, thinking perhaps she might be smiling at someone else, but no, it was him she was sashaying toward, her face alight. Their gaze held and he shifted a bit uncomfortably, not knowing what to expect. Women were not usually so bold.

She extended a gloved hand when she stopped in front of him. "I'm Dinah Gladstone," she announced, and even her voice sounded like the seductive purr of a satisfied cat.

She seemed predatory somehow, but wonderfully so. Pate now had an idea what it felt like to be caught in a web, although this was one good-looking spider.

"I'm visiting from Boston," she continued. "I'm staying with my Aunt Emmaline and Uncle Horace. They were here until a few minutes ago. Aunt Emmaline is bothered terribly by the sun and so they'd only planned to stay for a short while and socialize with friends. They wanted me to leave with them, but there's no reason I should miss the party, is there?"

Pate was coming up for air after diving into those huge emerald pools. A man didn't stand a chance. "Ahh, no. No reason at all. I'm so glad you stayed."

"Are you?" she asked coquettishly.

"Well, sure I am. I'm Pate Kavenagh. I'm from ... out in the country, and that's where I usually stay. I'm not much for stuff like this," he said, glancing around disparagingly for emphasis. "This whole thing is way too fancy for me."

She laughed, and its light tinkling sound was most pleasing to the ear. "You shouldn't be too hard on us," she told him, smiling broadly. "We women are grateful for any opportunity to wear our new summer bonnets."

He thought of Colleen's homemade bonnet, in which she looked uncomplicated, fresh-faced and pretty. Dinah, on the other hand, looked like she'd stepped from the pages of a city magazine, in all the best ways.

"I suppose that's true," he acknowledged, glancing up at her bonnet, "and you wear yours well."

She rewarded him with another dazzling smile. "Thank you! Now tell me you're not married, and this will turn out to be the perfect day. You're not, are you?"

He could see Colleen watching him from the cake table. "No, not married."

"Promised then?"

"Not promised either," he told her. "Not in the way you mean anyway."

He couldn't believe how daring she was, but the fact that she'd chosen him made his chest swell with pride. He could see the appreciative glances from some of the other men, and that pleased him. Let them be jealous. It'd give them something to talk about.

She clapped her hands together, not an easy feat while holding a parasol. "Wonderful! I've had my eye on you the whole afternoon because you're easily the most handsome man here." she said. Despite the fact that she was taller than most women, she still had to look up at him as he bested her by several inches.

He smiled again, darned if he could keep it off his face. "Thank you, and you're beautiful."

She laughed that tinkling laugh again. "And thank *you*! Now that everyone's been properly flattered, let's get down to more important things."

That took him by surprise. "Such as?"

"I didn't come over here to discuss the weather, Mr. Kavenagh. I made the trip across the lawn because I'd like to get to know you better. I can see you're shocked by what I say, but I'm a woman who speaks her mind. If I want something, I see no reason not to pursue it, and I want you."

He gaped at her.

She adjusted a tendril of her fiery hair. "You appeared to be a man who would find an honest woman refreshing. I'm not a silly goose who plays at life, sitting around nibbling curds as the nursery rhyme goes. Now, you say you're not obligated to that quiet little thing you had by your side earlier, so why not add a touch of spice to your life?"

It nettled him to have Colleen dismissed in such an ungracious manner. She was a good friend, and he was very fond of her. He might not have gotten around to deciding whether he would ask her to marry him, but he wouldn't stand by and have her denigrated.

"Now see here," he said, his smile evaporating. "Colleen is a fine woman, and I won't hear anything against her."

Dinah laughed. "Ahh, you're defending her. She must mean *something* to you."

"She means a great deal to me. Colleen and I haven't spoken about the future, not in so many words, but any man would be pleased to take her for a wife. I would hardly describe her as a *quiet little thing*. She happens to be bright and sweet, and a very kind soul."

Dinah bowed her head in acknowledgement of his comments, but was still smiling when she raised it again. "My apologies. But you have to understand, I now see her as someone who stands in the way of what I want. Is that right, would you say, Pate? Does she? Should I consider her an adversary?"

He realized he had arrived at a crossroads. Colleen was everything he'd described her to be, and most importantly, a stalwart friend. Nonetheless, that somehow seemed to pale in comparison to what he was feeling at the moment, in truth, had been feeling since Dinah Gladstone strode up to him. He'd never felt more alive, mostly with anticipation, if he was being honest with himself. At this moment, he wanted nothing more than to kiss this ravishing woman standing in front of him. Discard that confection she called a hat, and loose that thick, rich mane of flaming hair. He wanted to bury his face in its silky softness, lose himself in those emerald eyes.

"No, she doesn't stand in your way," he heard himself saying rather than intentionally setting out to do so. "Leave Colleen out of this."

What was happening to him? Poor little faithful Colleen, but truth to tell, she was no match for the magic dust being sprinkled over him by this bewitching young woman.

He felt Colleen's steady gaze from the cake table searing into him right this very moment, but it faded away as he looked at Dinah. If this was what it meant to fall in love at first sight, then it was happening to him.

"Perfect!" Dinah announced triumphantly. "But I also understand how things work, and I'm guessing you're a man who prides himself on doing the right thing."

Ouch! That stung because he was currently headed in the opposite direction of that noble assessment, but he tamped down his conscience. There would be plenty of time for regret, if there was any, like in about an hour or two, when Colleen finished at the cake table.

"How old are you?" he asked Dinah.

"I'm nineteen and a half, and every inch a woman," was her scandalous reply. "And I would guess you're in your middle twenties. Am I right about that?"

He nodded. "Twenty-four, and I'll bet if your aunt and uncle were here, they'd be warning you away from me."

She tilted her head in a most appealing way. "Oh? And why is that? Have you committed some terrible crime against society?"

"Most people around here would say that was true simply by being here today. The Kavenagh name is not the best in these parts."

She clapped her hands together again. "Even better. You're dangerous! I like that, and you know, you look the part. You're so tall and strong, dark, and those grey eyes of yours are rather mysterious. There's just something so alluring about a bad boy. How can I possibly resist you, Pate?"

This woman was full of surprises. "I'm sorry to disappoint you, but I've not broken any laws. It's just that our reputation isn't very good, and I've had to fight my whole life against it. I won't hear any talk against my family, and I won't dance like some puppet for the entertainment of someone who's looking to shock others by keeping my company. I'm not rich. I work on a farm, but I'm a decent person, as is everyone in my family. People can take that or leave it. I don't care either way."

She eyed him speculatively. "Nicely said, Pate, and I respect you for saying it. When I say bad boy, I don't mean I'm looking to take up with bank robbers or murderers. I like a man who has the courage to stand up for himself and be who he is, no matter what side of the blanket he was born on. You know who you are, I can tell that, and that's what I like. I'd take you any day over a dozen milksops with money. I've got plenty of my own money, so I don't need to look for it elsewhere."

"For the record, I was not born on the wrong side of the blanket," he corrected her, then made an effort to relax. "Who are you, besides a niece of the Gladstones?"

"I'm the daughter of Crandall, Uncle Horace's eldest brother. I was born in Boston, attended the best boarding schools abroad, and I am ready for the world."

Pate laughed. "But is the world ready for you?"

"I hope so," she said with a grin, "but ready or not, I'm here. So when can I see you?"

"Whoa there! Where I'm from, the man does the asking."

"Ask then," she told him impudently. "He who hesitates is lost."

Those were true enough words, but at the moment, he felt like backing up, just a little. He was already under her spell. He felt it, and it wasn't necessarily a bad place to be. In fact, the past few minutes were highly enjoyable. He knew, though, that the bubble was going to burst with a bang felt through all of Westmorland County once Colleen was back by his side. He'd handle that when the time came.

He wanted nothing more at this moment than to be close to Dinah, much closer since it didn't seem as though she'd mind that. Nevertheless, it wasn't quite so simple.

"I don't turn in the same circles as you do, Dinah. That much is obvious," he said, glancing down at his homespun attire. "I'm not a dandy."

"I told you, I'm not looking for a dandy. I've got eyes, I can see for myself what I'm signing up for."

"Signing up for?"

"It's a figure of speech, Pate. Now are you interested in us getting together or not?"

It was as if someone else was speaking for him. "Of course I am, but when? How? I somehow don't think you'd be comfortable coming to our farm, not in those clothes, and what I wear is what I wear. I have no plans to change anything about myself to fit into your world if you intend to invite me there."

She smiled. "I say we create our own world where neither side is welcome."

"And how long do you plan to live in this new world we'd be creating? Something tells me you'll be back to Boston, back to civilization, by the end of the summer."

"I have no plans to return in the foreseeable future. Now this is what I'm thinking. My uncle has a stable of fine horses, and I happen to be an expert horsewoman. I expect you know a thing or two about horses as well. I often go riding by myself, so I know of this small meadow that sits on the left, tucked away from view, a few miles past the fork in the road leading out of town. I can use a shortcut through the woods. Let's meet there. I promise you, Pate, you won't be sorry. Why, I can hardly keep my hands off you as we stand here and speak."

Pate felt a visceral reaction to her words. Boy, when he got up this morning, he didn't think something like this would be happening before the end of the day.

"I do know a thing or two about horses. I raise them, and I know where Crenshaw meadow is. What time should I be there?"

She blushed prettily. "If we're to have privacy, an early hour would be best. I'm an early riser, Pate, are you?"

"I am."

"Good, I'll meet you tomorrow at daybreak."

* * *

Pate wasn't sure how he managed it, but he did eat a plateful of fried chicken and potato salad, as well as three of Julia's buttered pan rolls a short time later. His stepmother was known for her delicious bread and rolls. He knew he should go to the cake table, despite the fact that he wasn't interested in sampling their wares, but his feet were reluctant to head in that direction. Instead, he lingered at Julia's table, where she was kept busy buttering fresh rolls for the hungry picnickers.

"Too bad Pa couldn't make it today," he told her, "but his side's still giving him trouble."

Julia looked concerned. "I didn't expect he'd come anyway, you know how he feels about such gatherings, but I don't like that pain he's having. It seems to be getting worse. I want the doctor to come out to the farm and see him, but he's not at all interested in having a medical examination. If it gets any worse though, I'll go for Dr. Mains and bring him back. Let the dust settle where it may. Who was that woman you were talking to?"

Pate could feel his colour rise. "Ahhh, a niece of some people who live here in Sackville. She's from Boston."

"She certainly had your attention," Julia teased him, "*and* Colleen's. She never took her eyes off you."

He nodded. "I could see her looking. I suppose I should get on over there."

He knew Julia wasn't fooled. Anyone with eyes could see he'd been taken with Dinah in a big way. She seemed like the type of person who would attract attention no matter where she went because she was so beautiful. He could see her now, chatting with a man whom he guessed must be a friend of the family, but he wasn't prepared for the blaze of jealousy that dashed through him. Dinah had been in his life for no more than an hour, and his strong reaction surprised him. Had he really taken the fall? All he could think about was seeing her again.

And since she was so unconventional, that could possibly mean she'd be no shrinking violet when it came to intimacy, but one could never tell. Even if that were the case, he wouldn't take advantage of her. No, he'd play it cool.

He was not unaware of his own circumstances of birth. His father had that talk with him a long time ago. While he'd never spoken about his late wife, he had stressed that he didn't want his own son to go down the same path he had in terms of young fatherhood. Both of his parents had been just fifteen when he was conceived, and his mother, still a girl, had died bearing him. That was a sobering thought.

He'd longed for a mother, and his grandmother had filled that void until she passed away nine years ago. No, if he should find himself in an intimate situation with Dinah, he would proceed with the necessary caution. That wasn't something he'd had to consider in his relationship with Colleen. She'd made it plain at the outset she was saving herself for marriage, and he'd respected that. Thinking about it now brought a rush of guilt. Colleen would not go to bed happy tonight.

He headed to the cake table, and the few seconds it took him to get there felt like the longest walk he'd ever taken. Colleen was working alone at the table now, busy serving an elderly couple with slices of yellow cake with boiled icing. He knew that's what it was because his grandmother used to make it, and it was the only kind of frosting he liked.

When she was finished, she turned her attention to him. "'Why don't I cut a piece of this for you?" she asked, indicating the large two-layer cake. "I know you like it."

She may as well have offered him a bowl of barn dust, for that's all the appeal it held for him at the moment. The food he'd already eaten now felt like a dead weight in his gut.

"No, I overate on the fried chicken and potato salad," he told her, and hoped she didn't notice he wouldn't meet her eyes.

She noticed. Apparently. "Who was that girl you were talking to, Pate?"

"She's the niece of a couple who live here in Sackville," he said, repeating the answer he'd given Julia.

The fact was, a lot of people were likely curious about the conversation between him and Dinah. Anyone he knew here had seen him and Colleen arrive together, knew they'd been a couple for some while now. Indeed, they were probably wondering why he'd given the other woman so much of his attention. Stop it, he told himself. How could anyone know she wasn't a family friend, although certainly not one of the Kavenagh's acquaintances? He also knew it was glaringly apparent that it wasn't that kind of conversation. Even he would have picked up on that, and Colleen routinely told him he was not as aware as he should be in the romance department. Maybe that was because so far no one had stirred his blood the way Dinah had when he first saw her. That was a difficult fact, but it was the truth. Colleen interested him, but it was quieter somehow, like a someday thing that he'd eventually get around to.

"Oh? Did you know her before today?" Colleen asked.

"We just met," he admitted, understanding as soon as the words were out of his mouth that he'd stepped into the trap Colleen had set for him.

"I would say you got to know each other very quickly then. She was flirting with you, Pate."

"Come on, Colleen. Don't start."

"And you were flirting back."

He sighed. She was right, of course, but there was no way he was going to have this conversation here, where everyone's ears were tuned for gossip.

"Are you through serving cake?" he asked, changing the subject. "It looks like most of it's gone, so let's head on home. I wouldn't mind getting out of here early. I've got a lot of work to do back at the farm, and I can't leave it for my father, not with him feeling so poorly."

Colleen was as pale as her white muslin dress, her hat now slightly askew, although he knew she wasn't overly concerned about such things. She was a simple girl who liked simple things, and he'd always liked that about her. She was calm by nature, although he guessed he was about to find out how far her good nature would extend in the next half hour or so.

They were silent as they made their way to the buggy and climbed inside. He was proud of the vehicle, had saved for two years to get it, and even the horse that pulled it was of good stock. He'd raised Pointer himself and kept his light chestnut coat brushed to a high sheen.

They hadn't gone far when Colleen turned to him. "Pate, I feel you have something you want to say to me, call it women's intuition."

He felt like the biggest cad in the world. He wanted to pursue a relationship with Dinah, but he wouldn't do it behind Colleen's back. He would do the honourable thing, no matter how much he hated to. She deserved no less.

He pulled the buggy to the side of the road and turned to face her. "There is something I want to say. I don't think it's going to work out between us, Colleen, and I have no right to tie you to me if that's the way I feel."

She turned on him with such indignation that it shocked him. "You liar! Everything was fine until that hussy came marching up and threw herself at you. I watched the whole thing. If you didn't think things were going to work out between us, why didn't you say something earlier?"

The thing was, he hadn't actually realized it until today, and besides, he asked himself, if he wasn't having doubts, how could another woman steal him away so easily? If he were truly in love with Colleen, something like this wouldn't happen.

"Colleen, you and I have gotten to be more like friends."

"I don't know too many friends who kiss each other goodnight. No, Pate, we were sweethearts. You knew very well I was saving myself for you."

"Well..."

"You knew that, and don't pretend you didn't!"

"All right, I knew, but I never asked you to, did I?"

"Pate Kavenagh! How dare you say such a thing to me! That's despicable! You know what? You want that tramp, you go and get her because any woman who would come up to a man she's never met before and throw herself at him in a public place is no lady. And don't think I was the only one who witnessed that spectacle. There were a lot more than me watching. But she is pretty, a lot prettier than me, and I can't compete with what she's got to offer. So don't bother with a flowery speech to let me down easy, because it's me who is deciding to walk away."

"Colleen..."

"I love you, Pate, or I should say I did, because my love is misplaced on a man who is not worthy of it. I take it back, my heart is no longer yours to mistreat. Goodbye, and don't you ever dare to darken my door again," and with that she flounced out of the buggy and began to march along the side of the road toward home, stepping around loose rocks as best she could.

"Colleen, now come on. Get back in the buggy. The road's dusty, and you're going to get your new dress all dirty."

She turned to face him, and his heart turned over when he saw she was crying. "Don't you worry a moment about the condition of my dress. Matter of fact, don't worry at all about anything to do with me anymore. You don't want anyone to see me walking because then they'd know what a scoundrel you really are."

"Colleen, get in the buggy, and I'll take you home. I knew this wasn't going to be easy, but..."

"Easier for you than me because I don't think we'd be having this conversation at all if you hadn't met that *Jezebel* at the picnic. Be honest with yourself, even if you can't be honest with me."

"I am being honest, and doing the honourable thing. I can't help how I feel."

"I can't help how you feel either, but I meant what I said. I never want to see you again after today. I hope she tears your heart out and stomps all over it because that's what you deserve, Pate Kavenagh!"

Chapter 2

Pate changed out of what he considered his Sunday best before heading for the barn. He knew his father would be there, and he wanted to talk to him, see if he was all right. His pa was as tough as they made them, and it would be a great relief to find him feeling better and going about his chores as usual.

Pate needed settling, he knew he did, and not just about the concern he felt for his father. He was entirely at loose ends. Never before had he felt as he did now. It was normal, he knew, to feel excited about meeting a woman, because that was the way of things. Everyone said so, although that wasn't the way it was with Colleen. They'd known each other from school and more or less gravitated toward one another and stayed that way. In over two years, she had never stirred his blood the way Dinah had the moment he'd first seen her. His reaction had been so powerful he could have taken her right then and there, although he'd never do such a thing, but it wasn't for lack of desire.

Colleen was different, gentler somehow, and while Dinah saw his family's shady reputation as a naughty adventure, Colleen truly hadn't cared what people said about her getting *mixed up* with a Kavenagh. When they'd first gotten together, a year after his Uncle Brogan's skirmish with the law, public bias against his family had been even stronger. It's what people had come to expect from the Kavenaghs. But it hadn't mattered to Colleen, defying her own family in the beginning to be by his side, though they'd eventually warmed to him. Her devotion had always counted for so much. Had he mistaken loyalty for love? He did care for her a great deal, but Dinah took his breath away.

His father was not at the barn, but he found him out back by the new paddock, leaning against the framework of the sizeable enclosure.

"Pa! Are you all right?"

Tabor turned to face him, pale, but with his jaw set. "Just a stitch in my side is all. Now, if you're done picnicking, you can help me get the rest of these boards in place. I want this paddock finished today."

Pate studied him. "Why don't you go on up to the house and rest. I'll do what needs to be done down here."

Fire flashed in Tabor's eyes. "Rest! The day I can't get my work done is the day I'm all finished."

Pate held his ground as his father had taught him to do. "You look about all finished *now*. You've had that pain for days. Go on up to the house and sit awhile. Julia should be along shortly, and she can make you some supper."

Tabor straightened, folding his arms against his chest, although Pate didn't miss the grimace. "When I'm all finished, Pate, you'll know about it. I'm not even halfway there. You and Julia get all excited about a little bit of pain. I pulled a muscle is all. Go up to the house and sit, you say! You go up to the house and sit if this is all too much for you. As for me, I've got work to do. Now, are you going to pitch in and help or not?"

Pate knew it was pointless to argue with his father, so spying the hammer and nails sitting on the ground beside a post, he grabbed them. Let his father hold the boards in place, and he'd swing the hammer. He could spare him that much.

When the last board was secured, Tabor was clearly hurting as he abruptly turned and left without a word.

"Pa!" Pate called after him. "Wait up!"

Tabor kept walking until Pate fell into step beside him. "Pa, you're sick and you need to see a doctor."

"No doctor!"

"Pa!"

Tabor wheeled on his son. "People get sick every day, Pate. What did people do before doctors started hanging out their shingles?"

"For one thing, they died."

"They also got over whatever was wrong with them. If everyone died that ever got sick, there'd be no room to bury them all. Now leave me be. I'm tired, what with Julia dogging me to see a doctor about my side. Now you. Get away from me, both of you, and let me be. I'll get over this a lot faster without being constantly pecked at."

Pate took a deep breath. He knew his father better than anyone. "You're not fooling me for a second, Pa. You're real sick and you need to see a doctor. You're not yourself at all."

Tabor stopped in his tracks, and it was a moment before he spoke. "Pate, you've got work to do in the barn. Go do it. I'm going to go sit on the veranda for a spell. Julia should be here any minute, and she can take up the nagging for you, give you a rest."

Tabor turned to go, but Pate blocked his way. "Pa, at least think about getting Dr. Mains to take a look at you."

"I'll think about it, yes," he said at length. "Now go and leave me be."

Later that evening, his father appeared to be somewhat better, but was still snarling at either Julia or himself whenever they came near, and God forbid, they should suggest he needed medical attention. He knew his pa had a ferocious bark that would frighten most people off, but he'd long ago become immune to it. Julia, somewhat less so. Her time with Tabor had toughened her up. He knew he would try the patience of a saint, but he could be right about this. Perhaps they ought to leave off him for a while. Give him a few days, and he might come out of it. Kavenagh men were strong, in every way, when he considered what they overcame daily to be here.

Pate had heard the stories of how the Kavenagh family came to settle in Canada, how his grandfather, Bart Kavenagh, Black Bart they called him, was a real bad man and that he'd been murdered. There were other whisperings too, about his grandmother, but he wasn't interested in listening to any of those. Why borrow trouble? There was already plenty of it to go around as it was.

As usual, he went to bed with the rest of the household when darkness fell. As tired as he was, though, he couldn't seem to find an escape from what was on his mind, besides his father. In the morning, he would ride out to meet Dinah Gladstone. Would she even show up? Would she ask her aunt and uncle about the Kavenaghs and be warned away by the couple, horrified their niece would even consider keeping one of them company? Would the uncle forbid her access to his horses if she insisted on going, which he assumed she might because she did strike him as headstrong?

Was it all a cruel joke? Had someone put her up to it as an act of retaliation for past Kavenagh shortcomings? Anything was possible for those with true vengeance in their heart.

As it turned out, he did get some sleep, waking with a start just after four in the morning. Throwing off the covers, he crept from his room and tiptoed down the stairs. Theirs was a household of early risers, and he already heard Julia stirring in the room at the top of the stairs.

Once in the kitchen, he freshened up at the washbasin, combed his hair and headed for the barn to saddle up. Breakfast was out of the question.

It was already a pleasantly warm day, so despite the early hour, and with his hat settled firmly onto his head, he set off at a trot out of the barnyard. The air smelled fresh and clean as he made his way along the country road to the rendezvous spot, fully expecting to either come upon her as she headed to the meadow or hear hoof beats behind him. Neither happened by the time he got there, and he recalled she was going to use a shortcut through the woods. He waited.

His father had given him his grandfather's old pocket watch, and he used it often. He checked it now and was not surprised to see that nearly an hour had passed, agonizingly slowly, since he'd arrived. He felt disappointment settle into the pit of his stomach. He'd been right. She'd played him for a fool, but that unsavoury thought had no sooner occurred to him than he heard hoof beats headed toward the meadow at a lope. She'd come after all!

She pulled up next to where Pate's horse was tied to a dead tree, and he knew he wouldn't forget the sight of her that morning. Her fiery hair was a mass of glorious soft curls cascading over her shoulders, tumbling clear to her waist. Her colour was high, her cheeks rosy in an alabaster face, her lips full and parted invitingly. Her eyes danced with mischief. If he'd thought he was in love before this morning, the sight of her now cemented that notion firmly in his mind. How could someone not love such a woman?

She dismounted with ease from astride the tall chestnut gelding, where most women rode sidesaddle and waited to be helped down if there was a man anywhere within a mile of them. Dinah Gladstone was her own woman all right. So was Colleen, come to that, only less aggressive, he acknowledged. He'd always admired Colleen's gentle strength...

"Pate! You came!" she announced unnecessarily. "I'm sorry I'm late! Uncle Horace was a bit difficult about my going out so early again, and on one of his most spirited mounts." She reached up and stroked the horse's neck. "I told Uncle it was a shame to geld this animal. I can't help but think of the fine babies he would have made."

Pate couldn't believe a lady would be so forthright about such a thing as castration, but there it was. He had great affection for a plain-spoken woman.

"Why did your uncle have him cut then?"

"He already has a good stud, and he also wanted to keep this horse. Two stallions among the mares is one too many, but I don't have to tell you that, do I? You being a horse breeder and all."

She walked over to his gelding, a handsome black, strong through the shoulders, long of neck and a short back. "What a superb-looking animal. I can tell he's very intelligent. Is he one of yours?"

"No, he wasn't bred on the farm. I bought him as a saddle horse last year. I call him Jacko."

She studied the black appreciatively. "I can tell by the look of him he can go. Something tells me when you're on him, you've got a lot of horse under you."

He smiled. What a smart woman. "You're right, he's quite a boy! He can run like the wind, possibly faster. I usually let him have his head, but this morning I didn't run him any faster than a lope."

She looked up at him, her smile wide. "I appreciate a man who's good to his animals, Pate. You're the kind of man a woman could become completely infatuated with. I'm not so sure it hasn't already happened. I'm dying to run my fingers through your hair. I love that you wear it long, well, to the top of your shoulders. And with that hat framing your face the way it does, you are certainly a feast to behold."

Her lips looked entirely kissable, so he cupped her chin in one hand and brought her closer, and as he thought, paradise lay waiting. Never had he thought it possible that kissing a woman would ignite such a fire in him. When he kissed Colleen... No, he wouldn't think about Colleen. Suffice it to say the two experiences were entirely different.

It seemed as though the kiss would go on forever, each pressing more eagerly against the other as it continued to deepen. Finally, with a groan, they broke contact, and she fell against him as he brought his arms more securely around her, his cheek resting against her forehead. They stood like that for minutes. Then, as if both were still starving for the taste of pure honey, they found each other's lips again until Pate thought he would burst from the wanting of her. He also knew they were quickly moving into deep water, his father's warning a small voice in the distant corners of his mind. He knew the consequences, even if she seemed impervious to them, and he did not want to father a child. Not at this stage anyway. Birthing him had cost his mother her life, and knowing that would haunt him forever.

He stepped back, holding her at arm's length. She looked up at him, perplexed, her lips swollen and parted. "What's wrong, Pate? Don't you enjoy kissing me?"

He smiled, one of his rare smiles. "You know I do. But things are moving a little too fast, don't you think?"

"Moving too fast? Didn't we come here to kiss?"

He chuckled at her brutal honesty. Of course, that's what this was all about, but Pate knew he was acting somewhat out of character in terms of spontaneity. He was a man with a wary nature when it came to such things.

"Let's sit down, Dinah," he said, indicating a fallen log over by the edge of the forest. "I'd like you to tell me all about yourself."

The spot he'd chosen sat high under a grove of maple trees, and so if anyone did happen by, they wouldn't be standing out in the open for all to see. True, the meadow was somewhat secluded, but prudence is often the companion of a cautious man.

Pate took hold of her hand once they were seated, and she leaned against him. Their familiarity gave the impression of a well-seasoned couple, which they were not, but there did seem to be an air of a kindred spirit about them at the moment.

"I am an only child," she began, cuddling against him as he slid his arm around her shoulders and drew her closer. "I don't have very much memory of my mother. She died when I was three years old, so I only have vague recollections of her holding me. They're like shadows in my mind that I can't put a face to. It's a knowing that she was there if I'm making any sense at all. It's hard to explain. Are you close to your mother?"

He explained his circumstances, and she lay her head against his chest. "That is so sad," she said. "And to think she never knew her child. But I'm guessing you're very close to your father."

"I am. He was fifteen when I was born, so it's almost like we grew up together. We can say anything to each other. He's my pa, for certain, but I would say he's also like a good friend. No one is closer to me in this world than my father."

She took hold of his hand and brought it to her lips, caressing it gently before she spoke. "I like that. I also adore my father. He completely indulged me after my mother died, but in a good way, I would say. As I grew older, I wanted an education, and he saw that I got one, even though he was discouraged from giving in to such desires. I attended private boarding schools, travelled extensively in Europe and have been trained in horsemanship by some of the best instructors in the world. Thanks to Papa, I've had every advantage. Aunt Emmaline and Uncle Horace question my independent ways, but I refuse to be tamed. I like me the way I am."

There was a long moment of silence. "Dinah, I have to ask you, what in the world do you want with me? I'm the son of a poor farmer. Ours is a small farm, and we work hard to make ends meet, although I've started to change that with my horses. I only have a grade school education, more, I guess, if you consider that I've read a lot, thanks to my Aunt Maggie. Someday I plan to have a first-class horse-breeding farm, but I have a long way to go. I'm a country boy, Dinah. I don't have fancy clothes, nor do I want them, the same as I don't want a fancy lifestyle. So what is the attraction? What could I possibly have to offer you?"

She pulled away to look at him in surprise. "Why, you're handsome and sweet."

"Sweet?"

"What I mean to say is you have a kind nature, which was obvious to me right from the start. You're very likeable. You and I can have a lot of fun together, Pate, and you should never underestimate fun."

"Really."

She laughed. "Why are you trying to talk me out of liking you? Certainly, I was attracted by what you look like, and I'm sure I'm not the first woman who's noticed how good-looking you are. I consider myself to be an excellent judge of character, and I don't think I got it wrong this time either."

He watched a bumblebee sail past and settle gently in the centre of a daisy. "That's it?"

She leaned against him again, and he returned his arm to its original position. "Well, Pate, I also like that you're dangerous, something you yourself confirmed to me yesterday at the picnic. You told me you did not have a good reputation."

"I said my family has a bad reputation, but that's all it is, a reputation. None of it is true. We're good, decent, hard-working people, like I said. We're not bad at all, it's just folks gossiping and making trouble for us."

"But something tells me you are your own man. You dance to your own tune, and I find that very attractive in a man. I also like the thought of challenging you on that."

"You think you can control me, Dinah?"

"Can't I?"

"I would say not, although your kisses are sweet."

"Do you think I'm pretty?"

He laughed out loud. "Now that's the silliest question I've ever heard. You're a beautiful woman, and you know you are. You don't fool me. You use your eyes and your body and your lips to tease me. Don't bother to pretend otherwise."

She laughed that tinkling laugh of hers. "All right, guilty as charged, but I won't apologize for my womanly wiles. Every woman ought to be aware of her charms and use them to best advantage."

"And yours are deadly. So tell me, what do you want to do with your life? I can't imagine you'd be content as some man's wife, doing housework, having babies."

"Oh, now, Pate, you're not asking me to marry you already, are you? Don't you think it's too soon for that? Do I have to sign up right here, this morning, to a life of drudgery, or can we have some fun first?"

He liked the way she hinted at a possible future with him. Getting married was the furthest thing from his mind at the present time, although it was nice to play with the idea. Life would be grand if a man had her to come home to every night. If two people were madly in love, all of the other stuff would take care of itself.

"You must have thought about what life would be like when you grew up. What were your dreams as a child?"

"What were my dreams? Like every other little girl, I suppose, to meet a handsome prince someday. That's what all of my fairytale books said would happen, and so I naturally assumed it would be no different for me if I tried hard enough."

"And so have you?"

"Met a handsome prince?

"Yes. With the way you look, I can't imagine I'm the first."

She giggled. "There aren't a great abundance to choose from, that's why I was so delighted when I found you. I was casting my gaze about the common, wondering if today would be the day I met my dashing young prince, and lo and behold, there you were. In all of my imaginings, I couldn't have found one better."

He laughed despite himself. "You're quite a storyteller, Dinah, and I will admit you make a man feel special. I would say your father misses you while you're away. I believe you are the apple of his eye, or am I wrong?"

"No, you're right. I am the apple of his eye, or I should say I was. He remarried not long ago to a frightful old thing who monopolizes his every waking moment."

He chuckled, enjoying her candour. "She can't be that bad. I think you don't want to share him. Didn't you have him to yourself for most of your life?"

She sighed, and he wondered if he'd been too forthright. But then again, that's what she seemed to prefer, and it was something that came easily to him. There were no secrets in the Kavenagh family. If someone had something to say, they were not inclined to hold back. He remembered his grandmother extolling the virtues of frankness when he was growing up. Oh, how he missed her, the only real mother he had ever known.

She sighed, speaking from beneath lowered lashes. "You are correct, Pate, and that is a situation I had every hope would continue until he brought Esmeralda home to meet me. Of all the women in the world looking for a husband, you'd have thought he could have found something better than her. It would've been nice if he'd chosen someone motherly. You know, someone I could love too, but no, home he comes with *her*. I can't imagine what he was thinking when he gave *her* a second look. I begged him not to get serious about her, but he informed me it was already too late. That Esmeralda was with child and would become his wife within the week. That's when I demanded passage to New Brunswick sooner than I normally would have because I had no intention of being present for the nuptials. I come to Sackville every summer anyway. It surprises me we haven't met before."

"I don't get down to Sackville much," he said evasively.

"Well, here I am. So you see, Pate, I'm completely available and all yours."

"And wouldn't it make your papa angry if you were to take up with a poor man from a family with a terrible name?" Pulling his arm back from around her, he made to get up from the log. "It's all starting to make sense now."

She was able to stop him, her strength surprising. "No! Pate! You've got it all wrong."

"I don't think so. I won't be part of your silly parlour games, Dinah. Things are bad enough without you trying to play me for a fool in order to punish your father."

She leapt to her feet and turned on him, her temper set alight. "That's not the way of it at all, Pate Kavenagh, and I don't care much for you calling me a liar. I've spoken the truth here today, and I don't see why you think I have a dishonest reason for wanting to be with you. Do you think so little of yourself that you don't believe I would find you attractive? I find you very attractive, and I don't care a whit about your station in life."

He still had misgivings. "You seem to put great store in the fact that I come from a family considered to be of poor character. That seems to titillate you. Calling me dangerous and a bad boy. I am neither."

Her chest was heaving, her eyes shooting sparks. "Stop trying to twist my words. I'm obviously not the milquetoast type of woman you usually keep company with. I've got a lot of spunk in me, and that scares you, doesn't it? You can't figure me out is the problem, and the truth is, you never will, so don't even bother trying. I've already told you, if I want something, I try to take it for myself. What is so terrible about that? Was I supposed to admire you from across the lawn, then turn away and tell myself I can't have you? Or should I take the bold step of walking up to you, such a simple thing really, and asking if you would be interested in getting to know me? It's not even a close call as to which action is preferable to me. I'll never be the timid lamb waiting on the sidelines, bleating my disappointment should I get passed over. You want to say no to me? Then say no, but it's up to me whether or not I accept it. I didn't and I don't, and I never will. If I lose a prize, it won't be for lack of trying."

Pate sat and stared. This was the first time he'd heard anyone express themselves quite like that, and he was used to women with a little fire in their bellies. Julia was not one to be pushed aside, that much was obvious if she was able to hold her own with his father. And Aunt Maggie was also a strong woman. As for Colleen... it was there too, but she didn't need to shout it from the rooftops. Hers was a quiet kind of strength he admired.

Dinah was flushed, her temper bubbling just below the surface, and her heightened colour made her all the more appealing. This was a lot of woman standing here, and she had ridden all the way out from town at an ungodly hour to be with him. And instead of being flattered, he'd all but held her in contempt.

He reached out his arms to her. "I'm sorry, Dinah. I was wrong with some of the things I said. I guess you can't know everything about a person in an hour or two, or expect to. I apologize."

In an instant, her gorgeous smile was back, and the tempest subsided. "Apology accepted. Now let's not be so darned serious. I came to be with you, Pate." She looked around, then pointed to a spot in the meadow where the wildflowers parted. "That's a good spot there. Come on," she said, taking his hand. "I want to lie with you. Right here, right now. I can't bear to wait another minute."

Chapter 3

"Whoa! Lie with you?"

"Yes, lie with me. Isn't that why you came here?"

Pate was astonished. In his limited experience with women, he was pretty sure this wasn't how it usually went. She was presenting him with a golden opportunity, but this wasn't the way he wanted it to be with Dinah at all. She was someone he hoped to bring home to introduce to his family someday, not just roll around in a field with. Boy, she really wanted to get back at her father, no matter how much she pretended otherwise, and he would not allow himself to be used in that way.

"I came here to meet you because I thought we could talk some more and get to know one another better. Kiss, yes, but not just have a round of *blanket hornpipe to* put it coarsely. I don't even know you."

She threw back her head and laughed. It was apparent she was having a good time at his expense. Pate felt like even more of a rube, and it made him angry. She *was* playing him for a fool. Someone must have put her up to it.

He started away, but she snagged his arm and managed to hold on. "Pate! What is wrong with you! I thought you said I was beautiful."

He snatched his arm away, but stopped. "Dinah, you are without a doubt the most beautiful woman I have ever seen. I'm not saying anything about that, but..."

"But what? You want to court me? Is that it?"

Removing his broad-brimmed hat, he pushed his hair back and then slammed it onto his head again. "Look, I don't know what game you're playing, or who you're playing it with, but there's something going on here and I don't want to be any part of it. I'm leaving."

She took hold of his arm with both hands now. "Pate, you've got this whole thing all wrong. I'm trying to show you how much I like you, that's all. I like the way you look, the way you speak, and I like spending time with you. Perhaps I got carried away. I will admit I have a tendency to be presumptuous, but it's only because of the way you make me feel. Please don't be angry."

He glanced around the meadow, shaking his head in bewilderment. "You don't talk like most women."

She grinned, her expression leaving no doubt as to her intentions. She didn't loosen her hold. "And I don't think that's very many unless I miss my guess entirely. It's not the biggest crime in the world if two people who like each other, and enjoy themselves together."

"You do that a lot, do you?' he asked testily. "*Enjoy* yourself that way?"

Her face darkened. "I don't think I like what you're insinuating. I, my dear man, am a lady."

Grey eyes, the colour of a winter ocean, settled on her. "Ladies don't go around looking for flat spots in the grass to lie with a man."

She lifted her chin impudently. "I would have thought you'd be flattered by such an invitation."

"I'm not. I might be, under other circumstances, but I'm not sure I trust you, Dinah."

She stepped closer, sliding her arms up and around his neck and pressing herself against him. "You can trust me, Pate. Can you forgive a lady one little slip? How can I be blamed for how you make me feel?"

He looked down into the face he was sure would make any man lose his heart, and he felt his own sprout wings and take flight. She even smelled wonderful, like August roses. He knew he was being hard on her, but old habits died hard. He still couldn't believe such an entrancing woman would be interested in him, a Kavenagh, a simple country boy, a hayseed, ploughboy, hick. He'd heard them all, and he'd be damned if he'd be fodder for anyone's jokes. Could

Dinah be different? Oh, how he wanted that to be true.

His lips descended gently onto hers, and he was swept away once more, his body jumping to life as he knew it would if he relaxed enough to allow it to happen. It would be wrong to lie with her, but who was he kidding? He wanted her in the worst way, like any man would want a woman. And then she was urging him downward, and he was letting her, the grass soft and springy against his shoulder, his hip, as they lay there side by side in the meadow. The sun warmed them as it continued to ascend in a cloudless sky.

The kiss seemed to go on forever, deepening even more if that was possible. She turned over onto her back, and now he was kissing her face, her hair as he adjusted himself and felt her beneath him, warm and willing.

And then he rolled onto his side again, away from her, and it took a moment before his breathing resumed its normal rhythm. He got to his feet.

"I've got to go, Dinah. There's a day's work waiting for me, more since my Pa isn't feeling well."

If she was piqued by what could be considered rejection, she was wise enough not to say so. Reclaiming her feet as well, they walked slowly to their horses, arm in arm.

"I understand," she said, straightening her jacket and riding skirt. "I must be away too. It was the perfect morning for a ride, but if I'm gone too long, Uncle Horace might send someone to look for me, and I'd die of embarrassment if that were to happen. So it's goodbye for now, my handsome paramour."

He chuckled. "Your what?"

"My paramour. My lover."

He shook his head but was unable to keep the grin off his face. "Friend, I suppose at this point, paramour for another time."

Her smile was knowing, her eyes a most tantalizing emerald green. "Paramour for next time. It will be our exquisite secret. You think about that when you're going about your farm chores today. Think about the delights that await you in Crenshaw meadow. You are mine, Pate Kavenagh, and make no mistake about it. Where would I find another one of you?"

He reddened to the roots of his hair. Unbidden, visions of what she would look like naked cavorted deliciously through his mind, and his body responded accordingly. Despite all of his high and mighty talk, he wanted her badly, but not for one time. He wanted her for always, the most challenging part of that would be to convince *her*. To somehow find a way to fit into each other's lives. If they were in love, they could do it. It occurred to him to consider what he would be prepared to give up to make that happen. He pushed it from his mind. He hadn't asked her to marry him, so all of that stuff would have to wait for another time.

She was what they called a free spirit. He'd read about that in a book once, and he knew he was the complete opposite. It would do him good to throw caution to the wind once in a while and live life. Allow it to happen instead of trying to steer it in the direction he constantly thought was best. He was downright predictable compared to Dinah.

"When can I see you again?" he asked her.

She straightened her hair, pulling a strand of grass from one of the fiery tendrils. "How about tomorrow at daybreak? Same place."

He hadn't expected it to be so soon, but fine. He would do it. It was about time he got on with becoming a real man, in every sense of the word, instead of running scared like some schoolboy.

"Tomorrow at daybreak it is," he agreed with a grin as he kissed her goodbye.

He had plenty to think about on the ride home, not a great distance to travel although he was not in any great hurry to get there. How could he have thought he loved Colleen? He did, he supposed, but this was more thrilling. One thing was for certain. No man would find time spent with Dinah to be humdrum. She was one exciting woman. He thought of how envious other men would be, namely those who had looked down on him his whole life. The bullies at school, the snobs who lived in Sackville, not that everyone there was like that, he amended fairly. There were plenty of friendly folks in Sackville, and thankfully, they outnumbered the snooty ones, although he was not there often enough to get to know any of them.

He hadn't gone far when he saw old Peterson Gault moseying up the road in his farm wagon. Poor Mr. Gault looked as though he didn't have many more years left on this earth, but he got himself into town practically every day. Time had caught up with his team. One old horse was left now to pull the wagon. Queenie had been lost to age two years ago.

Gault stopped beside him. "Out for an early morning ride, young fellah?" he asked Pate.

That had been Pate's nickname for as long as he could remember, young fellah, but then again, compared to Gault, he was a young fellah.

"The air is good this time of day, and it's a great opportunity to stretch this boy out," Pate said, leaning forward to pat the gelding's neck.

The truth was the horse had been deprived of a good run this morning, because that wasn't the purpose of this trip. Dinah had told him about the shortcut she took through the woods, and he knew of one himself to get to the meadow. He forgot about Gault coming home from the tavern in Sackville about this time, having stopped along the road at intervals to rest up during the night. Peterson Gault was low-key and likeable, although one of the worst gossips in these parts. Pate would take the shortcut tomorrow.

"He's a beauty for sure," Gault agreed with him about the horse. "I know you bought this one, but you're raising some nice horseflesh, Pate. Like that Freedom colt you got down there. I guess he'd be a three-year-old now, wouldn't he? How's he coming along?"

Pate thought about the horse that Brogan had named when he was in prison. He did not want to forget what that moment felt like, the full weight of that word's meaning. Every time he saw the colt frolicking in the pasture, he thought about it.

"He's a good one all right, and I'm going to keep him for stud. You're right, he's about three, so he's young yet."

Gault pulled a toothpick of indeterminate age from his shirt pocket. Sticking it in the corner of his mouth, he proceeded to chew it. Straightening in his seat to go, he suddenly remembered why he'd stopped in the first place.

"What's stirring at your farm, young fellah? I saw Julia hitching up the buggy when I rode by a few minutes ago."

Now that got his attention. Julia hitching up the buggy? At this hour? And then it dawned on him. His father must be worse.

"I'm not sure, but I should go right along and check," Pate told him as he nudged

Jacko into a lope and raised dust the last quarter of a mile to the farm.

Julia had just finished hitching the horse to her buggy when Pate rode into the yard.

She turned to face him, her jaw set. "Where on earth have you been, Pate? I've been looking for you."

"Out for a ride is all," he replied, hoping he didn't sound defensive. "Is Pa worse?"

"He's fevered this morning, and his pain is severe. I'm going to ride for the doctor."

Pate was off his horse in an instant, tying it to the rail under the spreading limbs of a massive oak tree. "I'll go for the doctor, Julia, and bring him back with me. You go on back into the house and see to Pa. Hopefully, Dr. Mains will be available to come."

"All right, Pate. Go as fast as you can. I'm frightened. Your pa is very sick. I hope the doctor gets here in time and that your father will agree to see him when he does. Travel safely."

Pate pushed the horse and buggy as fast as he dared, considering the less-than-stellar road conditions. It wouldn't help matters any if he overdrove and upset the rig. He tried not to think about his father and how sick he was. He had never seen Julia so distraught. Icy fingers slid around his heart and squeezed painfully, conjuring dark images, but Pate pushed them away. He couldn't even think about losing his father.

He made good time reaching the village, although to him it felt as if he was moving in slow motion the entire way. He was relieved to at last pull up in front of Dr. Mains' office, but when he rushed inside, he couldn't believe his ears when he was told the doctor was off somewhere delivering a baby and wouldn't return for an hour or two. So he waited. It wouldn't serve any purpose to rush back home and tell that to Julia. He had no alternative but to cool his heels until the doctor was available.

Three hours later, the doctor returned, clearly tired after having been up all night with a difficult delivery. Nevertheless, when he told Dr. Mains about his father, the young doctor didn't give it a second thought before he left with Pate for the Kavenagh farm.

Again, Pate pushed the horse as much as he dared, but it was early afternoon before they arrived and hurried inside.

Julia met them in the kitchen. "I'm very concerned about my husband, doctor. It started out with a pain in his belly, then down into his right side for the past few days, and I would say a slight fever. This morning, his fever is worse, and the pain is now unrelenting. He's continued to get sicker over the past few hours. He's not in a good temper at the best of times, but he's even sharper today and won't let me do a thing for him. He keeps saying it will pass, but I'm not inclined to believe it will."

Dr. Mains slipped out of his hat and coat without delay. "And I'm thinking he doesn't know you sent for me, am I correct?"

Julia nodded miserably. "I'm so sorry, but that is a fact. I hate to bring you all this way, but there will be an explosion when we tell him there's a doctor here to help him."

The doctor reached for his bag, an authoritative figure despite his short stature and young age. "He wouldn't be the first stubborn patient I've had. From what you've described to me, it sounds very much like appendicitis, and it is a medical emergency. I should have seen him two days ago, but I'm here now, so please take me to him."

Pate went with Julia and the doctor to the master bedroom where Tabor lay ashen-faced, grimacing in pain.

The doctor laid the back of his hand against Tabor's forehead.

Tabor opened his eyes. "Who are you?"

The doctor turned and pulled a stethoscope from his black leather medical bag. 'I'm Dr. Mains and I've come to examine you because you're sick."

"Well, doctor, you can trot right on back to where you came from. You made the trip for nothing because I've got the grippe or something like it, and it'll go away on its own. Now get on out of here and let me rest."

Dr. Mains glanced over at Julia, then back at Tabor. "I'm just going to listen to your heart a moment, Mr. Kavenagh. That's not going to hurt anything."

Tabor truly looked to be in agony. "Listen away then, before you pack up and get back down the road."

The doctor listened as he moved the instrument to the various positions on Tabor's chest, then looped it around his own neck as was his habit for easy access. Moving the covers, he pressed his fingers gently on Tabor's right side, and Tabor yelled.

Dr. Mains addressed the patient. "Mr. Kavenagh, you are a very sick man. It is my diagnosis that you have appendicitis, and it is an extremely serious ailment. Your appendix is swollen and hot, and in my estimation, ready to burst. It has to come out immediately. If we do not remove the appendix, it *will* burst and you will most certainly die."

Tabor was like a wounded bear. "I will not die! I refuse to die!!"

The doctor was not fazed by Tabor's temper. "You most assuredly will not survive, sir, if your appendix ruptures, and we don't have much time. As I said, I must operate immediately."

"Operate!" Tabor raged. "You mean cut into me?"

The doctor's voice was calm. "That is precisely what I mean, cut into you and remove the inflamed appendix. I can assure you I am a trained surgeon and well able to handle that task. Mrs. Kavenagh, you go at once and set your kettle to boiling so I may sterilize my instruments."

Tabor tried to rise up in bed, but fell backwards. "Julia, you will do nothing of the kind because I refuse to let this charlatan cut into me. You're worried about me dying from a bad appendix? It'll be him cutting me up that'll do it."

Dr. Mains studied his patient. "You're right, there are risks associated with any type of surgery, both during the procedure and after, but we have antiseptic measures we take now, which make for even greater success. You have to make up your own mind, but I can tell you with every certainty you're facing a bigger risk with a burst appendix."

Pate stepped forward. "Pa, you have to let him try to help you. I, for one, am not going to stand by and let you die if the doctor says he can do something to fix it. You said you'd think about seeing a doctor."

Tabor was breathing heavily. "Pate, mind your own business, son. I did think about it and have decided against it. It's not you he wants to cut into. I won't be carved up like a Christmas turkey. No!"

Pate moved closer. "Pa! Stop being so stubborn and let the doctor do the operation. Please!"

Tabor tried again to get up on his elbows. "Get out of this room, all of you!"

Julia was next to tears. "Please, Tabor. Listen to the doctor. He knows what he's talking about!"

Tabor turned on her. "And I know what *I'm* talking about! Doctors kill more people than they help. He doesn't know anymore what's wrong with me than one of those cows out there in the pasture. Matter of fact, I wouldn't even let him touch any of my cows. What do you think about that! And don't you give me anything to knock me out and operate without my permission because if you do, you don't want to be around when I get out of this bed."

The doctor took a step forward. "I can't operate on you, Mr. Kavenagh, without your permission. This is your decision in every respect, but at the moment you're making a poor one by trying to send me away. I can help you. I can save your life."

"Poor decision or not, it's mine to make, now leave. You're not wanted here."

Julia balled her fists. "Tabor Kavenagh, stop being so stubborn and listen to reason! You are as good as killing yourself if you lie in bed and let that appendix burst because the doctor says that's what will happen. Why do you want to die? Is life that terrible that you can't face it anymore? Women have babies every day and go through terrible circumstances sometimes to make that happen, but they face it and get through it. I've never known you for a coward, Tabor, so face up to what has to be done and let the doctor operate. If you're so set on dying, why not take the chance? What have you got to lose? I love you with all my heart, and I'm asking, no begging, you to let the doctor operate and save your life!"

It was obvious that Tabor's pain was getting the better of him, as his hand locked onto his side. "I am not a coward!"

Julia didn't back down. "Then stop acting like one! Tell the doctor he can operate."

Tabor gritted his teeth, clearly running out of strength or resolve to continue the argument. "Fine! You want to cut me so bad, doctor? Do it! But if I die, my passing will be on all your heads because you will have killed me."

Dr. Mains stepped nearer the bed. "Do I understand you to be giving me permission to operate on you, sir?"

Tabor turned fevered eyes on the doctor. "Are you deaf? Do what you're going to do and don't dally. If you're going to kill me, all I ask is that you be quick about it."

* * *

Julia had the water boiling as requested, and the doctor performed the surgery in the bedroom with Julia assisting him.

Dr. Mains administered chloroform, so Tabor wasn't conscious for the surgery, and it was all over in a little more than an hour.

"Everything went very well," the doctor explained to both Julia and Pate later in the kitchen. "And I can assure you he did the right thing by agreeing to have the surgery. I would say he was gambling with minutes. That appendix was ready to perforate when I got it out. Another five or ten minutes, it would likely have ruptured, and we'd be dealing with an entirely different situation. In my practice, and that of my father's, I am not aware of anyone who has survived peritonitis, which is the condition that results from a ruptured appendix."

When all was said and done and the doctor's bill settled, Pate took Dr. Mains home to Sackville. The poor man looked as though he was about to fall asleep at any moment because he admitted to Pate that he had been up for almost twenty-four hours straight. And yet, despite his lack of sleep, he had performed a delicate surgery with great precision. They were indeed fortunate to have such a brilliant and dedicated young man to see to their doctoring, and because of his age, he would hopefully be around to serve the community for a good many years to come.

When Pate turned the buggy around and headed for home, it was at a much slower pace, and he'd make sure Julia's horse got an extra helping of oats in her belly after a long and tiring day.

He had to smile at the way Julia had stood up to his father this afternoon, and he'd given in! That had shocked him. He'd sometimes wondered if there were any real feelings between the two of them, having separated for so long at one point, but he'd never seen his father back down like that before. He thought the world of Julia, and he guessed so did his father, although he wouldn't bring the matter up to him. It was none of his business anyway. He was grateful he still had his pa, and given what the doctor had said, he should make a full recovery, although he was cautioned to take it easy for a few weeks. That was not a problem. He'd simply pitch in and do what extra work there was to be done until his father was well again.

And he thought about Dinah, and their promised rendezvous tomorrow morning. He wondered if he could actually go through with what she had suggested. He respected her and wanted to go on doing so, but he had a lot to think about. Like he didn't want to cause her to be with child. He could just hear his father if that turned out to be the case. No, if they did end up being together in that way, he'd have to be mighty careful.

When he arrived back at the farm, he took care of the horse and buggy, and whatever chores were left over from the afternoon.

He looked up as Julia walked into the horse barn. "How is Pa doing?"

Julia looked more tired than the doctor. His father's poor health was an ordeal for everyone. "He was sleeping when I looked in on him a while ago. I pray his recovery goes smoothly, or I may be looking for another place to live. I may be looking for another place to live anyway, the way I spoke to him. Your father doesn't like to be crossed."

Pate smiled. "It took courage to do that, Julia, and I'm glad you did. Pa could try harder at times to be nicer. But I think I understand where some of that came from this afternoon. Remember, his father was murdered, stabbed to death, and to Pa, a knife to the side could be no different than a knife to the chest."

Julia's hand flew to her mouth. "Oh my! I did not connect the two. I'm sure it's something that's never very far from his mind. How dreadful!"

"I don't know if he's talked much to you about it, me either, really, but I know what my grandmother told me. My grandfather wasn't a very nice man, and from what Gram said, he was very hard on his sons."

"I do know about his past, what he's told me about it, and I try to take that into account during the difficult times. I love your father, Pate. He's a good man. A wounded man, but a good one."

Pate continued to brush the horse. "He's been a good father to me. He was only a boy himself when I was born, but he wouldn't let anyone take me away, even under the circumstances. I owe him a lot."

"It can be very difficult on both the child and the parents if they're too young. Having a baby can be life-changing. Now I must get back up to the house in case your father has awakened and feels he can take some nourishment. I'm going to do everything in my power to help him recover. I have supper ready for you too, whenever you're through with what you're doing down here."

It was about half an hour later that he finished the last of his barn chores and headed for the house, eager to look in on his father. He wanted to see for himself how he was coming along. He hated that his big, strong pa had been laid low, and he was hopeful he'd continue to come through this all right.

He was a few feet away when he heard his father yell, he presumed at Julia.

"Of course I want something to eat! Why wouldn't I!"

Yes, his father was coming along just fine.

Chapter 4

Pate slept that night, long and sound, as though he'd been deprived of sleep for a week. He realized with a jolt when he finally came to consciousness that the light was too high in his room for a four o'clock start. Oh no! He had overslept! Dinah would be waiting for him in the meadow!

The household was in silence, and that must have meant his father passed a peaceable night too, which, if that was the case, so did Julia. This morning was already much different in that regard from yesterday, and he was grateful all over again that his father had cheated the grim reaper. His beloved parent had survived almost certain death, and for that, he would be eternally thankful.

The fog of sleep now completely fallen away, he threw back the covers. Grabbing his clothes, he scrambled into them, hurrying down the stairs as silently as he could in order to freshen up at the washbasin. It was then that he found the nerve to check his pocket watch and was not surprised to see he was well and truly late. He'd have to give Jacko the fast run he was so fond of and hopefully make up for lost time. Once on the road, he did just that, the big black covering the distance to the meadow in ground-eating strides. As he neared his destination, he slowed the horse to a walk, although the animal had plenty of fast left in him.

It was warm for early morning, the sun already nudging the horizon in its bid for another spectacular rise. When he reached the meadow, he was relieved to see that Dinah hadn't arrived yet. Good! He'd hate to have her think this meeting wasn't important enough for him to be on time.

Tying his horse's reins around the branches of the dead tree, he made his way to the fallen log and settled down to wait. He didn't mind having a bit of a breather before she arrived, a few moments to relax if that was possible, because the idea of seeing her again sent excitement thrumming through him. Their conversation yesterday still rang in his ears, what was in all likelihood ahead for him today. If she wanted to lie with him, he'd made up his mind to do it. He was looking forward to being with her because in the intervening hours, he'd become more certain of his feelings for her.

When he heard her approaching hoof beats, his anticipation ratcheted up even further. He didn't care if she was late. It could be her nature to be a little tardy. It didn't matter. The one thing he cared about right now was that she had come. The most gorgeous woman, he was sure, in all of

Sackville or even possibly the entire province, had kept a date with him. She'd ridden here especially to see him. Life didn't get any better than this.

She tied her chestnut gelding beside Pate's horse, both with plenty of leeway to nibble the luscious grass that grew in abundance at their feet. The chestnut didn't appear to have been hurried, so she had obviously taken the time to enjoy her ride. That's what riding in the early morning was all about, drinking in the sweet fresh air and the beauty of the forest path by which she'd come.

He walked down to meet her, and it seemed like the most natural thing in the world to fall into each other's arms. And then they came together to share a hungry kiss, the world ceasing to exist as far as he was concerned. Finally, it ended, and they walked hand in hand to the fallen log.

"I was thinking you'd changed your mind about coming," he whispered against the top of her head as she leaned into him.

"I almost did," she told him.

His spirits immediately plummeted, although he wouldn't let on. "Oh?" he said simply. "Why is that?"

"For the same reason I'm late arriving, other than appreciating another incredible morning. Aunt Emmaline took a bit of a spell last evening, which is nothing new, but apparently she also had a difficult night because of it. Uncle had to send for Dr.

Mains, who gave her some sleeping powders, so I was finally able to slip away. I can't stay long, though. Uncle Horace was not in favour of my early-morning outing seeing as how Aunt Emmaline is ailing, so I promised to make it a short one today."

He caressed the top of her head, the texture of her hair against his lips most enticing. "I understand," he said, then related the story of his father's serious illness.

"That's dreadful, Pate," she said, expressing genuine concern. "Is he all right now? How is he feeling this morning?"

He realized with a rush of guilt that he hadn't taken the time to check on his father before hurrying off to the meadow. In essence, he had put Dinah ahead of his own father, then rationalized that if Pa were sleeping peacefully, he would not have disturbed him. It was better to let the man have the rest he needed in order to get well.

"He was asleep when I left, so that's a good sign considering what he's been through over the past few days. So you can only stay with me for a few minutes?"

She nuzzled against his neck, her lips finding their way past his hair to settle on warm skin, then trailed a path of fire to his ear. The dart of her tongue made him groan involuntarily.

"I'd say about an hour," she said after she quit his ear, "possibly two."

The sensations she was creating spiraled through him. He closed his eyes but opened them again when she moved, and he heard the rustle of fabric. She was slipping out from under her bright cardinal cloak, and when she came into his arms her skin was toasty from the bright red woolen garment. It was much too heavy given the warmth of the morning.

"Uncle insisted I wear the cloak in case I caught a chill," she explained, heaving it off to the side. "Now, unbutton my blouse, Pate, if you don't mind," she invited him with a playful smile.

Willing the tremble from his hands he slowly began the task and when he'd finished, she stood clad in her chemise, having dispensed of the riding skirt herself.

His gaze was immediately fastened to her ample cleavage visible above the plunging neckline of the lace-trimmed undergarment. Was there anything beneath it? There didn't appear to be.

"And now I'll help you, my love," she said in that same kittenish voice, except there was no fumbling on her part as she slowly, provocatively, undid the several buttons on his shirt and pulled it away to reveal a muscled, sun-bronzed chest.

Mesmerized as he watched her watch him, he didn't even offer to help when her slender white hand settled on his trouser buttons, the suspenders having already been pushed aside.

This was the first time he'd be seen naked by a woman, but overcoming his embarrassment, he stepped clear of the rest of his clothing and stood tall and proud before her. As though he'd always known how to, he reached for her chemise and pulled it gently over her shoulders, then dropped it in the grass. He was right. She was gloriously naked under the flimsy garment.

All right, so now he was standing without his clothes in a meadow with a beautiful woman in the same state of undress. However, despite the fact that he now felt awkward in the face of what seemed like her unashamed familiarity, they came together in one magnificent assault.

Theirs was the perfect hideaway, nestled amid tall grass in back of the fallen log. Pate now knew exultation, although he did remember the need to be careful. Despite her protests, he would continue to exercise caution at all costs. Twice, they moved as one. He was sure the earth must have shifted on its axis as he crossed a bridge he had firmly believed he would not take until he'd taken the vows of holy matrimony. He also knew in this moment he wanted Dinah to be with him forever. She was his now, the ultimate sacrifice of all the promises he'd heretofore made to himself. He hadn't known Dinah when he'd made them.

When his heart had resumed its normal rhythm, he moved to the side but gathered her against him. "I love you, Dinah," he said, toying with a tendril of her long hair.

She lay comfortably in his arms. "What is love, Pate? Moments like this? Us lying with one another in a meadow? If that's true, then I love you too."

His arms tightened around her. "I knew the moment I laid eyes on you that I wanted you for my own," he told her, his voice surprisingly husky. "And now I have you."

She raised up on one elbow and regarded him speculatively. "Do you have me, Pate? Can anything in this life truly be that effortless?"

He felt he'd already put in a good deal of effort considering the past two hours' activities, but he knew when he was being baited. Dinah liked to play word games with him, but that was all right. He could hold his own.

"I think when something is meant to be, it feels like that right away," he said. "Don't tell me you don't feel anything toward me because I won't believe you."

"I wouldn't be lying with you if I didn't feel something very special," she answered him, but it seemed he had already lost her attention.

"Do you regret giving yourself to me?" he asked.

He suddenly felt his words might be ill-chosen, but more importantly, something else puzzled him. Despite the fact that he'd never lain with a woman before, he knew from talk among other men that a woman's first time was not easy for her. There should have been a barrier, and he'd dreaded hurting Dinah. He disliked the idea that the act of loving a woman should cause her pain, that it was an ordeal to be gotten through. But it hadn't been like that today, and while he felt relieved, it also left him faintly uncertain. He didn't want to bring it up so he shrugged it off. It wasn't something he was going to worry about, not after the wonderful hour they'd spent together.

She laughed, and for some reason, he found that merry tinkling sound off-putting after such a tender question.

"Are you laughing at me, Dinah?"

"No!" she rushed to assure him. "I like the quaint way you have of putting things. I suppose in a way I did give myself to you."

Again, he felt perplexed. "What other way would there be to describe it?"

She smoothed the hair back from his brow, smiling demurely. "Pate, did anyone ever tell you that you have a tendency to overthink things? You're absolutely right, I did give myself to you, and I like to think you gave yourself to me, too. Is this the first time you've lain with a girl?"

He felt heat suffuse his face. Had it been that obvious? He somehow felt there had been a test and he'd failed it, although at no point had she seemed disappointed.

"Yes," he said simply. "Why do you ask?"

"No reason," she replied, pulling away from him. "Now, I must get back to Sackville. I did promise Uncle Horace I wouldn't be long, and I suspect I've overstayed that commitment by a goodly amount."

He felt like rolling over for a snooze in the sun-splashed meadow, but he, too, had to get back to the farm and the daily chores that were already overdue to be started. For one thing, the horses would be pawing down their stalls to get outside, and their mangers would be empty of hay.

"When can I see you again, Dinah? Tomorrow at daybreak?"

"Ahhh, no. I'm afraid I'll have to stay close to home for the next few days, although I'll be thinking of you, Pate. How about two days from now, which would make it Thursday. We'll come here again, that is, if it's not raining. If it's raining, then it'll be the day after that and so on. Until then," she said as she held him close, "remember this." Pulling back, she arranged herself so that he had full view of her nudity. "And I'll remember you, all naked and warm in the morning sun."

He groaned as he pulled her against him again. At the moment, empty mangers, impatient horses and even Aunt Emmaline's spell were the furthest things from his mind. However, after giving him a quick kiss, she deftly disengaged herself from his arms and, grabbing her chemise, stood to pull it over her head.

"You be a good boy now, Pate Kavenagh. And don't you dare look at any other pretty girls."

He grinned. "Why would I bother?" he asked as he watched her. "None could compare to you."

"And you remember that," she winked, then laughed that really special laugh of hers, and this time he laughed right along with her.

The ride back to the farm was quite different from when he had rushed headlong to the meadow earlier. He felt different. He had left the house this morning still a boy, and he was returning home a man. He had now known a woman, and again there was that pang of guilt. He'd assumed it would be pretty Colleen who would share that blessed right of passage with him. And now he had given that special gift to someone else. What would Colleen say if she knew her dream of a future with him, which he supposed she already guessed had been compromised, was now completely demolished?

Still, how many men could hope to meet a woman like Dinah Gladstone? Not many, he assumed. His heartbeat quickened at the thought of her. How on earth could he wait two whole days until he was with her again, because he had pretty much figured out that theirs would be a relationship of few words. It would be more, ahhh, carnal by definition.

When the farm came into view, he quickened his pace, leaving Dinah and the meadow behind for the time being. He checked his watch as he rode into the yard. It was approaching nine o'clock, so he continued down to the barn. When he got there, he was surprised to see the horses already in the pasture and heard the scrape of a shovel.

He hurried inside to find Julia cleaning out the stalls, the horses having already been watered and fed.

She glanced up when he walked in, leading Jacko, and began to unsaddle him. "Pate, you've come back. You missed breakfast."

He'd had an eye-opener of another kind, much preferred to pan-fried potatoes and beef.

"I wasn't hungry," he explained as his stomach growled noisily, reminding him that it was impossible to survive on stardust alone.

"All right, but the animals were, so I came down and put them out to pasture. Thought that while I was here, I might as well get busy shovelling out the stalls. The flies get so bad in here during the summer if the manure isn't taken out right away."

"Thank you, Julia," he offered lamely. "I didn't mean to be so late, but you can go back up to the house now. I'll take over from here and get something to eat when I'm finished."

Julia kept shovelling. "Colleen Sullivan was here about a half hour ago."

The bottom dropped out of his stomach. Colleen! "What did she want?"

"She wanted to see you, but I told her you'd ridden out early this morning. She asked me to give you a message."

Pate undid the stubborn cinch and, pulling the saddle free, set it aside, then the blanket. "Oh yeah? What is that?"

"She wanted to apologize for things she'd said to you. Said she wanted to see if you'd changed your mind."

He began to brush Jacko with long, firm strokes. "She knows I haven't."

"I'm wondering if you should drop by her place and tell her. She seemed to set great store in the fact that you two had been together for more than two years."

Pate continued to brush the black, bringing its already glossy coat to a high sheen. "Is that right?"

Julia stopped, leaning both hands atop the shovel handle. "That's between the two of you, of course, but she's a very sweet girl, Pate. Everyone thought you two would marry."

"You're right, Julia. It is between her and me, and that's all I'm going to say about it. She had no call to come here moping around."

"She probably felt she had a right since..."

"She has no right! I've decided it's over between us, and that's the end of it."

"Perhaps she hasn't decided that yet for herself." Julia persisted, he knew, out of fairness to Colleen. "If it's over, then it's over, but have compassion for her. That girl is in love with you, Pate. Has been since I've known her."

"Has she been telling you her life story?"

"No, a blind man could have seen that. Anyway, you can finish the barn work and then come up to the house. I'll reheat breakfast for you if you have a mind to eat it by the time you get done."

"Julia," he said, stilling the brush. "I didn't mean to be rude."

"You're not rude, Pate, just plain spoken, and Lord knows I'm used to that."

"It's just that I don't like Colleen coming here crying on your shoulder. She should not have done that. You've got enough on your mind. I'll drop by and speak to her later today. How is Pa this morning?"

"He's doing as well as the doctor said can be expected so soon after surgery. He has no fever, so that means, thus far anyway, there is no bacterial infection. That is the best news at this point in time. But I will warn you, Pate, your father is in a bear of a mood and ready for a fight. I've already got my dressing down for speaking up to him in front of the doctor, not taking his side, but all of that vitriol is wasted on me. I'm letting you know he's not yet got it all out of his system. And you know what that means."

Pate was busy brushing the horse's tail. "Yeah, I know. He's mad at me for speaking against him to the doctor. I'll go up and see him in a while, let him get what he has to say off his chest. I'm glad he's still here to do it. To Pa, any kind of pain makes for anger. Thanks for the warning, though."

He thought about Colleen after Julia left. On the one hand, he did feel sorry because he had a very good idea how much it would hurt to have someone end a relationship, especially if you cared a lot for that person. It wasn't that he didn't feel anything for her, he did, but now that he'd drunk from another cup, namely Dinah, he was well and truly satisfied. Better he discover there was no magic with Colleen before they'd gotten married as everyone expected them to. Divorce wasn't something he even wanted to think about, let alone be involved with. However, if someone did get married and all they did was fight and grow to hate each other, then divorce would be a good thing, although not easy.

It was close to two hours later when he went up to the house and found the plate of beef and pan-fried potatoes waiting for him in the stove's warming closet. Mind you, it would have been much tastier a few hours ago, but he was hungry enough that he was willing to forgo appetizing for filling.

Julia walked into the kitchen as he was finishing up. "Your Pa is awake, Pate, if you want to go up and see him."

Pate pushed away his plate and drained his teacup. "How is he feeling now? I didn't hear any hollering."

Julia smiled. "He's not feeling the best. He's been through an ordeal, and he's in a lot of pain from the cutting. I'm to give him another dose of laudanum in about half an hour. If you want to talk to him, it's best to go now because when he takes his medicine, he'll likely go right back to sleep."

Pate grinned. "He's still speaking to me, is he?"

Julia pulled a cautionary face. "Barely, I would say, so enter at your own risk. Really though Pate, don't expect too much. You know how your father gets sometimes."

"Yeah, I know."

Pate took the stairs two at a time and found his father lying awake when he walked in.

"How are you feeling, Pa?"

Tabor glanced at his son, then turned his head away.

Pate sighed as he entered the room and sat down on the edge of the bed in the direction of his father's gaze. "Not talking to me?"

Tabor remained silent, but Pate would say that his colour was much better than it was at the same time yesterday, when he'd been as white as a sheet.

"Pa, come on. I asked how you were feeling."

Tabor raised his eyes slowly, and Pate was surprised to see that he appeared to be as angry as he'd been when they'd brought the doctor. "I feel as though I've been cut into and part of me taken out. That's how I feel."

Pate stared. "The part that was taken out was killing you. That doctor saved your life, whether you want to admit it or not."

"I don't know anything of the kind. I believe I would have pulled through without him sticking that knife in me."

"Pa... He cut you, he didn't stab you with the knife."

"The way my side feels, I'd say he did more than stab me, but then everyone thinks they know more about how I feel than I do myself. You just wait. Your turn's coming. Someday you're going to be good and sick and I'll say to whoever's holding the knife, have a go at him and see what happens."

"It wasn't anything like that at all. We were trying to save your life."

"Is that right! What I heard while I was lying here was people who wouldn't listen to a word I had to say. People who called me selfish and cowardly, oh and stubborn. I believe that's what *you* said. I won't forget that, Pate. You showed me no respect at all. I am your father!" he surprised Pate by shouting. "You do as *I* say. I do not, and never will, take orders from you, sonny boy."

Pate stared. "Pa! I didn't want you to die. I was saying whatever I could to get you to listen so that the doctor could save your life."

Tabor gave a disgusted grunt. "Save my life. Isn't anyone tired of saying that yet? Who said I was dying? I was still very much alive. You had pneumonia two years ago and I didn't set the doctor on you with a knife!"

"That's because there was nothing he could cut out to help me. You can't compare the two things."

Tabor slapped his hand onto the bed for emphasis. "They're exactly the same because doctors don't know what they're doing! They guess at things, and you threw me to the wolves."

"Pa..."

"Don't you *Pa* me! You are my son, and I expect you to take my side when I'm down, not turn against me. I have done for you your whole life. Not once have I failed you. I would not turn you over to one of those medical quacks who call themselves a doctor. How do you know what they took out of me? You were so all-fired determined to have him cut into me, and you knew nothing about what he was going to do when he got in there. I will not forgive you for what you did. You turned on me! Your own kin."

Julia hurried into the room. "Tabor, don't get yourself all upset. You know the doctor told you to lie quiet because your body is trying to heal."

Tabor turned wild eyes on her. "This conversation is between me and my son. It has nothing to do with you, so leave."

Julia stood her ground. "Tabor, please quiet yourself. I'll be giving you another dose of laudanum in a few minutes, but in the meantime, try not to get upset."

Tabor pounded the bed with his fist. "Leave Pate and me alone, Julia!"

Julia threw up her hands and left the room, and Pate could feel his blood begin to boil.

"This is not a conversation, Pa!" he said, doing his best to rein in his anger. "This is a reprimand, and I have done nothing to deserve it. I had this crazy idea you'd be grateful we brought the doctor here. He's a good doctor. He's already done a lot of good in the community from what I hear."

"Then let him go and do his good deeds somewhere else. He is not welcome in this house again."

Taking a deep, calming breath, Pate stood to go. "It's no use trying to talk to you, Pa, when you're in this state of mind. You lie easy there and get better. You'll be back down at the barn in no time, and we'll be working with the horses again, you'll see."

Tabor was not to be placated. "No, I will not see. I've been meaning to speak to you about this before, but I've been putting it off for another day. That other day is here now. I think it's about time you found a place of your own. This farm does not belong to you. It never did. You're twenty-four years old now, and a man ought to make his own way."

Pate felt as though he'd gotten a one-two punch in the gut as he stood there reeling, staring at his father. "Pa, I thought we were running this farm together."

"We were, but like I say, it's high time you found somewhere else to farm. I'm a young man yet. I can run it as I always have. You've started raising horses, and you're cramping my pens and barn, using up valuable pastureland I need for cattle. Something worthwhile raising. Something that'll put food in our bellies. Go, and take your horses with you. I don't want you around here anymore."

Chapter 5

"I'm not going to pay any attention to what you're saying, Pa, because I think the laudanum is affecting your thinking. It wasn't that long ago you told me how much you liked us running this place together."

"I mean what I say, Pate. It's time you went."

Pate held his father's gaze for what seemed like forever, and when he saw no softening in his expression, he turned and left the room. It was funny at moments like this how a body felt disconnected, set adrift almost, and most certainly as though the rug had been pulled out from under them. Nevertheless, his father owned the farm, and he had spoken. He could be right. It was time he went off and made his own way. Garrett had done it when he was his age, and so had Brogan struck off on his own, gotten married, although he'd not been quite twenty. So now it was his turn, but as upset as he felt at the moment, he was not going to slam out of the house and run for cover. No sir! If his pa wondered if he could make it on his own, he'd show him he could.

His father was difficult. Everyone knew that, and he was also furious with his son at the moment. That would pass, but his decision would stand. When Pa spoke his mind about something, he was not in the habit of backing down. So be it.

Pate slowly retraced his steps down the stairs and into the kitchen, where Julia was elbow-deep in warm bread dough. He kept on going, out the back door and over to the paddock where this spring's two babies, a colt and a filly, were frolicking beside their mothers in the summer sun.

That's where Julia found him a half-hour later, leaning against the split-rail fence. "I couldn't hear what was being said, Pate, but at least your pa has calmed down. I've given him his medicine, and he's sleeping peacefully. We'll give him a wide path until he gets over this whole thing. Tend him, but don't try to have a conversation."

Pate kept his gaze on Freedom, the handsome three-year-old, his father's words echoing in his brain. Truth was, he felt numb. Where would he go? He had no real money, not enough to buy his own farm on which to raise horses. It would mean he'd have to sell off his animals to raise the funds needed and then start over again in some other part of the county. Property with buildings already on it wasn't that easy to come by, so he'd have to build. It was a daunting task, but others had done it and survived, and so would he.

"Pate?" she pressed. "Are you all right?"

He shrugged. "I'm okay, but I wonder if that laudanum has addled Pa's mind."

"I asked the doctor about that, and he said in the small doses he's taking, it was unlikely. What makes you think his mind is addled? He's in one of his poor tempers, is all. He'll get over it, he always does."

Pate pushed his hat back from his forehead. "Not this time, not where I'm concerned."

She looked at him sharply. "Oh? Whatever makes you say that? You've done nothing wrong, Pate. You went all the way to Sackville and back, twice, to save your father's life. When he gets well, starts to feel better, he'll see that and apologize."

Pate snorted. "Now, when have you heard Pa apologize."

"He does in his own fashion, you have to give him time. Try not to take all of this too personally. He's in pain. We went against his wishes, which is like waving a red flag in front of a bull when it comes to your father. You know that. He's got more than his fair share of that Kavenagh temper."

"It's more than that this time, Julia. He told me he wants me to leave the farm. He said he doesn't want me here anymore, that it was time I went and made my own way."

A swift intake of breath was her reaction to that particular revelation. "You can't be serious."

"I am, but you know I've been standing here thinking. It's high time I was out on my own anyway. I thought Pa liked having me here, he and I running this place together. He said so more than once, and now he wants me out of here. He said I disrespected him and he won't stand for it."

"I'm dumbfounded! I can't believe what I'm hearing. I'll talk to him..."

"No! Don't do that, Julia. I thank you for wanting to help, but leave it alone. I've got my pride too, and I don't stay somewhere I'm not wanted."

"You're wanted here, Pate. Your Pa's talking foolishness right now, and I know he'll regret it when he finally calms down about this whole thing. Give it time."

He looked at Julia. "Actually, I agree with him. Yeah, he's madder than a wet hen at the moment, but as hard as it is for him, I'm sure he feels he's doing the right thing by pushing me out of the nest. You know, it's easier to be pushed from the nest. It takes a lot more guts to jump. I've been thinking about who I could sell my horses to because I need to raise enough money to buy my own place. It looks like I'll have to let them all go."

"Oh no, don't sell your horses, dear. I know how hard you've worked over the past few years to get to the point you are now. You'd have to start from scratch again, and it would take another five or six years to rebuild your herd, that's if you can get good foundation stock. It wouldn't be fair."

Pate's attention shifted to the horses again, at the two babies of which he was so proud. Everyone who saw them said they were fine-looking animals with plenty of potential. He had an outstandingly good stud in Silver Billy, and his two brood mares were the same. And then there was Freedom. He was a champion in the making.

"Fair or not, people have had to face much worse," he said. "It's getting used to the idea is what's hardest. But don't worry. I'll be staying put until Pa is back on his feet and able to take on the chores. I won't leave him high and dry, and I certainly won't put any more on you than you're already doing. You're busy enough. But when I go, my horses go, and I guess I'd better start asking around."

Julia was quiet for a moment, then turned to him, her eyes glowing with warmth. "Pate, I believe I may have the solution. I mean, where you may want to go next. I know of a homestead that needs some work, but it has two barns, one large, one smaller, a nice house and assorted outbuildings. I happen to know it's available, and I also know you could get it for a very affordable price."

She had his attention.

"Around here?" he asked, his eyebrows furrowed and not quite sure what to make of what she was telling him. And then it dawned on him. "You're talking about your old home place, aren't you, Julia. But isn't it legally Pa's property since you got married?"

She nodded, a smile splitting her face from ear to ear. "I certainly am talking about the farm where I grew up and was living until your father and I got married. It's but a few miles from here, and it's in the condition I described. Like I say, it would take some fixing up, but you could do that with ease. I'm sure Brogan would help you. What do you say? I know there'd be no problem with the transaction. Your father would gladly agree."

"I say it sounds wonderful, but it's really *your* place."

"I haven't lived there since your father and I reconciled three years ago. But there's one thing I would ask if you're interested. None of us knows what's ahead, and I wonder if you'd be willing to give me a room there should I find myself in need of a home."

"I can guarantee you that with no problem," he was quick to assure her. "This is so generous of you but I'm still going to have to sell my horses in order to make it mine."

"I think you'll find my terms very reasonable, Pate," she said with a wink. "You would want to have the place in your own name, so in order to do that money has to change hands. That can be accomplished with as little as one dollar."

Pate laughed, his heart lighter in this last minute or two than it had been for the past twenty-four hours, not counting when he was with Dinah. That was different because he had been briefly transported to another world before crashing back into this one and being forced to face some harsh realities.

"I want you to set a better price for yourself than that, Julia," he told her, chuckling. "And I will sell a horse or two to cover renovation expenses. It's no hardship because why I got into horse breeding in the first place was to raise great animals that people would want to buy. Now that time has come. I have three that are all trained and ready to go right now."

Julia extended her hand, her eyes twinkling. "I promise the asking price will be more than a dollar, but it will be most fair. So, can we shake on it, Pate? It sounds as though I'm doing something wonderful for you, when in fact it solves a problem for me too. It lifts a big burden off my shoulders. Your father never considered leaving this place and said it was my decision what to do with it. I don't want to see it fall into rack and ruin and knowing it will be well looked after and thriving again will be worth the world to me. You'd be doing us a huge favour, too."

They happily shook hands, then briefly embraced.

Pate felt like a co-conspirator with Julia, and even though his father had hurt him, he wouldn't want to go against him. He was more hurt than angry at his father's announcement, but he wasn't accepting

Julia's offer out of revenge. He knew someday he would thank his pa for what he'd said to him. His father's words had been spoken in anger, but he'd accept the decision like a man and do what needed to be done.

"Naturally, Pate, I'm going to have to talk to your pa about it."

"I understand. He'll think you're babying me, but it doesn't matter. It's a legitimate offer and I'd be a fool not to accept if Pa's in agreement. Now you're sure this is what you want to do, and are not just trying to help me out? I want you to be certain."

Julia nodded happily. "I am one hundred per cent certain, and I know your pa will be too. I'm also delighted that we're solving a mutual problem in both our best interests. This is a very happy occasion."

Pate turned away again, resting his chin on his arms as he gazed back out over the paddock. "I hope so. Maybe when Pa's feeling better and isn't quite so angry with us all he'll be okay with it. Now, if you don't mind, I think I'll saddle up and ride out to take a look at your farm. While I'm out that way, I may as well stop in to see Brogan and Maggie and the children."

It seemed Julia couldn't stop smiling. "Good idea. I was out to the old place a month or so ago, after the roads dried up from all that terrible spring mud. Everything looked to be in good shape then, but you never know. Brogan says he rides up every now and again to check on the property, but

I think you dropping by today would be an excellent idea. You can look the place over, the grounds, the barns and the outbuildings. See what you have to fix and perhaps change. You could think up a new name for it, too. My father called it Maple Crest, and I was fond of that name, but it'll soon be yours, and you can come up with a name of your own."

"I like the name Maple Crest, Julia. I'll keep it if this thing goes through."

Minutes later, he headed back up the road. There'd be no running this time. A fast walk would do since it had turned out to be a pleasantly warm day. Jacko didn't seem in the mood to run anyway, so they ambled along at a leisurely pace. It occurred to him, too, that he'd be passing Colleen's home, so it might be a good idea to kill two birds with one stone. Make that three birds.

Apparently, he and Colleen needed to have another talk if she'd come all the way down to the farm looking for him. He was surprised she'd think he might have changed his mind. He knew how she felt, and it bothered him to hurt her like this, but a person had to follow their heart. Both parties in a relationship had to feel the same way, or it was no good. How was he to know that another woman would slip in so easily and steal his heart? He still couldn't believe it himself, but it had happened. All he could think about was Dinah.

He decided, as he rode along, to make Colleen first on his list this afternoon, get it over with, because it would no doubt be an unpleasant conversation. He was sure she was going to let him have it all over again, although she'd done a fine job of it on the way home from the picnic.

He rode into Colleen's yard and was relieved to see there was no one about, so he slid out of the saddle and looped the reins over the weathered grey hitching post. The Sullivan farm wasn't overly large, with a few cows, some chickens and a couple of horses. It being July already, he assumed her Pa and older brother were out making the season's first cut of hay. Which is exactly what Pate knew *he* should be doing instead of gallivanting up and down the road. He'd be late getting to it this year. There was too much going on at the moment, but he'd sharpen up the scythe at the first of next week and get started. He'd be doing it on his own this year, what with his father laid up.

"Have you come to apologize?" demanded Colleen, taking him by surprise as she came up behind him.

He spun on his heel and could tell by the tilt of her head that she was still upset with him. He knew Colleen. She was ready to accept his apology if he was inclined to make one, but not let him off the hook entirely. As sweet as she was, she could make a man squirm if you got on the wrong side of her.

"Is there someplace we can go and talk, where we won't be interrupted?" he asked.

She shrugged. "Same place that we usually go, over by the apple tree. There's no one around anyway. Ma is up at the neighbour's farm visiting, and Pa, Denny and Titus are up in the back field cutting hay. We could even go in the house if you wanted, spend some time inside where it's cooler."

"The bench by the apple tree is fine," he told her, and they walked there without talking.

He was no sooner seated when she demanded again whether or not he had come to say he was sorry for breaking up with her.

He shook his head, questioning his wisdom in even making the effort to talk to her again. It was because he held her in such high regard that he'd done so, but he also had no wish to reignite her anger. "No, Colleen, I haven't. Julia said you'd dropped by looking for me, and I'm not sure why, because I haven't changed my mind. I'm sorry that you haven't accepted it, but I don't know what else I can say."

Her breathing quickened; he could hear it.

"How would you feel if it were me who'd done it to you? Of course, I haven't accepted it. It was dropped on me so suddenly. I had been working on my trousseau, Pate, for when we got married. You know it was our intention to wed. You all but said so on more than one occasion."

"I didn't ask you to marry me, Colleen. It didn't go that far. Besides, you said you were breaking up with *me*."

"I didn't mean it, and you may not have proposed, but you knew darned well that's what I was expecting to have happen."

He couldn't argue with that, so remained silent.

"What did I do wrong? Tell me!"

He didn't see that one coming. "You didn't do anything wrong, Colleen."

"Why did you fall out of love with me then? How can that happen! Have you gone out with that bold tart from the picnic?"

He shifted his hips on the narrow bench. "I didn't come here to talk about Dinah."

"So that's her name. I'm assuming the answer is yes."

He could feel himself colouring. "I'm not going to talk about it, Colleen. I came to tell you I'm sorry it didn't work out, but it's definitely over between you and me."

He was shocked when she suddenly climbed onto his lap, quick as could be, and pressed her lips firmly against his in a provocative kiss. Now that was a twist. Colleen, of the heretofore chaste kisses, suddenly throwing herself at him. She was a good kisser, he had to give her that, but...

"Colleen, stop this now! It's not going to change anything," he said sharply, trying to pull away from her.

He stood up, and she had no alternative but to let go or fall unceremoniously on her backside.

Flushed, she pummeled him with her fists, her blows landing ineffectually on his broad chest. "You can't do this to me, Pate Kavenagh. I love you! I won't let you go, not to that red-headed hussy."

He caught hold of her wrists, holding them easily without force. "Don't start name-calling. What do you call what you just did? Climbing all over me like that. Hmmm?"

Yanking her wrists free, she backed away. "Doesn't it matter how I feel? That we've been sweethearts for over two years? You were mine, Pate, and she stole you away!"

Why had he come here! "It's over, Colleen. I didn't plan for this to happen, but it did, and I tried to do the honourable thing by ending it between us before I started seeing her. I didn't dally behind your back and make a fool of you. I can't help how I feel, but *it is* the way I feel. You'll always be special to me, but there'll be no wedding. I'd like to keep you for a friend, though."

"Friend! No, it will never be like that," she told him, tears shimmering on her lashes. "Do whatever you want then! You will anyway, whether I'm happy about it or not. Go to her! I won't bother you anymore. It's plain to see you've fallen for another, but don't you ever forget you broke my heart, and I will never forgive you for it. And don't worry, I won't come around to your farm anymore."

"I'm sorry, Colleen. So very sorry."

She was full-on crying now. "Go away, Pate. I don't know how you can live with yourself for being so cruel."

He moved to embrace her, but she flung herself away from him, and so he got back on his horse and left, his own heart heavy. It killed him to see her in such a state, the urge to take her in his arms and comfort her nearly overwhelming. His own sweet Colleen, he almost told himself, but that was a matter of habit. He had made his decision. He had chosen Dinah. Even with his limited experience, he couldn't imagine another woman exciting him the way Dinah did. But he didn't like to make people cry, especially not Colleen. She was like a ray of sunshine, everyone said so. Leave it up to him to break her heart.

It was about another three miles to Julia's old homestead. She had told him the stories of how grand it once was, her father, Henry Buckley, a proud, hard-working man who, along with her mother, had made their place one of the nicest along the road. They produced maple syrup and maple sugar, raised some of the finest chickens and turkeys around, and Henry sold milk, cream and fresh-made butter in his small wagon. The Buckleys were long gone now, and like any property, the farm required regular maintenance, or all too soon it would fall into disrepair. Still, there was a solid core to the place, and he couldn't believe his good fortune to have it offered to him.

He encouraged Jacko into a lope for the last quarter of a mile, and the big horse easily maintained the pace until they turned up the lane leading to the Buckley homestead. He'd seen it before, but he looked at it today with new eyes, seeing the possibilities. It was apparent at first sight that the fences needed some serious attention. Many of the posts had either rotted away or broken off under the siege of countless winters. But the pastures were large and the grass grew lush and deep on this balmy July afternoon.

He got off the horse and led it forward to the hitching rail and looped the reins. Jacko was a great horse, but he had a penchant for wandering, and he didn't need to be stranded if the horse took it into its head to trot on home without him. It was a habit he had so far been unable to break.

He set off for the barns. They, too, had been sturdily built and, outside of a few missing roof shingles, were in remarkably good condition. Same thing with the other outbuildings. The house needed some work done on the exterior. He knew Julia kept a few belongings inside, so he wouldn't go in until they came here together. He could barely contain his excitement. He felt it in every fibre of his being. He would be happy here. And now he would have a wonderful new home, hopefully by the end of the summer, to bring Dinah.

When he'd finished looking around, he headed back down the road to Brogan's to share his good news. They wouldn't exactly be next-door neighbours, there being a considerable distance between the two homesteads, but it would be close by country standards. Luke was twelve years old now, and he was sure he'd drop by from time to time to help him work with the horses. When he got old enough, he'd even hire him, although that was up to him to decide. If Maggie had her say, Luke would perhaps go on to higher education, but time would tell.

When he rode up the lane to Brogan's homestead his uncle met him in the yard, ready with a robust embrace once he'd dismounted and tied off his horse. Brogan had always been special to him.

Maggie, heavily pregnant with their third child, came up from the barn with an egg basket and three-year-old Jake by the hand, Luke following.

"You'll stay for supper, won't you?" asked Maggie. "We've got plenty. As a matter of fact, I've got cornbread in the oven and I've made a fine venison stew."

Pate laughed. "Actually, I could smell the cornbread as I came up the lane. If you're sure it won't be too much bother, I'll stay and take supper with you."

Maggie looked behind him. "Where's Colleen? I assumed she would be with you, the pair of you out for a ride on such a lovely summer day."

Pate's smile vanished. "Colleen and I aren't together anymore."

Luke plunged in. "Why not? Where did she go?"

Pate cleared his throat, ready for a lame explanation, when Maggie rushed to save the day. "Pate, you must be tired. Why don't you come in and wash up? Supper is ready to go on the table in another few minutes. Luke, would you mind setting out the extra crockery, after you've washed up."

The meal was indeed delicious, and there was plenty for second helpings. Both Brogan and Maggie were beyond thrilled when he told them about Julia offering him the Buckley homestead. He also told them about his father's health scare, omitting the difficult temper he'd been in both before and after the surgery. Some things didn't need telling.

* * *

By Wednesday night, Pate's desire to see Dinah had nearly reached a fever pitch, although he'd keep that information to himself. He'd given his father a wide path, and Julia hadn't said he'd asked for him, so it was better to leave sleeping dogs lie, as the old adage went. The most important thing was that Tabor was healing fast, his need for laudanum already diminishing considerably.

He couldn't help but think about how fortunate his father was to have Julia in his life. Not many women would be strong enough to withstand what she put up with.

Pate was awake in plenty of time the next morning. He crept out of bed before anyone else stirred, freshened himself, then slipped from the house as quietly as possible and headed for the barn. Jacko nickered when he heard him enter, and Pate soon had the big black saddled, and they were off. He felt bad denying the horse a good run. They'd have to accomplish that on the way back, but this morning he opted for the forest path and the shortcut that would lead him directly to the meadow. He'd give Dinah full credit for not being afraid to take her shortcut through the woods at this time of day, when animals were moving about, not yet settled down before the heat of the day.

He was glad to see her chestnut gelding already there when he rode into the clearing, his heart doing its familiar tattoo when he thought about being with her. Sliding out of the saddle, he tethered Jacko to the same dead tree and headed for the fallen log. But she was not there. Hmm.

"Dinah!" he called. "Where are you?"

There was no answer, so he began to search the immediate area but did not see her, nor did she answer him. Perplexed he stood at the edge of the meadow and trained his eyes on the surrounding countryside. Now where on earth had she gone off to?

Was she playing at some game in order to tempt him? No need to do such a thing because he was about as tempted as he was ever going to get. He couldn't be any more tempted if he tried.

Just then he heard a rustling sound in the nearby bushes, but still no Dinah. Could it be a bear? Was she all right? And then he heard her scream.

Chapter 6

His heart leapt in his chest as he started in the direction of her scream, but he didn't get far when she bounded out of the woods completely naked. He hit the brakes as she scurried over to him and threw her arms around him. Had she taken leave of her senses?

"There's a bee after me!" she shrieked, jumping away when indeed one of the fuzzy black and yellow insects flew dangerously close to an exposed shoulder, no doubt attracted by the rosewater she was wearing. "I think he already stung me, in the back. Look..."

He shooed the bee away, then looked as she pointed to the offended part of her anatomy. Her backside. A closer inspection did not reveal any sting marks.

"I think he came close, is all," Pate told her, trying but not succeeding at stifling a laugh. This was hilarious!

As appealing as the vision that stood before him was, it was not what he expected to come charging out of the woods at him.

"Are you sure it's gone, Pate? I don't want to get stung."

"No, it's long gone," he said, checking the air around them to verify his claim. "Why are you in the woods with no clothes on, Dinah? It's on the cool side this morning for you to be stripping off like that."

"Isn't that what we plan to do anyway?" she asked, having prettily recovered and was now smiling up at him. "Why wait? And the air's not cool. It's refreshing. It feels good on my skin. I get so fevered thinking about you. I got here early to get ready."

"Get ready?"

"Look at my hair. Do you like it?" she asked, waving a hand over her curls where she'd threaded buttercup blossoms, and it did look mighty fetching. "I'm playing the part of a wood nymph. It was a surprise."

He spread his hands. "You succeeded, Dinah. You look stunning. Every man should have a surprise like this first thing in the morning."

Each time he saw her, he was more enamoured with the wonders of Dinah. What other woman would even think of doing such a thing? Certainly not Colleen. That wasn't necessarily a terrible thing, he thought, defending not out of habit this time but natural inclination. Not all men wanted their woman to be running around in the nude, especially out in a field.

"So?" she asked, her smile lighting up her face. "Do I look like a wood nymph? A mythological spirit of nature? I'm supposed to be an alluring maiden who inhabits the forest."

"You look like all that and more," he told her, although he had no idea what in the world she was talking about.

Could be she'd had a touch of laudanum, but he quickly dismissed the notion. No, Dinah was what she claimed to be, a free spirit, but who was he to complain when paradise awaited?

He couldn't pull his gaze away. My, but she was a striking woman, or girl, more like, seeing as how she wasn't yet twenty. Long of limb, full bosomed and shapely in all respects, her crowning feature was her fiery hair that cascaded in a flaming waterfall to her waist. He couldn't think of anything better to look upon than her. He wouldn't mind starting every day like this.

Coming up close to him again, she slowly dispensed with the buttons on his shirt, then slid it off over his shoulders. Reaching up she removed his hat and tossed it to the side, running her fingers through his jet black hair. Next she fixed her attention on his trousers and he let her do as she chose, stepping out of them once she'd freed the buttons and sent them on their way. His boots were already on the pile.

Smiling invitingly she took a step away and he held out his hands to her.

"No!" she said, holding back. "I want to look at you. I have read about Satyrs, the mythological nature spirit from the woods, a

Greek god, but I haven't seen one in the living flesh. You are the male counterpart to my femininity. If there were an artist nearby bent on capturing the very essence of nature itself, he would have already begun to render our images on canvas. But then no one would believe he had merely painted what stood before him. They would think he had imagined such sweethearts so perfectly suited. We are the ideal halves of each other, Pate, and together we make a perfect whole."

He was spellbound. Not one to drink, he was sure now it would be a waste of time because he couldn't imagine experiencing anything more intoxicating than this enchanting creature. He felt like a drowning man as he watched her eyes devour him, from one end to the other.

When they came together minutes later in their private enclave, it was explosive, but when the dust finally cleared, he was glad once again that he had exercised caution. Creating a child between two people who were so obviously in love was an amazing thing. That was certainly true with Brogan and Maggie, yet he held that part of himself back, his father's wise advice at the forefront of his mind. Not that Pa felt his life was ruined by becoming a father. He'd assured him that was definitely not the case, but fruit picked too soon without the opportunity to properly ripen was not the natural order of things. No matter how swept away two lovers might be, he knew a relationship had to have a chance to mature before they created a child together.

They lay there in each other's arms, spent, and presently fell asleep. The sun had crept higher in the sky by the time they stirred, and their lovemaking now was unhurried and gentle. It had occurred to him more than once that she seemed quite experienced for one so young, but she brought him such pleasure he was not of a mind to question it.

Later, Pate pulled himself up on one elbow as he looked down into those huge emerald pools. "How did I get so lucky?" he asked as he teased wispy curls that lay on her forehead. "I can't believe I thought I was happy before you came into my life. A man would be a fool not to fall in love with you."

She studied him appreciatively. "I could say the same about you. You're every woman's dream, Pate. Didn't that girl you were with at the picnic try to do what I do to please you? You were her man, yet she let you slip right through her fingers."

He stiffened as she ventured into territory that was off-limits.

"Did I say something wrong?" she asked, looking up at him innocently.

"We're not going to talk about her. She's a fine girl, so let's keep her out of this."

"Oops, I guess I struck a tender spot. Sorry. Don't tell me you're still going out with her. *Are* you?" she asked sharply.

"I said we're not going to talk about her, so let's change the subject."

She was frowning now. "All right, fine, we won't talk about her, but I do want to know if you're seeing her. I believe I have every right to ask you that question. I do not like to share."

He willed himself to relax. "You're the one I'm keeping company with at the present time. I wouldn't think someone who looks like you, Dinah, would need to be jealous of another woman. You're by far the most attractive lady I've ever seen, which I know I've told you several times. So you win, satisfied?"

She smiled possessively, reaching up to trail her hand over a muscular shoulder. "Not where you're concerned. I simply can't get enough of you, Pate Kavenagh. Being with you is so pleasurable."

Leaning forward, he slid long fingers into her hair on both sides of her face, bringing her closer as his lips sought to claim hers. "I feel the same way," he said before kissing her soundly. "Now, as delicious as you are," he whispered, finally breaking contact, "I have to get back to the farm. My pa is recovering from his surgery, and there are chores to be done. You can come and help me if you want to, forest nymph."

She giggled. "Forest nymphs don't muck out horse stalls. I ride, I don't do the dirty work."

Her answer nettled him, but he let it pass without comment. He knew she was a city girl before he came to the meadow with her. He wasn't going to chastise her for something she wasn't accustomed to. Dinah Gladstone was spoiled, but that only added to her charm. If she were to become snowed under with drudgery, she wouldn't be the free spirit he loved, so he wouldn't do anything to dampen that enthusiasm. Today, a wood nymph, who would she be when they met again? A fairy queen? The female ruler of all fairies? The possibilities were endless and very enticing.

He smiled lazily. "No, I don't guess they do, but whatever you said I was…"

"Satyrs, a Greek god, the mythological spirit of the woods."

"He does muck out stalls, as you put it, and everything else that needs to get done. Such as in a few days, I'll start cutting our winter hay. Now I've got wonderful news that I haven't even shared with you yet. I hope to buy a homestead. Soon, I should have my very own farm, Dinah. It needs a bit of work, which I'll take care of in the next few weeks, but it's a grand place and you can come and visit me there."

She pulled her hand away. "You recall I'm only here for the summer, correct? But if you're all moved in before I have to go back to Boston, then I certainly will come by. But I like lying with you in this meadow. It's so romantic. I like the idea of being here with you, before most of the world even comes awake. And I adore all this sunny weather.”

“It’s nice to see the sun,” he agreed, “but that’s not good news for us farmers. We need lots of sunny weather, but we also need rain, and hopefully, we’ll get some before too long. The lack of rainwater is hard on crops such as hay and also on well water. Our well ran dry a few years ago, and it was a real chore hauling water from away. But, a person does what they have to do to survive.”

He could tell he’d lost her attention, but like a lot of city people, she didn’t understand that the food or meat on their table didn’t miraculously appear out of nowhere. Someone had to grow it, raise it. Then he remembered she’d said she would return to Boston. He was sure she’d told him she was staying in Sackville indefinitely. He decided not to press her about it, though. Plans changed, and they could just as well change back. When she realized how much in love with him she was, she’d see things differently. Isn’t that the way it worked? When two people were in love, they wanted to be together, so he wouldn’t waste any time worrying about it. Right now, he had to get back to the farm.

* * *

His heart was soaring on the way home, wings spread, like the raven that flew high in the sky above him. He took out his watch for

109

a peek and was stunned to see it was almost ten o'clock. He groaned. That would mean Julia was down at the barn seeing to the animals, and he urged Jacko into a lope to cover the remaining distance to the farm at a much faster pace.

Sure enough, he could hear the scrape of the shovel as he swung out of the saddle and looped his reins over the hitching post.

"I'm sorry to be so late, Julia," he apologized when he went inside. "Here, give me that shovel and go on back up to the house. You're busy enough without coming down here to work, other than the milking."

"We could hear the horses all the way up to the house, pawing in their stalls. Your father called down to me and asked why they were still in the barn so late. So I scooted down and let them out and filled their mangers and water tubs. And since I was already down here..."

Pate thanked her as he reached for the shovel, and she passed it to him.

"There's no harm done, Pate. I figure you've got more pressing business. This morning wouldn't have something to do with pretty Colleen Sullivan, would it?"

He began to scoop up manure. "No, it wouldn't," he answered her noncommittally.

"Oh," she said seemingly taken aback. "I was hoping you two had talked out your differences yesterday when you went over there."

"I know how much the family likes her, but I'm afraid it's over between us. Sorry."

"You don't owe us any apologies, Pate. It's none of our business. I'm sorry I stepped in it. Anyway, I'm going up to the house to get lunch underway. I've saved you some pan-fried potatoes and beef on a plate in the stove's warming closet. It's ready whenever you are."

He was deep in thought as Julia took her leave. Why hadn't he said anything to her about Dinah? What was the big secret? He knew it wasn't so much an official secret, as it was the unspoken necessity of secretiveness. It didn't feel right somehow to talk about Dinah. Meeting in the meadow and what they did there was not for the telling to anyone. That was their business. He was a grown man and did not feel obligated in any way to account for his time like some schoolboy.

He knew he was in love with Dinah, if that's what being in love felt like. He could hardly wait to see her again, and they had the usual date set for tomorrow at daybreak. But what then? It somehow didn't feel like a proper fit to bring her home to meet his family. For one thing, what would happen when the outspoken Dinah met his pa? It could be a disaster. For another thing, the time wasn't right. They barely knew each other, other than in the Biblical sense, so it was much too soon to say they were in love. Truth to tell, he couldn't think for the life of him when *would* be a good time. He recognized that with an odd sense of disquiet. It settled deep in his midsection and wouldn't go away.

But like Dinah had told him, he did have a tendency to overthink things. Embrace the moment, a little voice in a corner of his brain told him. Why try to label everything, explain it? If he was enjoying the company of a beautiful woman on *her* terms, he should do just that. Not think everything to death.

* * *

It had been a hot night and was still uncomfortably warm early the next morning. It felt as though rain might not be far off, but perhaps that was wishful thinking. When dawn broke, clouds hunkered dark and threatening on the horizon, obliterating the sun. Given the cloying warmth of the air, it felt as though there'd be thundershowers before the day was out.

* * *

Tabor spent a restless night, awake and asleep more times than he could count. He heard Pate leaving as he had been doing lately before dawn, and wondered where the young man was off to. He wouldn't ask, though. Pate's life was his own. He would not treat his son the way he had been treated.

His side was bothering him this morning, so he took a slug of laudanum from the bottle Julia had left on the bedside table. She was already downstairs getting breakfast started. He lay there for a while until he felt sleep begin to pull at him again. Closing his eyes, he gave in, and that was his last thought before he drifted off. He was drawn into a dream world where his father, Bart Kavenagh, ruled his sons with an iron fist, meting out what he called justice for any wrong, either real or imagined, in the cruelest of ways.

He was back in the old house in Hamilton County, Upstate New York, still a boy. He could hear the door handle turning, smell the whiskey on his father's breath when he came into the boys' room to make sure one of them hadn't run away. Tabor heard him make that ridiculous statement to his mother countless times, although in reality, he had far more sinister plans.

"Not tonight," Tabor yelled at his father as the nightmare deepened. He leapt from the bed and tried to run from the room. He could hear his own strangled cry as the old man got a death grip on the back of his nightshirt.

"No, Pa!" he screamed, running, running, but his father had the speed of a racehorse, the fire of a dragon and the strength of ten men as he fastened onto him more securely and pulled him back to the bed. "No, Pa!" he screamed again, fighting, twisting and turning. And then his father left him, grabbing Brogan, punting him across the room, his younger brother hollering his head off as he crashed against the wall.

"No, Pa!" Tabor shouted again, but his father was on him, raining down blows, smashing his fist into his face, tearing at his hair as he fought back valiantly. Knives, dozens of them, exploded into the room, imprisoning him as flames licked at him from beneath the bed.

"No, Pa!" he screamed, pushing at the knives, blood running freely as he fought to save Brogan, and yes, Garrett, who was watching from under the bed in this fiendish dream.

"I'll kill you all," his father screamed. "You will all be dead. I have no sons."

"No, Pa!" Tabor pleaded, but now his bed had shrunk to a tiny sliver that prevented him from hiding beneath it, Brogan now sitting in the corner of the ceiling, crying. Garrett had pulled the bed in upon him. Trapped! They would never get him out. More blood. More fire. And that awful smell of whiskey on Black Bart's breath. Oceans of it as he grabbed handfuls of bedclothes and tore them free, but he was in the middle of it all with nowhere to go. Hands grabbing. Cold steel. Knives everywhere. Terror. He had to save Brogan. Garrett was gone, the best hider of them all.

"No, Pa! No!"

Tabor woke up, drenched in sweat as Julia rushed into the room. "My heavens, Tabor. What is wrong? You were shouting. You're shaking. Are you all right?"

The nightmare felt as though it was still upon him, terror in the darkened room of his childhood, the whiskey breath, the face always much too close. No way out. Nowhere to run, although in his mind he had tried to escape a hundred times, and a hundred times he had been unable to. Dread, as old as the oldest mountain in creation, washed over him, his breath coming in shallow spasms. He felt as though he couldn't breathe. His hands balled into fists at his side, and he brought them down with violent force against the mattress.

Julia sat down on the edge of the bed. "Tabor, you're scaring me. Whatever is wrong? I think you've had a night terror, although it's been some time since you've experienced one. Are you all right now?"

Tabor was breathing heavily, and she could feel his heart racing beneath her fingers on his chest. Thankfully, he wasn't thrashing like he had in the past, which was a relief. He didn't need to tear his stitches and end up sick all over again.

There was one common thread to these night terrors, and that was his yelling: "No, Pa!" She knew his father was a tyrant, but no one knew to what extent, only that his sons, and Garrett, had suffered greatly because of him.

She realized to her astonishment that Tabor was weeping. Oh, the poor man. What torture was he reliving in those horrible dreams?

Sliding onto the bed beside him she snuggled up close and laid her arm across his chest in the best facsimile of a hug she could manage under the circumstances. "Tabor, tell me about your dream. What happened? Do you think that if you talked about it, it might help?"

He continued to weep softly, and she hoped she was doing the right thing by trying to hold him in this way. She felt he'd be embarrassed by his tears, so it was difficult to know how to handle this. As they lay there in the darkness, the shutters closed, she felt as though a barrier had been breached, and perhaps her husband could let go of some of the pain he'd carried around for most of his life. Perhaps it was the laudanum that had brought on one of his night terrors this time. Perhaps it might loosen his tongue.

She waited. She wouldn't push him. If he wanted to share anything with her, he would do it on his own terms. She wouldn't pester him about it. Tabor was not the type of man to be pushed anyway. If and when he felt ready to share any of his nightmarish past, he might do so.

She jumped when his anguish was verbalized in a loud cry, and it was an awful sound, like suffering that had festered for a lifetime. Was he close to excavating any of the horror he had suffered at the hands of his father?

Still, she held him, and then he began to speak. "He came to our room every night," he said so quietly it sounded like the roll of distant thunder. "He told me I was his favourite, although I knew he only said that for one reason. I was his Tabor boy. I fought him as best I could, but he held a knife to my throat. Threatened to kill me."

"Oh, Tabor," Julia whispered on a sob. "What a nightmare. The pain alone…"

"That's what it was, a nightmare, and the pain *was* terrible. I can't stand the stink of whiskey to this day. His breath was always sour with it. You've seen those scars on my neck. He put them there. Lots of nights, he was almost drunk when he made his visit, although it didn't stop him. He hurt Brogan, too, and Garrett. He especially hated Garrett because our mother whored around and brought him home in her belly, but he usually came for me."

"And you've been suffering with those nightmares all these years."

"My nightmare had been going on since I was old enough to remember. Brogan was three when he first started with him, Garrett younger. I saw everything. I vowed he would not hurt them again, so I let it be me. I was Tabor Boy and that seemed to be enough. It was the only way I could protect Brogan and Garrett, but I still fought against it."

She didn't even try to keep the emotion from her voice. "Tabor, that is so heartbreaking."

He didn't reply, and she wondered if perhaps he was finished sharing those monstrous memories. Those poor little boys.

Not much wonder her husband had such a rough exterior, it was self-protection. If he was crusty enough, no one could get close enough to hurt him ever again. Tabor was a handsome man, big and strong, and she was drawn to his quiet strength. But she'd also known he lived with something torturous, and she'd assumed it was because of the violent way in which his father had died at the hands of assailants. That would be enough to haunt anyone. Brogan seemed lighter somehow, and Garrett, although not undamaged, but then again, they'd had their older brother to look out for them. Perhaps Brogan and Garrett wouldn't remember, and the Tabor she knew would not tell them what he had endured on their behalf.

"How could my mother not know what was happening in that room?" Tabor asked, seemingly ready to continue unburdening himself.

She was thankful the floodgates had been opened. He needed to get some of the poison out because it was choking him to death. She couldn't believe this was happening, and she prayed a silent prayer that he would continue to allow it to come. If she had to lie here all day and listen to him, she would. She wasn't sure what to say next, afraid that if she said the wrong thing, he would retreat behind his walls again.

"She knew! She heard!" he said, answering his own question. "But she never came, and I hated her for it. It could be because he threatened her too, and she was afraid, but she had a duty to protect her children from him. She went off and saved herself, then came home pregnant for her trouble. When she did try to help, it was too little too late in my opinion. She should have been stronger. I couldn't do it all by myself."

Again he fell silent, and she let it settle around them until he felt strong enough to carry on, if that was to be the case.

She refrained from trying to please him with empty platitudes such as, "I know your mother loved you." She couldn't say something like that. It wasn't her right, even though it may have been true. She hadn't lived through the horror that was Bart Kavenagh. This man lying beside her had, and it was his story to tell.

When the silence stretched into long minutes, she thought he was finished emptying his soul, but it wasn't so. There was more. Worse.

"We came to Canada from Hamilton County after some thugs killed my father, stabbed him to death. We came here to escape those men, and we've been hiding here ever since."

"That was a wise move, Tabor. Wasn't it good that your mother wanted to finally protect her family? I believe I would have done the same thing."

He seemed to have calmed himself. He had stopped trembling, the effects of the nightmare wearing off. And hopefully it was cathartic. Instead, he spoke in a hollow, distant voice that was most unnerving. It was as though it was coming from a great distance, and she supposed it was. It was a voice that had waited many years to be heard.

"That whole story is nothing but a fairytale, Julia. My father kept the company of criminals, it's true. But there was never anyone who came to murder an unsuspecting Bart Kavenagh, although he deserved to die in the most painful way possible."

She was perplexed. "Your father wasn't stabbed to death?"

"That's how he died, all right. I know. I'm the one who killed him."

Chapter 7

Julia was thunderstruck, momentarily speechless. She was thankful it was dark in the room. Her husband had confessed to murder to her, but straight on the heels of that, she knew Tabor was not a violent man. The experience must have been horrifying, evidence of the insufferable burden he'd been carrying all these many years. That explained everything, and she immediately felt ashamed. The hatefulness she had accused him of was no more than pain, a deep and terrible scar on his soul.

She tightened her arm around his shoulders. "How did it happen?" she finally found the strength to ask, hoping she wasn't intruding too far.

"It wasn't planned, Julia, although I will not lie. It was always in the back of my mind. I know it's not easy for someone who wasn't involved to understand, but you just want the bad things to stop happening. I despised him, but in another way, I loved him because he was my father. I guess I loved what I wanted him to be, how I wanted him to act toward us."

He fell silent, and she did not feel inclined to press him. He would speak about it in his own good time, and possibly never again, but as long as the words kept flowing, she would try not to get in the way of them. She was aware her heartbeat had quickened and willed herself to relax. The last thing she wanted was to have him think he had frightened her, or worse than that, repulsed her. She did feel frightened. Not of him, but of what was being spewed into the room. Most of all, she was confused, but not repulsed by his confession. Not after what he'd told her about what Bart Kavenagh did to his children.

She realized she was holding her breath when he began to speak again, and she released it slowly.

"I stabbed my father, just as you've heard was done," he said after long minutes. "Some would say it was an accident, but my mother knew that once the police and courts got hold of it they might think differently. She said she didn't want our dirty laundry aired for the world to see, that's how she put it. That told me she knew all along what he'd been up to when we were kids. She saved my life by concocting the lie about how he'd been killed, but I hated her for not stopping him. Apparently, her lie was all too easy to believe because my father had been to prison more than once and was involved in shady dealings. He was not a good man, and not just because of what he did at home."

He paused again. She guessed that was the only way he could tell the story. Take his time because she knew instinctively it must be a painful excising. Daylight was beginning to sneak in through the shutter seams at the window, but she made no move to open them. This, somehow, was a recounting meant for dark spaces. Say it, and then leave it there and be ready for a new day. Let the light back in. But the day was already overcast, dismal, gunmetal grey clouds hanging low in the sky, heavy with rain. And so the perfect stage seemed to be set for the final chapter of this dreadful tale.

"I can remember it like it was yesterday," he said, as he punctured the silence in the room. "When I grabbed him, he pulled his knife and slashed the air in front of me with it, threatening me. He had that look in his eyes that I knew all too well. He meant business. I knew in that moment it was him or me, and I was determined it wasn't going to be me. Not if I could help it. I was nineteen, younger and faster than he was, and when he came at me again, I managed to wrestle the knife away from him. I know I could have simply wounded him when he lunged at me again, his hand on the knife too. And then it was against *my* chest, but I managed to turn it at the last second and pushed toward him. It went in to the hilt. He looked at me, dumbfounded, like he never expected that someone would beat him at his own game. And then the air went out of him.

Without a word, he collapsed on the floor. There wasn't even any blood, but I could tell by the look on his face that my father was dead."

"What did you do then?" she asked, curiosity overriding caution.

"Ma had heard the ruckus and come in. She saw what happened. She didn't ask how it started, because she probably already knew it would come to that someday. She told me to get hold of his shoulders, and she took his feet, and we carried him outside the front door of the small house where we lived and laid him on the step. She told me to keep my mouth shut, then she ran for the constable and said some bad men had come to our house, and when her husband answered the door, they killed him. No one knew that the knife in him was his own. He still had that surprised look on his face when the police came. I remember him telling me my Pa was dead, and to go back inside so I wouldn't have to see him that way.

"There was a big fuss about it at the time, people saying they knew Black Bart would meet a hard end someday because of the kind of life he'd lived, involved in crime like he was. The police didn't seem to care, no doubt glad he was off their hands. But Ma wasn't taking any chances. She told the constable that her husband had made a lot of enemies and that she was leaving the county because she no longer felt safe. That whoever stabbed her husband might come back for her or her children, and he agreed with her. She was good at putting on a face, tears and all, but I think she was as relieved as the rest of us that he was dead. We buried him the next day and then left for Canada before anyone could start asking questions."

Again, Julia's curiosity got the better of her. "Brogan didn't see it happen?"

"He and Garrett were helping a neighbour load wood down the road. There was only me and Ma. Pate was four years old at the time and I'd already put him to bed."

Her breath caught in her throat. "Oh no, Tabor. Your father wasn't…"

"He was trying to get at Pate. It was his crying that made me go in to check on him. I didn't even know my father was home. He must have come in the back way, but he knew what time I put Pate to bed every night."

"Did he harm him?"

"He didn't get that far, but I tell you, Julia, something tore loose in me when I saw what he was trying to do. Not my son! I would protect that child with my life."

"So Pate saw everything? Even the stabbing?"

"He was half asleep, and I don't believe he remembers. He's not spoken about it and of course *I* never will. So there you have it, Julia, your husband is a murderer."

She raised up on one elbow to face him in the darkness. "You are nothing of the kind, Tabor Kavenagh. You are a good man."

"That's not the way I see it."

"Surely you understand it was more or less self-defence."

"More or less."

"It was a knife fight, it could have gone either way, couldn't it?"

"I suppose, but...."

"You didn't prey on your father, lie in wait for him to come into the room. You didn't plan to do it. In my mind, that's what a murderer does."

"A big part of me wanted him dead! For as long as I can remember, all I'd wanted was for him to leave and not come back."

"And another part of you loved him. I can't imagine how confused you must have been growing up. I know he was your father, but he deserved what he got. Any man who would do such a thing to his own children, attempt to do to his grandchild should have been horsewhipped, or face a firing squad."

"But as terrible as he was, I took him away from all of us. I didn't even cry when he died. If I'd been a better son, things might have been different, because when he wasn't trying to flatter me, he'd tell me over and over what a bad boy I was. He must have said that to me a thousand times, and I believed him."

"And what child wouldn't!" she said with emotion. "From your account of the whole sordid mess, he tortured you for years. You bore the brunt of his evil ways. You were a child, Tabor, and you suffered greatly because of him."

He was silent for a moment. "He was plenty hard on Brogan and Garrett, too. He told me once he'd kill Garrett if he got the chance. Called him the bastard, and turned Brogan and me against him. You know, besides us, there wasn't one single person at Pa's funeral. Nobody liked him because he was no good."

"It's so sad I can hardly take it all in."

"Most of the time I think I'm just like him. He used to call me a chip off the old block."

She could make out his face in the shadows, and he turned miserable eyes on her as she spoke. "Tabor Kavenagh, you are nothing like him. You may resemble him, but that's the only thing you share. You are an honourable man. I will admit that you are hard to get along with at times," and she was relieved to see a tiny smile pull at his lips, "but now I completely understand why. You have been living with a horrendous secret, but I hope you can see by its telling here today you were not to blame. He was going after your son! He had to be stopped. He pulled a knife on *you*, and I believe if he'd had the upper hand that night you wouldn't be lying here today. It is unfortunate it had to be that way, but he left you with no alternative. I can tell you one thing, I would have acted in the very same way had it been me. He may not have lived even as long as he did. He's the one who put himself in that situation. I don't think there's a man alive who would have showed the restraint you did for as long as you did. The blame is entirely his."

"I tried to talk to him, you know. Warned him, but he laughed. I think he thought he couldn't be touched. He loved having a despicable reputation. He was the worst kind of bully."

Julia ran the back of her hand over his forehead in a soothing gesture. "You know, Tabor, I didn't know your mother but I wonder how strong I would have been against a man like that."

He sighed, sounding exhausted. "I've asked myself that too, but Julia, what kind of a mother knows something like that is happening to her children, and lets it go on? I think she was glad to have him away from her. I think it was as simple as that, as awful as that sounds."

She thought for a moment. "You could be right, but we'll never know. He certainly was depraved. Did she try to make it up to you? Talk to you about it?"

"We were not a family of talkers. The least said the better was how we went about things. Sweep everything under the mat and leave it there out of sight."

"To fester. Poison needs to be cleaned out, a wound cannot heal otherwise."

She could see by his expression he was thinking about what she'd said. "Funny thing. I wasn't planning to tell you about any of this. If it weren't for that nightmare... But

I guess stuff's going to come out eventually whether you want it to or not. So, how do you feel about me now that you know all of this?"

She looked surprised. "How do I feel? I feel enormous sympathy for what you went through as a child, the nightmare you all endured for so many years."

"I don't want to be felt sorry for."

"I don't feel sorry for you as a man," she said, lying back down beside him. "I feel terrible about the circumstances, what your entire family was put through because of your father. As far as you are concerned, I admire your strength, how you've carried on all these years, and raised a fine son. You're good and kind and I couldn't love you more, Tabor Kavenagh. It took a lot of courage to have this conversation today, and what I'm feeling most at this moment is gratitude that I have such a wonderful man for my husband."

He sighed deeply, wearily. "You won't think I'm so wonderful when I tell you I would have lied to that constable if he'd asked me anything about my father's death. I guess I lied by not telling him how it actually happened, but I was not going to hang because of that man, my father."

"In my mind, it was self-defence, pure and simple. He started it. You didn't have a knife."

"They wouldn't have believed me, Julia. Our family had a terrible reputation there, too, just like here, thanks to my father and my mother. No, I had a child to raise, I couldn't take the chance."

"Tabor, that is one of the worst stories I've ever heard, so unfair. It's also grossly unfair the way some people are around here toward the Kavenaghs."

"We were new to the area back in 1857, and people thought we were strange because we kept to ourselves. They made the rest up I guess, except for Brogan's shenanigans when he was a lot younger. Anyway, we are who we are."

"You don't have to apologize to anyone," she said kissing his cheek, "and my sterling opinion of you stands."

He smiled. "I'm going to try to be different, Julia. Not so angry all the time. When I'm talking, or yelling, it's like I'm listening to my father and the way he spoke to *us*, and that makes me even madder. But I'm going to try to show you how much I love you, do a better job of it. Matter of fact if I didn't have this sore side, I *would* show you, but I don't want to bust anything open and have to go through all that again."

She smiled lovingly. "We'll save that for another day. You look tired, Tabor."

"Hmmm," he agreed, his eyes already closed. Within minutes, he was snoring softly.

* * *

The meeting in the meadow was to be of much shorter duration this morning. It looked like the heavens might open at any time, and Dinah didn't relish the prospect of getting drenched on the ride back to Sackville. Pate didn't care. In his opinion a little rain didn't hurt anything.

"Let's sit and hold each other," he suggested when he sat down beside her on the fallen log. "Since we're only going to be here for a few minutes, I mean."

She looked up at him impishly. "You have no wish to pick the luscious fruit from the vine this morning, Pate?"

He laughed. "The fruit is luscious as you put it, but do you really want to lie with me in wet grass?"

"We could be quick about it," she suggested, then laughed that happy laugh of hers.

He pulled her against him. "Not today, sweetie. This is going to be a day for sitting," he said, resting his chin on top of her head.

She smelled like rosewater, and he had grown to love the scent of it on her. It did make him want to divest her of her garments, and he liked the fact that she wore fewer clothes than most women did, or he assumed they did. Outside of what she'd had on at the picnic she didn't seem to have a predilection for corsets, hooped crinolines and voluminous petticoats like he'd seen in a magazine. He knew. He'd undressed her more than once and there was just a chemise under her outer garments. Perhaps she dressed lightly because of the activity they would be engaged in, but knowing her as well as he did, she would seek to flout convention at every turn. Whatever, he liked her precisely the way she was, but he appreciated what was under those clothes even better.

He was tempted to take her up on her suggestion to make love. His body was certainly in favour of it. However, his brain was in charge this morning, and it seemed right to leave things as they were at the moment. All the more to look forward to next time.

"All right, Pate," she said, "but I hope you're not getting tired of me and what we do here in the meadow because it's very special to me. But I do have a bone to pick with you."

That took him by surprise. "Oh? And what would that be?"

She sighed and leaned more heavily against him, "I haven't had a decent night's sleep since I met you, and I'm getting tired of it. Excuse the pun."

"The what? Why haven't you been able to sleep?"

"Because all I do is think about you, silly. You're on my mind constantly."

"We could spend more time together outside of this meadow," he suggested, wondering when that would be because farm chores took up most of his days and into the evenings, and he would begin work on his new property before the end of the summer.

Haying would also occupy a good portion of his time over the next few weeks. However, would he manage to do his early-morning chores, be at the meadow with Dinah, and get to the hayfields before late morning? It was a pity there was only one of him.

She sighed. "I wish that were possible, Pate, I do, but I, too, am simply kept busy at home. For example, I'm helping Aunt Emmaline this afternoon prepare for the church bazaar. There is a lot of baking to be done, but the next few days are going to be spent collecting and pricing items for the rummage sale. That's a popular item on the agenda."

"What's a church bazaar?"

"You don't know what a church bazaar is?"

He felt she was laughing at him again, but decided to ignore it. "No, I don't. I'm not one for going down to Sackville much."

"They have them everywhere. This one is being held to raise money for the missionary society. There's going to be a silent auction and they're even putting on a lunch this year. I am good at making pies, so I've promised to bake no less than twenty pies if you can believe it. I'm not afraid of a good challenge."

He thought of how proud he'd be to walk in with Dinah on his arm. He could buy a new pair of trousers and get Julia to wash and iron his best shirt.

"I'd like to take you to that bazaar, Dinah. It sounds like it'd be a lot of fun."

"Ahhh, you can't! What I mean to say is that I'll be working as a volunteer that day, selling pies. I seem to recall you telling me you try to avoid stuff like that."

She was right, of course, but he'd make an exception for her. He could get dressed up and go and buy a pie or something, talk to her a bit, then leave. The important thing, if he was being honest, was to let people know she belonged to him.

"Forget what I told you at the picnic," he chuckled. "I'll make an exception for you. I wouldn't mind having one of your pies. I could even help. What do you say to that?"

"Thanks, Pate, that sounds like a wonderful idea, but I know how busy you are, and I'll be kept hopping that day too. It won't be possible to stop and chat. I'm afraid Aunt Emmaline wouldn't stand for that at all. A dereliction of duty is what she'd call it, and I don't want to get on the bad side of her with them being so kind to me. It's not my doing, you understand. So it's best to leave me to my work. I don't like to mix the two. There'll be other opportunities. You do understand, don't you?"

He sighed, then regarded her skeptically. "I understand you don't want me there."

She swiveled around until her cheek lay against his. "You're right, I don't, but for no other reason than I do not like to put my private life on display for all the world to see. What we have here between the two of us is very important to me. Putting it out for public scrutiny feels gauche and awful. You're mine, Pate, and I want to keep you all to myself. Is that so terrible? Call me selfish, but I don't want to share you, not with anybody, and certainly not at a church bazaar with all those old biddies sticking their long noses in. You don't know how protective my aunt and uncle are! They'd start asking questions. Is that the man you're sneaking off to see every morning? My uncle could very well forbid me the use of one of his horses. He's funny that way. Besides, I won't apologize for wanting to keep my treasure all to myself."

He relaxed, and when she began to tease him with her lips, the feeling of uneasiness slowly fell away. He loved what she said and the way she said it. This gorgeous woman sitting on his lap had just finished telling him he was all hers. It was about the best few words he'd ever heard, and he groaned as the kiss deepened.

* * *

He made it home about a half hour before the storm hit, and he hoped she did as well, otherwise she'd get that dreaded soaking. He smiled. If she did, it was nobody's fault but her own because he'd given in to her pleading and spent the remainder of their time together this

135

morning in the tall grass. How had he thought it wouldn't be a good idea?

After he finished unsaddling Jacko and cooling him after the fast ride home, he set about the rest of his barn chores before running through the rain up to the house.

"Hi, Pate," Julia called to him cheerfully. "Hope you didn't get too wet."

"Nah, a few drops on my way up here. It's good to see the rain though, we sorely needed it."

"That we did. I have your breakfast in the warming closet on the stove, and when you finish eating, your father would like to speak with you. I was up there a few minutes ago, and he asked you to come up after you'd eaten."

He regarded Julia speculatively. He had planned to avoid his father until he was in a better frame of mind. The last thing he wanted this morning was to have another fight with him.

"He's not feeling poorly again, is he?"

"No, he's coming along very well. He says the pain from the surgery is less every day, which is good because he doesn't want to take any more laudanum. I'm glad. I think the less he takes of that kind of stuff, the better."

"Good then. I'll eat then go up and see what else he's found to growl at me about," he said with a grin as he retrieved his plate and sat down at the table.

Julia was a good cook. She was one of those people who made anything taste good with the right amount of salt and pepper, and a lot of practised know-how.

* * *

The window shutter now open, he could see that his father's eyes were closed when he entered the bedroom, so he turned to leave.

"I'm awake, Pate. Come on in, I want to talk to you."

The last conversation they'd had stuck in his craw, when his father had kicked him off the farm, although he'd tried to put a positive spin on it to make himself feel better.

Tabor indicated with a hand gesture that he wanted Pate to sit down, so he did.

"I want to apologize for the way I talked to you the other day, son. I know you were trying to help me, and I think it's about time I thanked you for all you went through to get that doctor here in time. I'm not much for doctors, but you and Julia are likely right. I could have died if he hadn't come and done that surgery. We'll never know, but I shouldn't have taken it out on you."

Pate could feel tears spring to his eyes, and he furiously blinked them away. "Are you still throwing me off the farm?"

Tabor took a deep breath and released it slowly. "That got all mixed up in how I was feeling the other day, and it came out wrong. I didn't mean it to sound the way it did."

"But you want me to go."

"Not like that, no. I've been thinking for a while now, it's time you got your own place, but not because I don't want you here. You'll always be welcome in my home, but it is time for you to spread your wings, son. You're twenty-four years old. You're a man now, and you'll take a wife, raise a family. This farm is small, too small for the dreams you have, which is what I'm trying to tell you. You want to raise horses, and you're doing a fine job of it, but you and I both know we don't have the pastureland here to support all of those animals. I want a few cows, a couple of pigs, a horse and some chickens for eggs and a Sunday dinner or two. The truth is, you've already outgrown me and this farm. You just don't want to admit it."

His father had hit the nail squarely on the head, as usual. Tabor Kavenagh was not known to talk much, but when he said a thing, it went straight to the heart of what needed to be told. More people should have the same gift, those who loved the sound of their own voice so much they rattled on forever.

"I guess you're right, Pa. Julia was going to tell you about what she wants to do with her old homestead. She's offered it to me at a reasonable price, but in the end, it's up to you legally."

Tabor nodded, grimacing slightly as he adjusted himself more comfortably in the bed. "She told me all about it, and I think it's a great idea. I had that in the back of my mind all along, but I saw it as Julia's decision. If she wanted to offer it to you, that was her choice, something she had to come up with herself. You'll have all the room you need there to raise your horses on the scale you've always hoped for. That would solve her dilemma, too, of what to do with the place, and I wouldn't have to keep paying the taxes on it. That farm will go to you. So are we all right, you and I? I don't want there to be hard words between us, Pate. I shouldn't have made it sound like you were no longer welcome here."

"Don't worry about it, Pa. I've known for a long time that there wasn't a future here for me and my horses, because of the acreage. But there is up at Julia's old place. I'll be here until you're better, but you can come when you're all mended up and see what you think of everything. I know you know what it looks like, but I could use your opinion on a few things. What do you say?"

"I say that's a good idea. Be more than happy to do that."

Pate stood. Pulling the curtain aside, he glanced out the window. "Too wet to do anything today, I think I'll go and take a nap. I haven't been getting much sleep lately."

"I've noticed," said Tabor with a ghost of a grin. "But that can wait for a few minutes. There's something I've been meaning to say for a while. Sit back down, son. I want to tell you about your mother."

Chapter 8

Pate sat back down, immediately interested. All he knew about his mother was that her maiden name was Mollison.

"You told me a long time ago that you and my mother were fifteen when you had me, and that she died in childbirth."

Tabor nodded. "Would you like to know more?"

Pate watched his father. "Sure."

"Her nickname was Tricia, short for Patricia. That's what I called her, too, and she was an only child. We fell in love young, and I knew right away I wanted to marry her someday. We should have waited until then, but we didn't and of course, she became pregnant with you.

"Tricia was a small woman, with dark hair and nice light blue eyes, a real beauty. But she wasn't strong, and you were a big baby. The midwife in our town was considered to have great skill in birthing babies, but Tricia died. I was devastated at the time, and I remember her fondly all these many years later."

"Why did you keep me after she died? Didn't her parents want me?"

Tabor looked at him curiously. "Why did I keep you? You are my son, Pate. Tricia was my wife. Why would I give my child away to someone else to raise? There was never any question that I would bring you up myself, and of course, my mother was there to help. It was a tough time, I'm not going to lie to you, but I have no regrets that you were born. I loved you from the moment I saw you. I was proud to be a father, but at the same time scared of doing it right because I wasn't yet sixteen when you came along."

Pate thought about what he was like at fifteen, all gawky arms and legs and not yet comfortable with his height. He hadn't known which end was up, let alone being responsible for a newborn baby.

"I'm glad you raised me, Pa. I knew even when I was small that our situation was different from other families, and I thought of you and me as more like friends. I was glad to have you for my pa," he rushed to explain, "but it felt different. I thought of Gram as my mother, but I was way closer to you."

Tabor smiled sadly. "Like I say, I'm not sorry the way things turned out. Oh, I don't mean Tricia dying. We were deeply in love, and losing her was a very hard thing for me to accept. How I felt at that time has never left me. Someone going sudden like that is the worst, but you already know that, having lost your grandmother."

Pate nodded. To be sure, he'd cried over his grandmother when he was alone. He wasn't one to share such things.

"What about my grandfather, your pa? I don't know much about him, just that I've not heard anything good about him. Was he really that bad? I was four when he got killed, but was he good to me?"

His father was slow to respond, as though choosing his words carefully. "To answer your question, your grandfather was not a good man to anyone, and that's all I'm going to say about that."

"I don't have any memories of him, except one."

Tabor's eyes narrowed. "Oh?"

"I guess you could say two memories. I remember one time he carried me on his shoulders, and he was so tall I was scared being up that high. The other time was the night he died."

"You remember that, do you?"

"Yes, I do. Everyone was running around, yelling. I was scared that night."

"There was a lot of commotion for sure."

Pate looked at his father. "Do you miss him?"

"I miss having a father, but no, I don't miss him."

Pate ran his fingers over the patchwork quilt. "It's something like I feel about my mother. I don't miss her because I didn't know her, but I miss having a mother. Julia would have made a good mother."

"Julia would have made a great mother, I agree with you there. I should have married that woman years ago, not waited until she was beyond her childbearing years."

"I guess," said Pate, wondering why his father was so talkative this morning.

He seemed different, lighter somehow. Conceivably, he was feeling better than he had for a while, and if that was the case, it was good news. But since he seemed open to talking, had in fact invited this conversation, he had a few more questions he wanted to ask.

"What about my grandparents on my mother's side. I don't remember them at all."

Tabor sighed, suddenly interested in the ceiling.

"Pa, if you don't want to talk about that, it's all right. I thought…"

"No, it's good you asked. All of this stuff should have been out in the open years ago. You have a right to know where you came from, Pate. Who your people are, all of them."

"I take it they didn't want me."

His father met his eyes again. "Tricia's parents were getting ready to head west in 1853 as part of the westward expansion in the United States. I believe they were going to either California or Oregon. Tricia's pa didn't care for me getting his daughter pregnant like I did, and me from a bad family. The whole idea was to get her away from me. Shortly after your mother died, they washed their hands of the whole thing and headed west anyway. They probably didn't think there was much point in trying to stay in touch with their one grandchild, seeing as how they were going to the other end of the country in wild, unsettled territory. If they got to where they were going, they're out there homesteading somewhere. I'm sorry, Pate, I wish it was a better story to tell you."

"Where was my mother from? The same place as us?"

"Your mother's family, the Albrights, were Lowland Scots, and she was born in Scotland in 1838. She came with her mother and father to the United States when she was three years old. Actually, you're named after her in a way. She liked the name Patrick, the male version of her first name, but decided on the pet name for Patrick, which is Pate. She used to hold her belly and say: "Hello, baby Pate". She did that all the time. At least she got to hold you, in a way, before she died."

Pate stored that information away for another time when he could reflect on it in private. "What was she like, Pa?"

Tabor became pensive as he stepped back in time. "She laughed a lot, she was very happy. *We* were very happy."

Pate welcomed the ensuing silence in order to digest this new information. He couldn't envision his father's grief at losing his young wife, although if he thought about losing Dinah in the same way, he could begin to picture what it might feel like. Yet his father had bravely carried on. In that moment he realized the debt of gratitude he owed his father. Suddenly overcome with emotion, he dared not speak.

He thought about how he'd grown up feeling loved and wanted because of his father. Brogan and Garrett had also spent a lot of time with him when he was a youngster. He'd always been surrounded by family.

"It doesn't seem fair that she was taken like that," Pate said after a few moments, his eyes bright with unshed tears. If his father noticed, he was tactful enough not to mention it. "Funny how a tiny baby doesn't know anything, or I would have been able to meet my mother."

The words came to rest gently in the room, sad musings that would be left to lie in peace. So he pulled himself away from that troubling reality and tried to recall more scattered memories from Hamilton County. But he couldn't, other than what he'd already shared, and a vague recollection of their escape to Canada.

He turned to his father. "Something else I remember from back then. It just occurred to me."

He wondered why his father suddenly looked so guarded. He got the distinct impression that there was more, but he knew he would not ask. It wasn't necessary to turn over *every* stone in the field. Most were best left where they were.

"What is that?"

"I remember being on that ship and falling sick. I remember you holding my hand. Anyway, I've been here since I was four years old, so it feels like I've always lived in this house. Thanks, Pa, for telling me about my mother. I knew she had to be special. I don't suppose you have a picture of her?"

"I do. I've been meaning to show it to you for a long time, but I wanted to have this talk first. Wasn't sure whether you'd even want me to bring it up. I didn't want to make you feel bad. Julia dug it out for me a while ago, and it's lying on the bureau over there."

Pate went to the bureau and there was the tintype portrait of his mother. Taking the metal plate reverently in both hands he studied it closely. A pretty girl looked back at him, unsmiling but serene, her long dark hair parted in the middle and arranged in curls alongside her face. She was wearing a striped dress with a lace collar, simple attire.

"Pa, she was really pretty."

Tabor smiled. "Indeed, she was, but she looks so young to me now. That photograph was taken when she was fifteen. We were little more than children, having a child. You have your mother's eyes, except yours are grey and hers were pale blue. When you look at me, sometimes I can see the same expression I used to see in hers."

Pate continued to stare at the image. So this was his mother, something coming to life within him as he suddenly missed her. He could feel tears gathering in his eyes again, but warned them away.

"That's yours to keep, Pate," said his father. "You take it and put it in a safe place because it's the only portrait I have of her."

"I would love to have known her," Pate said, drawn once again to his earlier regret and not able to tear his gaze away from the photograph. "Had the chance to call her ma."

"And she would have been a wonderful mother to you. She often spoke about having a little boy of her own. It seemed she preferred that over a daughter. She got her wish, but didn't live to know the joy of watching you grow up. It was not meant to be, so I did it for her. Now, son, I'd like to rest if you don't mind. I'm all talked out for today."

It was true. Pate had never heard his father say so much. This had been a day for shining a light on the past. Thanking him, he left to go to his room.

* * *

Once back in his own bedroom, Pate's mind was spinning like a top. So much had happened in the past few days. Just when he thought he'd come to grips with the changes in his life, more came upon him. He picked up the photograph again. So this was his mother, the woman who had carried him for nine months. Her son. But fate had other plans, and he was immediately thankful to still have his father.

His pa had told him he'd had to become a man overnight after his son was born, and certainly that would have to be the case. He was also relieved that their dust-up about leaving the farm had been smoothed over. It had been an eventful few days, and he was glad it was over and things could return to normal, for a while anyway.

He thought about what Colleen would say when she saw the picture of his mother, then remembered she was out of his life. Strangely, he would not show the picture to Dinah. If she was critical or belittling in any way, he wouldn't take it well.

Nevertheless, he remembered with a rush of pleasure their time in the meadow this morning. If he thought the first few times were spectacular, they couldn't hold a candle to his experience today. He was completely swept away by this redhead from Boston. She was worldly and sophisticated compared to him, and while that bothered him to a certain extent, he was not ashamed that he wasn't a citified dandy. He was satisfied with his station in life, although he did have big plans for the future.

Like his Uncle Garrett, he was going to make his mark. For Garrett, it had been building fine carriages, and amazingly, he now owned his own carriage shop. He, Pate, would raise horses to pull fine carriages, and he would one day be a horse breeder of distinction. Look what he'd accomplished in only a few years. He was even more excited about what was ahead. He looked back at his mother's photograph. Even though she had long ago crossed over Jordan, he would make her proud, both her and his pa.

He propped the precious tintype up on his chest of drawers where he could see it from his bed, then lay back down and soon fell into a deep sleep.

He slept soundly, many lost hours to make up for, and when he wakened, it was to mid-afternoon sunshine pouring into his room. His first thought was of Dinah, and half asleep, somehow believed he'd overslept and missed his rendezvous with her. He leapt out of bed, trying to get his wits about him. And then he realized it was the same day and he'd already seen her. Smiling to himself and relieved that he hadn't missed their date, he laid back down, content to lie here and think for a while.

First up was the curious difference in his father. It perplexed him as to what had changed over the past twenty-four hours. Hadn't he heard him speak to Julia in his usual demanding voice just last evening? That same harsh edge? He'd figured that would last for a while until he got over his upset about the doctor. His father wasn't hateful all the time, but that sharpness was there. Like he was angry, but not sure about what. Oh, well, he wouldn't look a gift horse in the mouth.

He checked his watch. Three o'clock.

He got up, looked out the window, and was surprised by how fast the yard had dried up now that the sun had taken back command of the sky. The fields would still be wet though, so nothing to be done there. And since it'd be an hour or so before he started the evening chores, he decided to saddle Jacko and take him for another run, really stretch him out this time. There shouldn't be anyone much on the road, so he could give the horse his head, let him get some of that pent-up energy out of his system.

He could hear his father snoring, even with the bedroom door closed, and he was glad he was getting some much-needed sleep. Downstairs, he found Julia cleaning up the makings from a pot of stew she'd prepared for supper. The aromatic smell of the cooking beef made his mouth water.

"You going to be home for supper, Pate?" she asked him when he walked into the kitchen. "I'm going to make some biscuits to go with this stew."

The thought of her melt-in-your-mouth biscuits made him salivate all the more. His favourite thing was to dip them in the stew juice. Oh, were they good!

"Sure, I'll be here. I'm going to take Jacko for a run, then I'm coming back to do the chores. I'll be home in lots of time."

She winked. "He gets plenty of exercise, but I've not known you to go so early in the morning before."

He smiled. He didn't mind Julia's gentle teasing. She didn't mean any harm. But she was no fool. She knew he was going to meet a woman, and he had no doubt she knew exactly who it was. She would have seen Dinah talking to him at the picnic but was wise enough not to mention it to him. She'd listen to him if he was of a mind to talk to her about it, but he wasn't, not yet anyway.

"That's the best time of the day," he winked back, and she laughed good-naturedly. "I've really taken to it."

He lifted the cover off the stew pot and inhaled deeply. "Hmmm, that smells so good. I'm starving now, so suppertime can't come fast enough to suit me."

"That's three hours away. If you're hungry now, why don't you grab a couple of those molasses cookies I made earlier?"

He didn't wait for a second invitation as he dipped into the ceramic cookie jar on the counter.

"Do you want some milk to go with those?" she asked, taking a glass down from the cupboard. "I've got a pitcher right here that I fetched from the spring house. It's nice and cool. Why don't you have a glass before I put it back?"

Pate sat down at the table while she poured a tumbler full and set it before him. "You notice you don't have to twist my arm for any of this," he said as he drank deeply of the sweet whole milk, then made quick work of his first cookie. The second cookie followed, as he finished the milk and got to his feet.

"You sure know the way to my heart, Julia. Delicious! Thank you!"

"So you rode out and took a look at the homestead, but I haven't heard anything about it since you got back. What do you think? Is it going to fill the bill? Can you do something with it?"

"Julia, it's absolutely perfect. And I don't think there are going to be a lot of repairs, a few loose roof shingles, and the back stairs need to be replaced. And there'll be a lot of work to bring the fences back. Other than that, I'd say it was in good shape. I didn't go inside."

"Oh, darn. I didn't give you the key. Sorry, but you'll be out there again soon, and you can poke around inside all you like. I'll move the rest of my stuff out, what personal belongings that are still there. But Pate, if you think you can use the furnishings, bedding and such, I'll let them go with the property. It's up to you."

Now that was welcome news. "I'll take whatever you want to leave, but I'll give you something extra if you're going to include furnishings."

"Pate, whatever I leave will go with the price we all agree on. I'll be happy you'll have the use of it. Now, if you're going to go for that ride and have time to do the milking before supper, you'd better be on your way. You've eaten enough of my biscuits to know they're at their best when they first come out of the oven, and your father likes to eat at six. So that's when they'll be ready. Off with you now!"

Once saddled up, he and Jacko hit the road, and while the purpose of the outing was to give the big black a good fast run, he decided he'd save it for the way home. He wished he were riding to meet Dinah, but instead of the usual time of daybreak tomorrow, it'd be a couple of days because she would be tied up getting ready for that bazaar. He missed her already. She promised to meet him at the usual time on Sunday, but explained she had to be back for Sunday services. If she'd wanted him to go with her, she would have asked. She hadn't.

No matter, he wasn't going to let anything get him down today. He felt well rested and in a cheerful mood. He thought again about his mother and knew as long as he lived, he wouldn't forget the moment he first saw her. There was a lot to think about, an ocean of thoughts that had been stirred within him, but it didn't have to be covered all in one day. It was all so new, and he was sure there'd be other questions he'd like to ask his father once he'd had a chance to sift through things.

The air was a bit cooler, fresher, rid of the mugginess of the past few days as he and

Jacko went at a brisk walk. The horse knew what was coming. A highly intelligent animal, he marked his time, his tension apparent. He was ready to go at any moment, but he kept his stride, knowing Pate would give the signal when the time was right.

Pate carried on along at a satisfying pace, another mile or so and then he'd open up and let Jacko fly. He smiled as he talked to the horse, the black's ears alert, not missing a thing. It was a shame this horse had been gelded, but he'd bought him because he was a handsome animal and wanted him strictly for a saddle horse. Had he remained a stallion, he would have kept him for breeding, not that Silver Billy wasn't a great stud. He'd used him several times before the owner was finally willing to sell him, and what a stud he'd been. He'd sired Freedom, the three-year-old that'd been bred to a solid black mare. Midnight Muse would give him many fine babies, but none better than Freedom.

If he got home soon enough, he'd spend some time with the three-year-old. That horse was smart, and on his father's advice, he'd decided not to geld the young colt. He was glad he'd listened to his pa because Freedom was a very special animal. He'd make a great stud when the time came.

He'd almost gotten to the turnaround point when he heard a wagon rattling up behind him. He knew by the slow pace and the clomping of the old workhorse that it was

Peterson Gault ambling home from an afternoon spent in Sackville. He'd likely been getting supplies, oats for his horse and the like.

Pate moved over onto the shoulder of the narrow road and let him catch up. Gault was a good neighbour. Everyone knew he was fond of drink, but no one held it against him. Some said he'd never recovered from the loss of his family to typhoid. He'd had his share of hardship, and he was a personable old fellow.

Within minutes, Gault pulled up beside him to pass the time of day, and of course, share any gossip he had learned along the way. He'd seen him a few days ago, so he wasn't quite sure what news he'd gathered in the meantime, but it was courteous to sit and pass a few minutes with him.

"How are you doing today, young fellah?" Gault asked him when he'd *whoaed* his old horse to a stop. "Heading up to Brogan's?"

"I don't have time for a visit today," Pate explained. "I promised Julia I'd be home in time for supper."

"I hear your pa is ailing. I heard the doctor from Sackville saved his life. I didn't know your father would allow himself to be cut open like that."

"You're right, but we talked him into it."

"A lot of people would say it was a dangerous thing to do, that you might have killed him. Being sick doesn't mean they have to start cutting into you. My father was not much for doctors. I don't guess I mind them too much, but I wouldn't let one of them cut me. I hear they're good for other sicknesses, though."

"Dr. Mains saved my pa's life. He said Pa had something called appendicitis. His appendix was sickened somehow. Turned poisonous. Anyway, he cut it out of him, and now Pa's doing fine. The doctor said he came close to dying, and would have if he hadn't done surgery on him."

"He's mighty lucky. So, how's the horse business?" Gault asked him, giving Jacko a good looking over. "I like that animal you're riding. Who'd you say you bought him from?"

"Richard Dempsey over in Westcock." He patted the gelding's neck. "This ole boy is as fast as the wind. You should see him run."

Gault was immediately interested. "I'd be mighty interested in seeing him go. Why don't you keep on going up the road a ways, and I'll sit here and wait while you run him to me. I don't want to see the back of him go, I want to see him head-on, mane and tail a flyin'. What do'ya say?"

Pate shrugged. "Sure, I was going to run home anyway, so I'll take him on ahead a short distance and then run him back past you."

"Sounds good to me."

Pate started ahead, Jacko, understanding what was about to be asked of him, was dancing in anticipation. Continuing on, Pate went three or four hundred yards beyond, then turned. With barely a cue, Jacko leapt ahead and bore down, his hooves pounding the dirt road under him, Pate leaning into the ride.

It happened so fast that there wasn't a moment to react. A rabbit dashed out of the underbrush beside the road and streaked across to the other side, spooking the horse. Jacko hit the brakes, hard, managing to keep his feet under him, but Pate was hurtled out of the saddle at speed, flew over the front of the horse and slammed headfirst into the ground.

Jacko, still frightened by the rabbit, dashed away, redoubling his speed, coming upon Gault, who was watching from the wagon.

"Whoa!" Gault hollered at the riderless horse, climbing down as fast as he could, but the animal sprinted past him, likely on its way home.

Gault got back up on the wagon and clucked to Missy, the old workhorse seeming to understand he should hurry. A few minutes later, they came upon Pate lying unconscious in the middle of the road.

Chapter 9

Gault knelt by Pate's side, but he could not rouse him. Moving as fast as his tired old legs would allow, he climbed back up onto the wagon seat and headed for Brogan's homestead, not more than a half mile up the road.

Brogan was in the yard splitting wood when Gault came rumbling up behind him, hollering whoa to the horse that was surprisingly spirited considering her age.

"Come right away, Brogan," Gault yelled. "Pate's up the road a ways, and he's hurt. He was thrown off his horse, and he's not moving."

"Turn this thing around," Brogan shouted to Gault, "and let's go get him. He's knocked out you say?"

"Out cold. I tried to wake him, but he was lying where he landed in the middle of the road. He was showing me how fast his horse could run, and I don't know what happened, but he came off somehow. Something must have scared it because that horse sailed past me as though the very devil himself was at his heels."

"Was it Jacko?"

"A big black is all I know. The horse didn't look hurt, just spooked."

"That sounds like Jacko, and I'm sure he went right on back to the farm."

Rounding the turn, Brogan could see Pate sprawled face down on the road, his hat a few feet away.

Brogan jumped to the ground when the wagon clattered to a stop and ran to where his nephew lay unconscious. Resting his fingers against Pate's carotid artery, he could feel the throb of a pulse, and he breathed a sigh of relief. From what he could feel, his neck wasn't broken, but he looked more dead than alive at the moment.

"All right, we've got to get him into the wagon. Turn this rig around, Gault, and back in, and I'll take down the end gate. Then you and I will lift him onto the wagon bed, face up so he can breathe properly, and take him to my place. We'll have to drive slowly, though. I don't want to jostle him any more than we have to. Then one of us will have to ride for the doctor."

Given Pate's size, he wasn't easy to move, but they managed to get him aboard as carefully as they could, and made the slow trip back to Brogan's homestead. He hadn't had a chance to tell Maggie what was going on, but she was waiting in the yard for them.

She looked anxious. "How's he doing? I heard Mr. Gault here yelling that Pate had been thrown from his horse." She rushed to the side of the wagon when it stopped moving. "Oh, Brogan, he looks terrible. Are you sure he's even alive?"

Brogan felt for a pulse on Pate's wrist but couldn't find anything discernible, so he tried again at the neck. "It's faint, but he's still breathing."

Maggie put her hand on Pate's forehead. "Are you sure, Brogan? It doesn't look like he is, and he's so cold. We need to get the doctor right away."

Brogan took his time as he felt Pate's arms and legs for broken bones, his chest, but wasn't able to locate any. "I'd say he took the brunt of the fall on his head. This is bad, Maggie. This is real bad."

Unbeknownst to the adults, Luke had young Jake by the hand, and they'd walked over to the wagon.

Luke was tall enough to look over the narrow sideboard. "Is Pate going to die?" he asked, stricken. "I don't want him to die."

Maggie turned to the children. "Pate's been hurt, but I'm sure he's going to be fine. Now, Luke, you take your brother and go down to the barn to look for eggs."

It was clear Luke didn't want to leave, Jake now standing on tiptoes to try to see over the sideboards of the wagon. "I already got the eggs for today, Ma."

Maggie put her hand on Luke's shoulder to steer him away from the wagon. "Take your brother to the barn, Luke, and look for more. I think that old red hen is hiding her eggs again, so you two go and look for them.

Go on now," she told him in a sterner voice in order to get them to leave.

If Pate was almost gone, she didn't want the children there to watch him die.

Luke thought the sun rose and set on his cousin, Pate. It wouldn't do him any good to have to remember him like this. It was frightening enough for the adults.

The men were about to carry Pate into the house when Julia pulled into the lane and hurried up into the yard. She climbed down and ran to the wagon.

"Oh my lord!" she shrieked. "What happened?"

Gault recounted what had taken place.

Julia listened, stricken. "I knew something was wrong! I heard the hoof beats coming into the farmyard and saw the empty saddle. I hoped he'd been tossed and was walking home. Something told me to hitch up the buggy and go look for him. So I took the stew off the stove, told Tabor I had to go out for a while and ran. I didn't want Tabor to know what I was doing in case it was something serious because he'd just as likely try to come himself and tear out his stitches if he did." She looked at Pate. "Is he gravely injured?"

Brogan felt for a pulse again. "He's still unconscious. Can you go to Sackville, Julia? He needs a doctor, and I don't think it'd be a good idea to take him all that way in the back of a wagon. We're going to get him into the house so he can lie quiet until the doctor can get here.”

“I’ll go as fast as I dare, and hopefully he’ll be available when I get there,” she said, rushing back to her buggy and expertly turning it in the cramped space.

And with that, she was off. Julia was a good horsewoman. She wouldn’t go at breakneck speed and risk an accident, but she knew the road, such as it was, and how to handle a horse on it. She’d press the animal when it was safe to do so, but with caution.

Gault watched the young man. “He don’t look more than half alive, does he? The good Lord knows I’ve seen death up close before, and he’s as white as any dead man. I hate to say it, but he’s not breathing very good. Do you think we dare to move him before the doctor gets here? It might be best to leave him right where he is.”

Brogan kept his finger on Pate’s neck, then shook his head worriedly. “His heart is beating, but it’s weak. I can’t even get a pulse at his wrist, as you saw. I think you’re right, Gault. We shouldn’t move him any more until the doctor gets here. It’s a fine day, warm, so it might be best if we leave him stay right here. I’m no doctor, but I’m thinking moving him too much might not be a good idea.”

Maggie nodded her agreement. “I’ll go and get a couple of good warm blankets, that’ll help keep him comfortable.”

Gault studied the young man. "I think he might be past knowing what's comfortable, but you never know. As I've heard said, as long as there's life there's hope."

Brogan lifted one of Pate's eyelids, but his eyes were rolled back, which was thoroughly disconcerting. "Pate!" he said, speaking sharply in the hope his nephew might somehow be reached in his state of unconsciousness, but he did not stir. "Pate!" he called out again. "If you can hear me, lift a finger, anything to let us know you're going to be all right."

Pate lay motionless.

"I was unconscious one time," Gault said. "They tell me I was out for a good fifteen minutes, and I didn't remember a thing afterwards. And as you can see, I lived."

Brogan's jaw was set. "How long you figure he's been out now?"

Gault considered the question. "I'd say a little more than an hour."

Brogan studied his nephew. "How did he happen to be going so fast?"

Gault touched Pate's boot, as though that would somehow awaken him. "I came across him riding, and he was telling me how fast the big black could go. Of course I said I wanted to see it. That's when he rode up the road a ways, then turned and was going to get him moving good so's I could see it better than if I was watching from behind."

Brogan listened intently. "And you didn't see what happened? Pate's an experienced rider. He knows horses, has since he was four years old."

Gault was already shaking his head. "Like I said, I didn't see a thing. All's I know the horse came flying past me with an empty saddle and never slowed."

Brogan sighed heavily. "It's obvious he hit his head when he came off. I'd say something spooked the horse. Jacko's a good horse, but too spooky for my liking. He'd jump at his own shadow. But that's what Pate liked about him, being a young fellah and all. The harder a horse is to handle, the better he likes it. That's why his owner sold him to Pate in the first place, he came out from under him a time or two when something surprised him. I'm guessing, but I'd say a rabbit ran in front of him, or a partridge flew up and scared him. It would fit for what I know about this animal. A horse like that can kill you 'cause you don't know when he's going to explode or stop short. I like the excitement of a fast horse, too, but I don't like knowing he's going to jump at every little thing."

Gault rubbed his week-old whisker stubble. "I didn't see him run when Pate was on him, but if how fast he was travelling when he went by me is anything to go by, he's one of the fastest horses I've ever seen. We should have had a stopwatch on him."

Brogan's jaw muscles tightened. "And where has that speed got him now? Lying on the back of a wagon, half-dead. I know we can't blame the animal, but right now I don't care how fast the damn thing can run."

Maggie returned with two patchwork quilts and passed them to her husband. Brogan kneeled in the wagon bed beside Pate and arranged them in place before climbing down.

Maggie watched Pate, who was still as death. "I hope those won't be too warm for him."

Brogan leaned over the sideboards and felt Pate's head again. "He's as cold as ice. I'd say the quilts are a good idea."

Gault studied Pate. "They say that's shock, being cold like that. They say you can die from it."

Brogan didn't take his eyes off his nephew. "Yeah, well, you can die from a lot of things. Pate's young and strong. If anyone can survive a fall like this, it's him. Pate!" he tried again in a louder voice. "Move your fingers if you can hear me!"

There was no movement.

A moment later, Luke and Jake arrived back from the barn. "How come Pate's laying in the back of the wagon?" asked Luke with the natural curiosity of a child. "Is he sick?"

Maggie took Luke by the shoulders. "Luke, you and Jake were supposed to be looking for eggs."

Luke held up empty hands. "We did! We couldn't find any."

Maggie pointed toward the house. "All right then, you take your brother and go inside. You and Jake can each have a cookie out of the jar, and please stay there until we come back inside, all right?"

Luke was stubborn. "But, Ma, isn't it too close to supper? You said..."

Brogan turned to his son. "Luke, do as your ma tells you. The reason Pate's lying in the wagon is because he's not feeling very good at the moment. When the doctor gets here, we'll be taking him into the house. We'll talk about all of this later. Now go, and take Jake with you."

The children left.

Maggie watched Pate. "I'm going to go in and make the bed ready in the spare room for when the doctor gets here."

Brogan nodded solemnly. "Good idea. It could be the better part of two hours before they arrive back here, if he's even available when Julia gets there."

Maggie was next to tears as she looked at Pate's deathly pale face before turning to go back to the house.

Brogan tucked the quilts up high under Pate's chin, every few minutes checking his neck artery.

Gault pulled a pouch of tobacco from the pocket of one of his raggedy shirt pockets and his pipe from the other. Filling the device, he set it on fire with a match, drawing vigorously on the old pipe until it was fully lit.

"He doesn't look like he's breathing, Brogan. It's mighty shallow."

"I know it is. Come on, Pate!" Brogan shouted at his nephew. "Don't you dare die on me!"

"They say hearing's the last thing to go," Gault offered from within a cloud of pungent tobacco smoke. "I talked to my wife right before she passed on, and I swear she heard me. I told *her* not to dare to die, but she went anyway. I guess what's going to happen will happen no matter what we have to say about it."

There was no sign of the doctor by the time suppertime came around, so Maggie fed the children. She knew she couldn't shield Luke from the reality of Pate's condition, although Jake was much too young. Naturally, there were questions, and she answered them as best she could, trying to remain in a positive frame of mind as she did so. It would not do anyone any good to focus on what appeared to be a dire set of circumstances. Luke was twelve now and old enough to face death if that's what this came to. She'd do what she could to protect them from such a harsh reality, but she couldn't wrap them up in cotton and keep them from the real world.

After they'd eaten, she had Luke take his brother back outside and gave them permission to play in the haymow until it was bedtime. That would keep them busy for a while.

It was close to a half hour later when they heard the rattle of buggies coming up the road, two of them. The doctor had generously brought his own, so Julia wouldn't have to make a return trip after dark, should that be necessary.

The yard was crowded when both vehicles made their way in. Dr. Mains climbed out with his black leather bag and hurried toward the patient, Julia close on his heels, her face full of hope. It evaporated when she saw Pate still lying unconscious.

Brogan helped the dark-haired doctor up onto the back of the wagon, where he felt for a pulse and looked into Pate's eyes. He then felt his neck, for any swelling he said, before addressing the others.

"How did this happen?" he asked no one in particular. "Does anyone know?"

Gault repeated his account of the mishap.

The doctor listened intently. "He came off a horse travelling at a very high rate of speed. You found him face down, so it looks like he must have landed on his head. I see that his nose bled some, which would seem to confirm that. We don't know if he tumbled at all, or if there were any subsequent blows to the head other than the initial impact. One thing is for certain, he is deeply unconscious. He could even be in a coma."

He pulled out his stethoscope and listened closely in various spots on Pate's chest. "His heartbeat is slow," he said as he returned his instrument to the bag he'd set beside Pate. "Can we take him into the house? It was a good idea not to move him any more than you had to before I got here, but evening is coming on, and I don't want him to become chilled. He's already in shock, and I'm quite certain he has a concussion, if not a fractured skull. I'm very much afraid it could be the latter."

Very carefully, they pulled Pate forward until Brogan could take his shoulders, and the doctor got hold of his legs. They pulled him out feet first and carried him into the house, to the room that Maggie had prepared. Once he was settled onto the bed, the doctor turned to the others. "All right, I'd like you to leave me alone with him now so I can get him undressed and do a more thorough examination. I'm going to need a nightshirt for when I'm finished. Do you have an extra one of those?"

Maggie was already scurrying from the room, returning a few seconds later with a freshly washed nightshirt. It would fit because Brogan and Pate were about the same size. She closed the door behind her at the doctor's request.

Gault headed for the door. "I think I'm going to go now. I've got a couple of stops to make along the way, and then I want to get ole Missy home. She's old and tired, like me, and I've pushed her kinda hard today. She'll be wanting her supper and a nice soft bed to lie down for the night. I would ask that someone let me know about Pate. If he di... When he comes better, I mean."

Everyone thanked him for getting help so quickly for Pate, Brogan shaking his hand. "You saved his life, Peterson. He could have lain on that road half the night for all we know and got run over by one of those freight wagons that run through here."

Julia spoke with emotion. "It was God's providence that put you two together today, Mr. Gault. I do not believe in coincidences. You were there when Pate needed you, and we are all deeply grateful."

Gault attempted a weak smile, but it was clear the afternoon's events had taken a toll on the old man. "That's one thing you can say about old Peterson Gault," he remarked about himself, "I'm on the road a lot. I get to see more than most folks do that way, but I'm mighty happy I could help. And I pray he lives to see morning, yes, I do. Pate is a fine young man."

Julia and the others agreed. "The finest," Julia managed around the lump in her throat.

There was barely enough room for Gault to turn his rig around, but he managed it, and within minutes, he and Missy were on their way as he continued on up the road.

Just then, the bedroom door opened, and the doctor came into the kitchen. "You did a good examination of him, Mr Kavenagh, I assume it is," he said to Brogan. "I can find no broken bones, and I looked at his neck again. If it were broken, he would have already died from his injuries, but he's breathing. I don't like the look of his pupils, though. They indicate to me that something is going on within his brain."

Julia's voice was soft, as though she was hardly daring to ask the next question. "Do you think he's going to die, Doctor?"

The doctor shook his head slowly, with a sigh. "I don't know. There's just no way to tell, and there's nothing I can do for him except check his breathing, hope for signs that he will regain consciousness, or... Tell me again how long it's been since he was thrown off his horse."

Brogan cleared his throat. "It was about four o'clock that Gault came here, and I believe it happened about fifteen or twenty minutes before that. He said Pate was unconscious when he reached him."

The doctor watched Brogan as he spoke. "And I doubt he regained consciousness while Mr. Gault was on his way here to ask for help. That seems highly unlikely. So, let's see," he pulled out his pocket watch and flipped the lid. "It's a quarter past seven now, so that would make it more than three hours." The next few hours will be critical. If he doesn't regain consciousness by morning, it would be my educated guess that he may not come around at all. He may very well remain in a coma. He's a big man, and he would have fallen hard. The injury might be too much for his brain, but time will tell."

Julia didn't try to hide her tears. "It sounds as though there isn't much hope."

The doctor regarded her speculatively. "We can't say that, not yet, but unfortunately, the longer he remains in a state of unconsciousness, the less his chances are of surviving this, or being functional again if he does. Medicine is just beginning to understand this type of trauma, but as of now we have no way of knowing the full extent of the injury. We can't look inside his skull and see what's happening. All I can tell you is that his pupils indicate he suffered a blow to the head, and that much we've already guessed."

Maggie spoke up from her seat at the table. "Can you stay with him, doctor?"

The doctor smiled at her kindly. "I'm not going anywhere for the next few hours. That timeframe should be very telling as to what the final outcome will be in this matter."

Brogan ran his hand through his hair. "Isn't there a chance he could wake up and be all right? He's not the first person who ever got knocked out."

The doctor nodded thoughtfully. "And he won't be the last. Certainly, he could awaken with no lingering effects other than a miserable headache, and that's what we're all praying for. But unfortunately, there's simply no way to tell, and that's the worst of it. I'm sorry."

Julia was clearly distraught. "Doctor, Pate is my husband's son, as you know, and I have to tell him what's taken place. He has a right to know. But when I do, I know he'll try to get out of bed and come here to him. But it hasn't been very long since his surgery, and he's not healed enough to travel over those rough roads, even in a buggy. I don't know what to do. I'm sure he's already wondering where I am. Wondering why Pate isn't home. That means he'll get out of bed to see what's going on, and he could open his incision."

The doctor ran his hand slowly over his face. "I see your dilemma. It would be very risky for him to be out of bed, let alone driving for miles in a buggy over those roads. But of course he would want to be with his son, as would I, or any of us."

Julia fixed a loose hairpin. "Nothing will keep him away, and I can't very well not tell him. If Pate doesn't recover, he would never forgive me. It's an impossible situation."

The doctor was already going for his bag, returning a minute later to the kitchen. "Would anyone here happen to have a jar of petroleum jelly?" he asked.

Maggie got to her feet. "I have some here for when Luke burned his hand last year. It's right over there on the shelf. Why?"

The doctor looked pleased. "That's good. Please pass it to Julia here, and I'll give her this," he said, handing her a roll of bandaging. "You rub the jelly on your husband's incision, put lots on, but be gentle about it. Then wrap him as tightly as is comfortable for him, but as securely as possible. That will give him stability. Now I would advise you not to tell him about this present state of affairs until you've done what I've told you. If he asks why, say it's what I instructed you to do as part of his care. Once that's in place and you have him downstairs, tell him what's going on. If you drive very carefully, he should be all right, but take it slow. No crashing or rushing to get here. When he arrives, we can help him in, and he can sit by the bed in a chair. It won't be the best, and he may want to lie down, but he'll be with his son."

Brogan stepped forward. "I'll ride down in the buggy with you, Julia, tie Dutch to the back. That way, I can help get Tabor into the buggy and make sure he doesn't get too hot-headed to drive here in a hurry. Then I'll ride the gelding back behind you. Come on, let's go!"

It was coming on dark when Maggie heard Julia's buggy drive into the yard, Brogan following on horseback. She watched from the doorway as Brogan swung out of the saddle, tied the horse off at the rail, then sprinted to the buggy to help Tabor indoors. His older brother looked drawn as they made their way into the house, and he was immediately taken to Pate's bedside.

Julia sank into a chair across from Maggie. "I take it there's no change."

Maggie shook her head sadly. "No. He's about the same. We need a miracle, Julia. We surely do."

The doctor and Brogan returned to the kitchen so Tabor could be alone with Pate.

Brogan looked at the doctor. "Is his breathing still shallow? Is his heartbeat as weak?"

The doctor accepted a glass of cool spring water from Maggie. "His heart rate is very slow, which is to be expected under the circumstances. I hope it doesn't get too slow. It needs to be able to pump blood to the rest of his body. If he does survive, and regains consciousness, you have to prepare yourselves that he might not come back all the way. I recently read a paper on that. As I was explaining to you earlier, medicine is making advancements in our understanding of this type of injury. It has been observed that patients who present with the same symptoms as Pate could remain in a vegetative state for the rest of their lives. I'm not saying that's what's going to happen here, but there are a lot of unknowns."

Brogan blinked back tears. "Then it would be better for him to die if he doesn't pull out of this. He wouldn't want to live like that. No one would. It would be worse than death."

The doctor understood, laying a hand on Brogan's arm. "All we can do at this point is pray, and hope for the best. I can tell you one thing, it truly is in God's hands whether he lives or dies, and if he does survive, whether he comes out of it with no long-term effects."

Julia stood up. "I have to get back to the farm. I have a whole barn full of animals to feed and bed down for the night. And I think that horse of Pate's is still saddled."

Brogan's eyes flashed angrily. "Shoot the damned thing!" he said before striding out of the house.

Maggie watched her husband go. "He'll be all right. He needs to be alone for a while."

Julia dabbed at her eyes as she rose to leave. "These hours of waiting seem endless."

The doctor set his empty glass on the table. "They do seem that way. He's definitely in a race against time."

Chapter 10

Minutes later, Brogan was back. "I'm going to the farm with you, Julia. I don't want you travelling alone in the dark, and you're certainly not staying there by yourself all night. You need to be here with us. So I'll go down with you and help get the chores done, same with the morning."

Julia breathed a sigh of relief. "Thank you, Brogan, that would be so much appreciated. I wasn't relishing being down there alone with no news about Pate until I came back tomorrow. Also, I have a pot of stew we can bring back with us to help feed everyone. There are also biscuit makings too that I can bake here."

It was now fully dark as the pair set off, and an hour and a half later, they were back, coming inside with hopeful eyes, only to be told there had been no change.

Brogan sighed dejectedly. "How is Tabor holding up? He won't leave Pate's side, I know he won't."

"But he needs to rest," Julia worried. "It's a large bed, so why don't we move Pate over a bit and let his father lie down for a while. Perhaps it would be best if you suggested it, Brogan. I know he won't want to give in, but there's no sense in both of them suffering. He got here, I don't think it matters where he waits."

Brogan agreed. "I'm going in now, and I'll suggest it. The doctor may have already done so anyway. Then I'll go out and see to your horse, Julia, and the doctor's."

Julia realized she was still holding the stew pot and biscuit dough and passed them to Maggie.

"Thank you, Julia, I'll put the stew right on the stove and get those biscuits in the oven," Maggie told her. "I'll bet you and Tabor haven't eaten for hours. I know I'm getting hungry myself, me and the baby, I should say. Luke loves your biscuits too, but he and Jake have already gone to bed, so we'll save a few for morning."

Julia smiled. "You know, Maggie, I think I'll do up another double batch of biscuits, and we can bake them all at the same time. I don't think what we have now is going to stretch as far as we need them to."

Maggie and Julia had no sooner set about preparing the food when they heard another vehicle approaching.

Maggie looked up as she stirred the stew. "My goodness, who could that be at this hour? We're all here."

Julia went to answer the knock at the door and was surprised to see Colleen Sullivan standing there. "Colleen! What are you doing out and about so late, dear? You didn't drive down here by yourself, did you?"

The girl shook her head, her cheeks wet with tears. "My pa drove me. Peterson Gault stopped in and told us Pate had been thrown from his horse, and he might not live. Oh, Julia," the girl sobbed, stepping into Julia's open arms.

Julia soothed the young woman. "He is seriously injured, Colleen. No one saw the accident happen, but the doctor thinks he must have hit his head to injure himself like this. But he's still very much with us, although unconscious."

Colleen sniffed noisily. "But Mr. Gault said he was expected to die."

Maggie was beside the girl now, too. "The doctor has not told us that for sure, Colleen. Pate is still breathing. He has not come back to us yet. We can't give up. We're all praying as hard as we can that he'll regain consciousness."

Colleen wiped ineffectually at her eyes. "Can I see him?"

Julia took her by the shoulders. "You can see him, Colleen, but try to calm yourself first. His father is in there with him, and he himself is not very well. It won't help anyone if you become hysterical and upset everyone. The doctor wouldn't let you stay anyway if you were to be like that. Take some deep breaths and get hold of yourself, and I'll take you in."

Taking the recommended deep breaths, Colleen wiped her eyes, fixed her nose with a white cotton hanky, then squared her shoulders. "I'll be all right, Mrs. Kavenagh. It was the news of it, Mr. Gault telling us Pate wasn't long for this world. I'm ready now."

The bedroom was bathed in the soft yellow glow of a single oil lamp on the bedside table, the doctor sitting on a chair next to the bed. On the other side of the bed sat Tabor, his face tight, holding his son's hand. Brogan turned from where he was standing at the end of the bed when Julia and Colleen stepped into the room.

Julia kept her arm around Colleen. "Doctor, this is Colleen Sullivan, a friend of Pate's. She's come to see him."

The doctor rose, vacating his chair, and Colleen moved closer, scrutinizing Pate with troubled eyes. She remained calm as promised, although tears did fall.

The doctor inched his empty chair toward her. "Here, Miss Sullivan, please sit down. I'm afraid there's been no change in his condition over the past several hours."

Colleen sat down, then reached ahead and took hold of Pate's other hand. "How come he can't wake up?" she whispered to the doctor.

The doctor remained standing beside Brogan at the end of the bed. "Because his head's hurt, dear. He's what we call unconscious."

Colleen watched him closely. "I've heard of a vinaigrette concoction that can bring people around when they faint. Why wouldn't something like that work?"

The doctor smiled indulgently. "This is much different from simply fainting. If it were that easy, we wouldn't have let him lie here all this time. This is much more critical, and all we can do is wait. I'm doing everything I can for him, but as to when or if he wakes up is not in *my* hands."

Brogan left the room to see to the horses still hitched to buggies in the yard, advising Julia before he did so that Tabor wished to remain seated, spreading his hands in an *I tried* gesture of defeat.

When he'd finished outside, he helped himself to a bowl of Julia's stew and some biscuits. He even managed to get Tabor to take some sustenance, and of course, the doctor.

Half an hour later, Maggie set the rest of the stew on the back of the stove, and what remained of the biscuits in the stove's warming closet. "I'll set these aside because Pate will want something to eat when he wakes up," she said, forcing a cheerfulness into her tone that it was obvious she did not feel.

Julia looked at the clock on the mantle. It was just shy of eleven o'clock. Pate had been unconscious now for something like seven hours, and it was without a doubt the longest seven hours of their lives.

Just then, there were loud voices in the bedroom. Julia's eyes flew to Maggie as they clearly heard Tabor declare, "He squeezed my hand!"

They raced into the bedroom, Maggie's more of a fast waddle because of her size. The doctor was standing by the bed, holding Pate's hand, with Colleen hovering behind him.

"Pate! Squeeze my hand!" Dr. Mains instructed his patient. "Squeeze it as hard as you can."

Everyone watched, their eyes glued to Pate's right hand, and clearly saw, as did the doctor, Pate squeeze his hand. Moments later, his eyes began to flutter open partway.

The doctor turned to Brogan. "Fetch me another lamp if you can, Mr. Kavenagh. I want to have a clear view of his eyes, see if they will track me."

Colleen stepped to the back of the room, out of the way. "Track you? What does that mean, Doctor?"

"It means follow me. I want to find out if he's actually seeing me, as opposed to erratic eye movements."

Brogan was back in a few seconds with a larger lamp from the kitchen and held it as the doctor set about to determine Pate's present state of consciousness. They all watched as Pate, opening his eyes a little wider, did indeed follow the doctor's commands of right and left, up and down, straight ahead and follow my finger, all valid indicators that his brain was functioning as it should.

The doctor was smiling broadly, revealing prominent teeth. "This is an excellent outcome," he announced. "He's understanding my commands and that's highly encouraging at this point."

Pate's eyes fell shut for long moments, and then he stirred again, moaning, struggling to raise up on one elbow, but the doctor restrained him gently. "No, Pate. You lie still. Settle back now and don't try to get up."

Pate appeared to be confused as his gaze, heavy-lidded, slowly surveyed the room and came to rest on his father. "Pa," he said, looking at him with a bewildered expression.

Tabor continued to hold his son's hand, reaching ahead to smooth a strand of hair from Pate's forehead. "I'm right here, son. Everything's going to be all right. You're going to be fine."

Pate's tongue was thick, as though waking from a long sleep, his eyes partially open, dazed. "Why is everyone looking at me? Where am I? What's going on?"

"He's really confused," Colleen whispered, but aloud she said: "Pate?"

"Dinah?" Pate asked, looking around the room, oblivious to the curious glances among those assembled there. "Where are you, Dinah? Did something happen?"

Colleen looked as though she'd been struck in the face, backing up with an expression of utter devastation. She was breathing heavily as she pivoted and ran from the room.

Closing the bedroom door behind her, Julia was hot on her heels as Colleen headed for the kitchen door and tried to wrench it open.

"Colleen! Wait," Julia called after her, finally catching up. "You can't go running off into the night."

"I can and I will. Dinah is that hussy from Sackville, and it's plain as day to me she's who he wants. But where is she tonight? Not by his bedside, and that's a fact."

"I haven't met her, but in all fairness, she likely doesn't know about Pate's accident."

"I love him, Julia," she wailed. "I love him! I was going to be his wife, and now he's given his heart to someone else."

"I'm so sorry you had to be hurt in this way," Julia said gently, "after you came all the way here to be by his bedside. It's most unfortunate the way things turned out."

"He said her name just to hurt me!"

"Oh, Colleen, I don't believe that for a second! You saw for yourself he's confused. He suffered a blow to his head, dear. He's clearly not himself."

"And I suffered a blow to my heart. I've been made a fool of in front of everyone."

"This has got to hurt so much," said Julia in an effort to comfort the girl. "I know how much you care for Pate. You're heart is broken right now, but I'm sure once you've had a chance to give this more careful thought, you'll be as thankful as we are that he's still alive. He's come back to us, and we've been waiting hours for such wonderful news."

Brogan came out into the kitchen. "Come on, Colleen, I'll hitch up Julia's buggy and drive you home. That's all right, isn't it?" he asked his sister-in-law.

"Of course! Absolutely."

Colleen flung herself at the door again, her colour high. "I'm walking home!"

Brogan grabbed his hat. "Oh no, you're not. Come on, Colleen, it'll take a few minutes to get the rig ready, and then we're off. I know you're upset, and we're all tired and on edge. It's been a hard few hours, but things will look better in the morning."

Julia headed back into the bedroom once Brogan left with Colleen, and even in those few minutes, she could see an improvement in Pate's colour, although he was a long way from being fully recovered. Maggie was in the middle of explaining to him what had happened, as far as they were aware, as told to them by Peterson Gault.

Pate watched his aunt seriously until she'd finished speaking. "I don't remember any of that. When was all of that supposed to have happened?"

Maggie gratefully sank into the chair the doctor had previously occupied. "Shortly before four o'clock this afternoon, I believe."

Pate still appeared to be trying to focus on the people standing around his bed. "What about Jacko, my horse? Was I riding him? He's the big black."

Maggie pulled a face. "It was the big black horse. You don't recall anything as to what caused you to come off him? Did he stumble? Did something scare him? The doctor here says it looks like you went off over the horse's head. Peterson Gault says you were trying to show him how fast the horse could go, and apparently, he was flying. Does any of this sound familiar to you?"

Pate looked crestfallen. "What's wrong with me? None of that makes sense. I don't remember any of it at all."

The doctor stepped forward. "Now don't be too hard on yourself, Pate. You have some memory loss, but that's to be expected, too, I understand in instances such as this. We believe it has to do with the inner workings of the brain."

"But I want to know what's going on."

The doctor took hold of Pate's wrist to check for his pulse, but Pate pulled his hand away. "What are you doing?"

The doctor picked up his wrist again. "What's going on is just what we're explaining to you, and what I'm doing at the moment is checking your pulse. And then I'm going to listen to your chest. You're going to be all right, Pate. I know this feels overwhelming right now, but I think it will pass, although you'll have to take it easy for a few days — a week or so."

"I heard another woman's voice in the room earlier."

Julia smiled at Pate. "That was Colleen, dear. She came by as a friend to make sure you were all right."

"Oh, Colleen," he said. "That was nice of her. Now, tell me more of what you know. I want to try to remember."

Julia tweaked his toe under the blankets. "Do you remember I made a stew and biscuits? You were most anxious to have some when you got back home."

Pate looked at her blankly. "Stew? Biscuits? What day is this?"

Tabor never took his eyes off his son. "It's late Friday night. Now tell me, Pate, do you remember the picture I gave you yesterday morning?"

Pate turned toward his father. "My mother. You gave me a picture of my mother. I set it up on my chest of drawers," and for the first time since coming conscious again, a brief smile flitted across his face. "I remember that!"

The doctor folded his arms. "Young man, I would say you're making a remarkable recovery. Remarkable! Two hours ago, I wasn't sure whether you'd pull out of this or not, and here you are getting better by the minute."

"I don't like not remembering everything, like how I came off Jacko. I'm trying to puzzle that out."

"You'll likely never know," the doctor told him, "so don't get yourself worked up about it. Focus instead on what's important, and that is getting past this."

Pate sighed. "How long does this headache last? It's hurting something fierce."

The doctor shrugged. "A few days, I'd say. You won't feel your best either, that's why I want you to take it easy. I can guess you'll be raring to be up and out of this bed in very short order, but listen to me when I say you had a severe jolt to your system. You will feel the effects of it for some time, I expect. You'll feel faint, so no riding for a week or so. Can you promise me that? And I understand that the horse you were riding is something of a speed devil, so especially don't get up on him for the foreseeable future, and ideally not again. I would suggest that another fall, another blow to the head, such as you had today, and you may not be as fortunate as you were this time."

"Can I ride in a buggy?"

The doctor smiled. "You're a stubborn one, aren't you? I guess that's in your favour. I suspect you've got somewhere important to be, have you?"

Pate nodded, wincing. "Yes, doctor, I do. And by the way, thank you for your help. How much do I owe you?"

The doctor chuckled. "We'll settle up when you're recovered, and that includes not taking any silly chances. Now, I must be on my way."

Brogan had just returned. "It's almost midnight, doctor. We can make room for you here if you want to stay 'til morning."

The doctor smiled tiredly. "Thank you, but no. I'm used to coming and going at all hours because, for some reason, babies seem to want to be born in the middle of the night. So I'll be on my way. Thank you all for your help and hospitality."

Tabor spoke up tiredly. "Thank you, doctor, for everything you've done. I owe you a debt of gratitude."

The doctor inclined his head toward him, his expression revealing that he understood Tabor to be a recent convert to his medical skills. "You've got a strong son here, Mr. Kavenagh, and I'm happy he's back with you all. I'm happy for everyone, but most of all you, Pate," he said, returning his attention to his patient. "I'm mighty glad to see you doing as well as you are, having regained consciousness less than an hour ago.

"Again I say it's nothing short of remarkable, and it's what gives me the determination I need to carry on. There are times when it's difficult to be a doctor, while other times it's downright gratifying, although I can't accept too many thanks for what happened here tonight. I think we owe a lot to the good Lord up above for bringing this young man back the way He has."

All agreed.

Brogan went out once again to help hitch up the buggy, and the doctor was soon on his way with a wave of his hand.

Pate's colour continued to improve as he reclined against the pillow, closing his eyes. "I'm hungry," he announced to the room. "You said something about stew and biscuits, Julia?"

Everyone laughed.

Tabor and Julia stayed the night, as did Pate, and understandably, there were no early risers the next morning, save for the children. Luke, a mature young man for his age, fed Jake and took his younger brother to the barn with him, where they fed and watered the animals, and turned Dutch out for the day in the pasture. They were in the process of collecting eggs when Brogan walked into the barn.

"I thought I'd find you here, Luke. You did a fine job getting things started for the day." He turned his attention to his youngest son. "Finding many eggs, Jake?"

At three years old, Jake was the size of a five-year-old, following in his older brother's footsteps. Both were the image of their father, dark-haired and light-eyed like the Kavenaghs.

Brogan squatted down, and Jake ran over and put his arm around his father. "I got thwee eggs, Papa."

Brogan smiled. "You got *three* eggs, Jake. Can you say *three*?"

The child cocked his head to one side. "Yes, Papa, thwee. I got thwee eggs."

"Good for you, Jake," he said, pulling his son into a hug.

Every day with his wife and children felt like a gift. It wasn't long ago his world had come crashing down around him, and then he'd been given a second chance. Just as Pate had gotten a second chance last night. Jake put both arms around his father's neck, and Brogan hugged his child all the harder. Things could be taken away so easily.

* * *

By Sunday, Pate felt almost entirely like his old self, except for a lingering headache, and he hadn't quite gotten all his strength back. His father even appeared to be doing better, insisting on coming downstairs for breakfast. Julia, it seemed, couldn't stop smiling, a fresh batch of biscuits coming out of the oven as the menfolk trooped into the kitchen. She also had salt pork sizzling in the cast-iron frying pan and fresh eggs crackling beside it. Pate could smell the coffee when he first woke up, and he happily threw his legs over the side of the bed and hauled on his trousers.

He'd take it easy today to pacify Julia and his father, but make no mistake about it, he was going to the meadow at daybreak tomorrow morning. He wasn't sure what he'd be up to once he got there, but he'd see about that when the time came. And he wasn't going to ask anyone's permission, accident or no accident. He wasn't sure how he was going to get there because he wasn't inclined to ride Jacko for a while. It was unnerving to think he had lost a whole block of time because of that fall, and he'd like to try to figure out what had caused the spill. He might never know, but if he had to guess, he'd say something ran out from the undergrowth onto the road. That was the one thing that made sense.

He remembered another incident a couple of weeks ago when he'd been riding Jacko on the road. Mind you, not at the top speed that by all accounts he'd been doing the day of the mishap, but travelling along at a good pace. A partridge, no doubt with chicks nearby, had flown up unexpectedly, and Jacko, startled, had leapt sideways and almost unseated him. That was one thing about the big black. Jacko owned the road when he wanted to do speed, but he turned into a big chicken the first time anything wanted to share that road with him.

Pate knew it would always bother him that he was missing that piece of the puzzle, but the memory of that unfortunate day would fade soon enough. He had other things on his mind. It felt like a lifetime since he'd seen Dinah. He missed her with a keen longing, and he hoped she felt the same way.

He missed those emerald eyes of hers and running his fingers through her thick, glossy hair. He liked listening to her laugh, the way her body responded to his. He missed everything about her.

He thought about Colleen coming to Brogan's the other night. Poor Colleen, the last thing he wanted to do was hurt her. She was so sweet, so kind, but she hadn't stayed long.

"More biscuits?" Julia asked him, breaking into his thoughts. "There's more in the warming closet. I kept them warm so the butter will spread better."

He was ravenous. "I sure do, Julia. They are so good."

His father seemed suddenly contemplative, his eyes on his plate. "What are you going to do with that black, Pate?"

"You mean Jacko?"

"Yes, I mean Jacko."

Pate was surprised by the question. "I don't understand. What would I be doing with him, other than feeding and exercising him? I'm not going to ride him for a while, if that's what you mean. I'll wait 'til I'm a hundred per cent," he assured his father, "or leastwise until my head stops hurting."

His father chewed a piece of fried pork and swallowed it before he spoke again. "And then go out and let him try to kill you all over again."

Pate gaped at him. "Jacko didn't do anything wrong. He must have been spooked."

"That isn't the first time he's spooked, Pate. You said so yourself when you bought him. I've seen him almost bolt because of a shadow. He's a spook, and that makes him a dangerous horse."

"He's not dangerous, Pa. He's nervous, is all. He'll come out of it eventually."

"An unpredictable animal like that is dangerous. And since you like to go fast on him, that makes him tenfold more dangerous. You're lucky to be alive. I don't need to tell you how easily it could have gone the other way."

"Jacko's my horse."

"And you are my son, and in my opinion, the two don't go together."

"I like riding him fast. He's a good horse."

Tabor buttered another biscuit and then set it on his plate, more interested in the conversation at the moment than biting into the quick bread. "He's not a good horse if he almost kills you. It's not hard to figure out that something scared him the other day. You bought him because he's a challenge, but I want you to think about down the road a ways. Is it worth getting crippled over? If he doesn't land you on your head again, which, after what has already happened, would in all likelihood kill you, you could break your neck or your back. I don't have to go into all the ways that horse's behaviour can hurt you. You know very well what I'm saying. I also know you've worked with him to help him get over that nervousness, but he's an accident about to happen. I doubt you'll take it out of him."

It had crossed his own mind that Jacko was as flighty now as he'd been when he first got him. But oh, how he loved to sail along on that horse's back. There was no feeling like it in the world. On the other hand, he didn't care for what had happened on the road either, not one bit.

Tabor set about eating his biscuit as he waited for his son's reply.

"I know what you're saying, Pa," Pate said after a moment, "but I'd sooner cut off my right arm than part with that horse."

Tabor swallowed. "And I say you may part with *more* than your right arm because of that horse. I don't want him on the farm, and I don't want you to take him with you when you go to your new place either. But he is here at the present time, and Julia goes down there and tends that animal when you're not around. I have forbidden her to do that from now on because he can get fractious. He's a beautiful animal, it's just his disposition. I want you to think about it and make the decision. He has to go, Pate. I'm not going to stand by and watch him kill or maim somebody some day."

Pate drained his coffee cup, the pleasure now gone out of his meal. He liked owning the black, was proud of how fast he could go, but of course, his father was right. It had occurred to him on more than one occasion, as he was racing along the road, what would happen if Jacko spooked at something. He wouldn't relate his previous experience with the partridge. He didn't need to add any powder to the cannon.

"I know you're right, Pa," he said finally. "He is unpredictable. I'll make some enquiries. He's young yet, and I could try to sell him to one of the racing outfits starting up in the province. He's a great trotter, so he won't have any problem proving himself."

Tabor looked at his son. "I think that would be best," and that was the end of the conversation.

Chapter 11

After they'd finished eating, Pate went down to the barn to take care of the chores. He had to admit he was slower going about them than usual, but he already felt miles better than he had yesterday, and glad to see the animals again. He couldn't imagine doing anything else with his life other than animal husbandry and working with horses in particular.

He made his way to Jacko's stall, the powerful black horse waiting for him. There was no question that the two shared a bond, and Jacko nickered softly when he heard Pate approaching. It was as if he knew he'd hurt Pate and seemed almost apologetic as he nuzzled him.

"I'm sorry, boy," Pate said, leaning his face against the horse's soft nose. "I'm sorry it happened. I'm sorry you have to go, but I'll find you a good home. I swear I will."

He thought again about finding an owner who would race the horse. Would he work him too hard? But then again, he reminded himself, the black loved to run; he couldn't get enough of it. He couldn't take that away from him, and he was sure whoever did get him would take good care of him because with his kind of speed, he was a valuable animal. He simply wouldn't sell him to somebody who wouldn't treat him well. The alternative was to put him out to pasture and let him run to his heart's content. However, such pastures were for animals that had earned their rest after a lifetime of hard work. Jacko was too young to be put to grass. He had a lot of living yet to do, and Pate knew it was his job to make that happen.

It would break his heart to see the best horse he'd ever owned go out of the yard, but that's the way it would have to be. His father had been right, and he'd told him so. It wasn't practical to take the kinds of chances he'd been taking. It was downright stupid. He wanted to live his life to the fullest, not be stuck in a wheelchair for the rest of it, or worse. So in the end it would be the best thing for him *and* the horse to part ways.

"Looks like you and I won't be doing any more racing," he told the big horse, "but until then, you get to run in the pasture and kick up your heels. How does that sound?"

Jacko nickered again, perhaps unable to understand what Pate had said, but liking the sound of his voice.

"Remember, old son, you haven't done anything wrong. You were only being a horse. It's natural for you to avoid something you're not familiar with, to stay away from danger. To run from it as fast as you can. I guess you have to leave because you're too much of a horse. So you're going to go and be a horse somewhere else, but I'm sure going to miss you."

* * *

By Sunday morning Pate felt as bright as a new dollar — a new dollar with a headache that didn't seem like it was going to go away anytime soon. He knew he and Dinah would have their usual outing at daybreak. He reckoned what they had could be called a courtship, although it didn't rightly feel like that. He imagined if her aunt and uncle thought their niece was being courted, they would prefer she have a chaperone. How Dinah would scoff at the need for one of those. What rules were there left to break anyway? They were already having sexual relations, or more politely what some would refer to behind their hands as amorous congress or basket-making. He thought of the reservations he'd had at the outset of engaging in this type of behavior, but Dinah had swept away all of his concerns.

He held fast to his father's warning of being cautious. His father was no fool, and certainly not inexperienced himself in that regard. He'd been three years older than Luke when he got caught. Preposterous, but those things happened. No one talked about it, but that didn't mean people weren't people. Love was just that, love. He actually

199

would have preferred to wait. Get married and then partake of the pleasures of the flesh when one didn't have to be so careful, but this fruit, ripe and luscious, had dropped into his lap and the feast was very much to his liking. He did intend to do right by her. It just seemed too soon to talk about marriage. They'd get around to having a serious conversation about it sooner than later.

He felt oddly reticent as he hitched Pointer to the buggy and set off. It was a wonderful morning, and it seemed that despite the good drenching they'd gotten last week, drought-like conditions were again upon them. Mosquitoes, most often a summertime curse, were all but non-existent this year. Not that he was complaining. It made their sojourns in the meadow all the more pleasurable not having to contend with stinging insects.

Dinah was waiting for him as he drove up, still fully clothed. He remembered with a smile her humourous misadventure with the bee. He thought of her naked body. Now that got his senses stirring.

She regarded him curiously as she waited for him to climb down and slowly make his way to her. "What's wrong, Pate? Why are you travelling by buggy?"

"I had a bit of a spill last week," he told her in an offhand manner.

He didn't need her worrying about him. He'd had enough people fussing over him these past few days to last for a good long while.

She scrutinized his face. "I think I do see a bit of a bruise on your forehead. Please don't tell me your horse was injured. He's such a splendid animal. I wouldn't mind having him for my own, but I know you'd never give him up."

He guessed he didn't have to worry about her fussing over him. "Jacko is fine, not a scratch on him."

She looked genuinely relieved. There was nothing wrong with loving animals. He certainly did.

"Thank heavens!" she exclaimed, clapping her hands together. "You look fine though other than a bruise. You're so big and strong, what could happen to you?"

He found himself piqued that she would dismiss his own welfare so casually. A little concern wouldn't hurt. "I did get bumped around a bit."

"A bump on the head is nothing, Pate. I once broke an arm in a jumping accident, now *that* hurt. But it wasn't the horse's fault. I miscued him. As long as Jacko wasn't hurt. Now that would be a real tragedy!"

He thought of Colleen who'd rushed to his bedside. She'd been genuinely concerned for his wellbeing. Anyway, no use crying over spilt milk.

"I can't stay long today," she announced starting to undo the tiny row of buttons on her white cotton blouse. "So we'll have to hurry."

He stilled her hand. "Why don't we just talk today, Dinah. We spend all our time lying together, and while that's most pleasurable, I'd like to get to know you better."

She threw back her head and laughed. "I would say you know me very well by now. I believe you could even say I hide nothing from you."

Pulling her hand away she continued unfastening her blouse.

He walked away, sitting on the log, oddly disquieted. "Tell me about the bazaar. Did you make a lot of money?"

She stood with her hands on her hips, although wearing a bedazzling smile. "A beautiful woman is taking off her clothes in front of you and you want to talk about a bazaar? How much money we made on pies and a rummage sale? Are you teasing me, Pate Kavenagh?"

He folded his arms and settled back. "No, I'm not teasing you."

The truth was he'd thought he was fit as a fiddle, when in fact driving the horse and buggy here had tired him more than he realized it would. He needed to sit for a few minutes and collect himself, and he seriously questioned he'd be interested in anything more strenuous than that today.

"Then start taking off your clothes, or do you want me to do it for you? I will, you know, because it's fun. It's like digging for pirate's gold every time I undress you. Don't tell me you're tired of seeing *my* body."

"Not at all," he told her, and that was the plain unvarnished truth. "I love looking at you."

"Then what's wrong? You want me to be the only one parading around naked?"

"You have a beautiful body, Dinah, and you know it. And you don't mind showing it, which I also enjoy."

She pulled the blouse over her head, revealing her lace-covered chemise beneath. He felt a surge of energy charge through him. It seemed he was in better shape than he thought he was. Leave it to Dinah to fix what was wrong.

She unbuttoned her riding skirt and let it pool at her feet, clad now only in her thin undergarment. She began to dance suggestively for his entertainment, and he was a rapt audience. How had he come across such a delectable creature? A woman who stated without apology what she wanted out of life and offered up her body to him on a silver platter.

"I wish there was music," she called over her shoulder, laughing her tinkling laugh.

Extending her arms, she swayed to an imaginary tune, obviously basking in his unblinking stare.

He took his shirt off.

"Now that's more like it, Pate. I told you we must hurry today, and the minutes are ticking away. Come to me," she coaxed him seductively. "Come to the witch of the woods and let me cast a spell over you, my most handsome prince."

She pulled the chemise off over her head, twirling it above her like a baton, luxuriating in her nudity.

He divested himself of the rest of his clothes and within moments they were lying together in the tall grass. It was soon over in a glorious explosion, in keeping with her urge to have him hurry. It had worked out perfectly, for her. Pate rolled to the side, a headache of mammoth proportions crashing in his temples. He felt nauseated, knife-like pain radiating behind his eyes.

Dinah was already on her feet, getting dressed. "I'm afraid I can't meet you for a few days, Pate. Aunt Emmaline tells me my father is coming home for a visit tomorrow and he plans to stay for the better part of the week."

Pate struggled to sit up. "Great. I'd like to meet him," he said playing devil's advocate. "Let me know when I should be there."

"Are you out of your mind? That bump on the head must have loosened something. My father is very possessive and he does not want me spending time with young men he hasn't properly investigated. So how in the world would I explain you?"

He bristled. "How would you explain me?" he said sharply. "What is that supposed to mean?"

She knelt down beside him. "Ohhh, my little tiger has a ferocious growl."

He swiveled his head to look up at her, and that made his headache worse. "Your little tiger?"

She laughed, enjoying herself. "All right then, my big tiger. Sorry, I misspoke. You know how I feel about you, Pate. Believe me, you don't want to meet my father. Or I should say I don't want you to meet him because I know the two of you would quarrel, and I do not want the two most important men in my life fighting over me."

"You sure it's not more than that?"

She giggled. "What, that you're not from one of Sackville's founding families? That you don't feel your blood is blue enough to suit me? You know I'm not like that, Pate. I'm being honest with you when I say I don't want to bring anyone home to meet my father, or my uncle and aunt for that matter. They're very protective of me."

He remained annoyed despite her protest. "I'm not out to harm you, Dinah. Quite the opposite."

She swatted away a butterfly that was flitting in front of her face, again likely drawn by the scent of rosewater. "It's not going to happen and all I ask is that you understand."

He felt disgruntled as he found his trousers and hauled them on, followed by his shirt.

"What is wrong with you, Pate! You look as though you swallowed a bee. Why are you in such a poor twist today?"

He *was* in a poor twist as she put it. Dinah was rushing him when he didn't feel like being rushed, and she didn't seem to want him to come any closer than this meadow. And it nettled him that Colleen had hurried to his bedside and then left before she even found out if he was all right. He didn't understand women, and probably never would.

"For one thing I have a headache," he told her even though he hadn't planned to, because the last thing he wanted to do was complain.

"Oh boohoo, you have a headache," she tossed back at him as she stepped daintily into her riding skirt and reached for her blouse. "Don't take it out on me. I rode all the way up here to be with you and you act as though you are doing me a favour by showing up."

He sighed deeply. This wasn't the way he wanted it to go at all. He didn't want to argue with her, but she too seemed to be on edge. It could be she was out of sorts because her tyrannical father was coming to town, and from the way she described him he did sound like he kept her tightly under his thumb. He knew Dinah well enough by now that she'd naturally push against such restraints.

Pulling on his boots he sat back down on the log, and rested his elbows on his knees. Her face looked uncharacteristically pinched as she began to fasten her blouse, and he wondered absently as he watched her why there were so confounded many buttons on it. Style he guessed was the answer, and she did wear it very nicely. If he didn't know any better he'd say their meeting today was not going to end on a good note unless he did something to turn it around. Fast. Dinah didn't strike him as the type to get over something easily, so he had to get in the way of this before she really got out of sorts.

"You are ravishing," he told her, trying his best to ignore the dull pain in his head and the lingering queasiness.

The doctor had told him to take it easy and not exert himself, or something to that effect, and what was he doing? Right. He deserved everything he got.

She looked up at him, the sparkle back in those emerald eyes. She surprised him by leaving the rest of her buttons undone and joining him on the fallen log.

"And you are so handsome!" she said, helping herself to his lap. "I was starting to think you'd become resistant to my charms, Pate Kavenagh, and that's not the way to my heart. I think you're one of the best-looking men I've ever met, so strong and muscular."

He hadn't tucked in the tail of his shirt, and she slid her hands up under it and splayed them over his chest, her breath catching in her throat.

"Take your shirt off again," she said thickly. "I don't like playing hide and seek. I want to see you in full view so I can have it etched in my mind for when we're not together."

He did as she asked, pulling it over his head and tossing it aside, and she moved against him until her lips were on his. It was then that he recalled they hadn't even kissed yet this morning, just gotten right down to business like some old married couple he thought.

Her lips tantalized him as the kiss deepened, picking up momentum until they both pulled away, breathless. "Pate, you take my breath away. I've never felt anything like this before."

He was tempted to say 'I would hope not,' but said nothing, only agreed. He and Colleen had kissed before, but nothing like this. She had held back, likely as she believed was expected of her as an unmarried lady. He hadn't even tried to take it any further because he'd respected her.

But he respected Dinah too, in a different way. Her hands were upon him again and he groaned under her exploration. If Dr. Mains could see him now he would advise him against such amorous pursuits, but the doctor wasn't here, and he would survive this. He'd lie with her again, or die trying.

Later they lay satiated in each other's arms, and he was careful not to mention his pounding headache. It would ease when he got up and got on his way, but for the moment he was going to stay with her as long as she wanted him to.

"You know, Pate, I was thinking. We should ride on up here in the nude, we spend so much time getting in and out of our clothes."

He had to chuckle at that. "Now that would be something to see. You want to set tongues wagging, go ahead and do that. You'd be like that Lady Godiva woman, except that your hair is red. It would cover you, though, if you let it all down."

She kissed his throat, still in his arms. "You, sir, wouldn't be as fortunate. Your hair isn't nearly long enough to make you decent."

He laughed. "You'll have to stop wearing clothing that has so many buttons. Like, why are there two hundred buttons on that blouse of yours?"

She giggled. "There are not two hundred buttons!" she scolded him, swatting at his shoulder. "There's only about twenty," and then she laughed some more.

"When there needs to be seven or eight."

"Point taken. I'll wear only my chemise next time, and nothing else. And what do you think my aunt will say when she sees me riding out like that, or God forbid, my uncle?"

"Tell them you're coming to meet the god of the forest, or whatever it was you called me the other day."

"Ahh, but that's exactly what I am doing. Joking aside, there is something different about you, Pate, something very special. Something amazing shining out of your eyes. It makes me feel spellbound sometimes. I like that you're not some city dandy all dressed up in a silk top hat."

"You don't think I'd look good in a silk top hat?"

"You'd look good in anything, but I like that you're a man of the land." She reached for his hand and held it securely in hers. "I like the roughness of your hands, their size. You have a quiet strength about you, a powerfulness that I haven't seen in any other man, except for my father. I thought my father was a role model of the highest order, until lately, when he up and married that tart. Now I'm angry with him and I have no wish to see him. I think he knows that, too. He understands I'm a woman now and not afraid to speak my mind."

He touched the end of her turned-up nose with the tip of a forefinger. "I think you're telling me falsehoods, Dinah Gladstone."

Why did she stiffen? "Oh?"

"I don't think you're nineteen at all. I think you're much older. No nineteen-year-old I ever met speaks the way you do."

She relaxed. "I already explained that. I didn't grow up in an isolated place like Sackville. I have been abroad at a boarding school and travelled the world. I studied horsemanship for several years at my school in Switzerland and have competed in various parts of Europe and the United Kingdom. I have lived a lot of lives for a nineteen-year-old, as you put it."

"And yet you choose to spend time with a farm boy."

"You're hardly a boy, Pate. You're a man in every sense of the word."

"And you're a woman, not a girl."

"And I'm not a virgin..."

Yet again, she shocked him. There were so many twists and turns to Dinah that he never knew what was coming next.

"I already guessed that," he said.

"I had my first affair when I was fifteen years old, with the son of an earl at an equestrian competition in Brussels. My, but that was interesting. My second affair was with the younger brother of my father's business partner."

"Umm, maybe you shouldn't tell me anymore. I don't need to hear about your escapades."

"Why, am I disappointing you?"

"Well..."

"You feel that way because you're decent and nice, and you expect everyone to play by the same rules. I never have, but those were my two *escapades,* as you put it. Don't tell me you haven't deflowered more than your fair share of innocent maidens because I won't believe you."

He chortled. "You make me sound like some kind of Casanova roaming around the countryside preying on unsuspecting women. Actually, I haven't deflowered anyone, as you put it. I told you my first time was with you."

"Like I said, I don't believe you. Someone who looks like you?"

He couldn't help but think about sweet Colleen and their promise to wait until marriage to know one another, even though he hadn't been in a hurry to walk down the aisle. But he couldn't have lived with himself if he'd taken liberties with her. Used her. He thought too much of her to go about it that way.

"Believe it," he said. "I wouldn't be interested in lying with just anyone. It would have to be someone I was close to, or felt some connection with."

She snuggled closer to him. "I wouldn't have guessed that was the case. Now I feel extra special, like you're all mine. So it really was your first time with me?"

"I already told you it was. I hope I didn't disappoint you, you being so worldly and all."

"Not so worldly, Pate, a little more experienced is all. I felt at loose ends, not having a mother, and then being away from Papa all the time. It gave me the feeling I could do whatever I wanted. I've felt like that since I was a girl, perhaps because I was sent away and someone else took care of my parenting. But then, I was the one demanding an education, just as if I were a boy, so I guess I can't have it both ways. They say I'm bright, and I'm not so sure that's a good thing. If it's true, it means I think more, analyze more and am not at all accepting. Anyway, it's made me who I am, and I won't apologize for it."

Silence fell between them, and Pate also felt the need to share. "I saw a photograph of my mother for the first time the other day. She was very pretty. It was taken the year I was born, so that means she was fifteen."

"There, you see? You can't judge me for having an affair when I was fifteen, because your own parents were the same age when they created you. So it's not so far-fetched that it couldn't happen. I, for one, am glad they had you, because if they hadn't come together the way a woman and a man are supposed to, there wouldn't be you. The world would be a poorer place, Pate, if you weren't in it."

He felt his heart swell. "That is one of the nicest things anyone has ever said to me, Dinah. Thank you. I'm sorry you don't have a good relationship with your father, at least not lately. My father has been the best pa that a man could ask for. I have always felt wanted by my family."

She was quiet for long moments, her hand tracing designs on his shoulder as they continued to relax in each other's arms.

"I've never felt like this before," she told him. "So cherished, so welcome to be part of someone else's life. I've had many exciting experiences that I believe most people would envy, but all it has left me with is feeling empty. That's why I say you're so different. You fill me up, Pate. I do believe you have stolen my heart.

"Does that mean you'll marry me?"

"I thought you'd never ask."

Chapter 12

Pate raised up on his elbow to look her more fully in the face. "You mean to say you'll marry me?"

"Yes, I'll marry you, Pate. I don't think we need to be in a big hurry, though. I think we should wait a while."

He lay back down, trying to process this unexpected turn of events, but no less eager. "I thought you said you like to do things in the moment, strike while the iron's hot."

She chuckled. "Usually I do, but I'm in no rush to walk down the aisle. It doesn't matter anyway, we already know each other in every way. The difference would be that I'd have a ring on my finger. I'd be Mrs. Pate Kavenagh. Hmmm, my name would be Dinah Kavenagh. That has kind of a nice ring to it, don't you think?"

Pate gathered her close once again, his heart full. "It certainly does. And we'll have children. I'd want a daughter who looks like you. A little red-headed Dinah."

She giggled. "Slow down, Pate, or you'll soon have us grandparents. There's a lot to be done for a wedding, and ours would be a big one. My father would make sure it was the highlight of the social season. You see, since I'm from Boston, that's where we'd be wed and naturally make our home. I know my father, he'd build us a fine house on Beacon Hill. That's where we live, and I know he would want us to settle down close to him. And he'd find you a job, a good one. Since he's into shipping, he'd naturally want you to come and work with him. He laments that he doesn't have a male heir to take over his company. If this new child he's expecting is another girl, then *our* first child, if it's a boy, would naturally assume that position. But there's no reason why you couldn't be his right-hand man."

His mind was whirling. He'd have to contend with all of that so he could be with Dinah?

"That's a lot to think about," was all he could find to say.

"It is, but that's what's in store for any man who wins my hand. It will be a good life. We'd be turning in the best social circles in the city, and you'll make a whole new set of friends. There's a wide, wonderful world out there beyond the confines of this tiny little place."

"I like this tiny little place."

"It's a nice place to visit, Sackville I mean, and of course I love my aunt and uncle's company. They've been very hospitable to me during my summer vacations with them. This summer, they completely understood I needed time away from my father and his new bride, and they've provided every comfort.

"They're very proud of my father and what he's accomplished. He left Sackville at a young age to strike out on his own and made good for himself. He's one of the wealthiest men in Boston. I'm proud of him too, knowing all that, but angry with him at the moment."

Pate felt completely adrift, like he'd found the pot at the end of the rainbow and it was filled with lead instead of gold. He loved this woman in his arms, but did she come with too high a price tag? His pa had always told him that people should know their place, and this was the first time he understood his meaning. Nevertheless, if it meant having Dinah, he could learn new things, couldn't he? Yes, by darn, he would!

He kissed the top of her head. "We're talking about a year or so down the road, I expect," he said, his voice a low rumble in the intimacy of their embrace.

She sighed, a happy, contented sound. "At least that, because my wedding dress will have to be made, and I would insist on approving every seed pearl and crystal that went into its design. I want to be the most extraordinary bride in all of Boston! And then there'd be my trousseau. I'd need an extensive wardrobe for our month-long honeymoon. Think how exciting it will be to sail around the world! You'll see things you never imagined existed."

"I have some idea what exists out there," he teased her. "I read, you know."

"Ahh, but you'll see for yourself what delectable sights there are far beyond the pages of a book. Don't get me wrong, books are splendid, but also limiting. We'll go to Paris, London, Austria, Madrid. The possibilities are endless."

"Or we could elope, leave all of that stuff behind and live our lives on our own terms. Now, if you were a daring girl, which I think you are, I'd say that's what you'd choose."

She was silent for a moment, as though contemplating the idea. "Now, that would set everyone on their heels, wouldn't it. Think of the look on their faces when I told them I was a married woman and turning my back on all those trappings. Oh, it does sound deliciously wicked."

"More wicked than coming to lie with me in the meadow?"

"Not more, but equally as wicked," she said. "The more I think about doing it that way, the more I like it."

Pate chuckled. "At the rate we're going, we'll leave from here to go and get it done. I like the idea of doing it that way, too, eloping, I mean, but unfortunately, I have to wait until I get my new homestead up and running. That won't be until the end of the summer, what with Pa sick and all. Can you wait that long for me?"

She kissed him lightly on the lips. "I'd wait for you forever, Pate, but let's keep this secret all to ourselves. Now I must be on my way, and I can't come back until Wednesday. Until then, my love."

* * *

Pate was over the moon as he watched Dinah ride off, hopelessly late for church, he assumed, and he hoped she didn't get into too much trouble on his account. But she had agreed to be his wife, and what was even better, he was changing her mind about all of that high society stuff.

He'd have done things her way, though, if it meant having her for his wife. What would the people around here think if a Kavenagh made good like that? Left to go live in Boston. It would take some getting used to, but who knew? He could like it once he got accustomed to that way of life. She'd even promised him before she left that they would have their very own riding stable stocked with fine horses. Once she'd mentioned the word horses, well that could change the water on the beans. Whichever way it went, he'd make peace with it.

When the initial rush began to subside, there came the usual sobering second thoughts. He couldn't imagine leaving his pa and Julia behind, or Brogan and Maggie and the children, everything he had known since he was a child. But that's what he'd asked *her* to do, and she had readily agreed, so there was no reason why he couldn't do the same.

219

People had given up more for the people they loved, and he did love her. Still...

There was nothing sweeter this side of heaven, he was sure, than holding her in his arms. One day soon, perhaps as early as a few weeks, he would know her as his wife, and it would feel like the first time all over again. They'd have a family, the children he'd thought about having someday.

He felt the familiar urge for speed as he climbed into the buggy and turned Pointer toward home. However, he had no wish for another mishap, not with his head aching the way it was. No, thank you. On top of that, since he was soon going to be a husband, and hopefully not long after that a father, he would have to start taking things a little slower. Be more responsible. He set off at a reasonable pace.

He hadn't gone far when he came upon Brogan travelling toward Sackville on horseback. Both hauled up.

"Where are you headed?" he asked his uncle.

"Maggie's come to her time, and I'm going to fetch the doctor. Running into you will save me from stopping at the farm to let Julia know. She said she'd go be with Maggie, so if you could run her up there for me, I'd appreciate it."

"I'll be home in a few minutes," he told Brogan, "and I don't mind doing that at all, then I'll come back down and do the chores."

Brogan was off, Dutch carrying his master to Sackville effortlessly with his long-legged stride.

Julia was lifting a baking sheet of molasses cookies out of the oven when Pate came hurrying in with news about Maggie. Ten minutes later, they were on their way to Brogan's homestead. After dropping her off, he turned the buggy and started back for the farm, his head spinning from the events in the meadow this morning. It was hard to believe such a short time had passed since he'd met Dinah at the picnic on Dominion Day. When something was meant to be, things usually fell into place quickly. Didn't they?

It was late morning when he returned from Brogan's, pleased to see his father relaxing on the front veranda.

"How are you feeling, Pa?" he asked, stepping down out of the buggy. "You sure you feel up to sitting out here?"

Tabor's smile was fleeting. "Feeling strong enough, I suppose. Julia said you were taking her up to Brogan's because Maggie was ready to have her baby."

Pate leaned against the veranda rail, folding his arms loosely across his chest. "That's right, and now I've got to get down to the barn and take at those chores. I'm a little behind this morning."

Tabor's smile stayed in place this time. "You've been a little behind a lot lately. You got a young woman stashed away somewhere we don't know anything about?"

Pate could feel his face catch fire, but he wouldn't give away his secret.

"I'm not saying a word," he told his father.

Tabor chuckled. "You don't have to, son. It's written all over your face. You have a mind to marry her?"

"Someday, yes," he said simply.

"That's good, but remember what I told you in the meantime. Try not to let the stork get ahead of the preacher."

"Pa..."

"Nuff said. I raised you right, so I'll not worry about your decisions. Now I think I'll wander on down to the barn and look around."

"But, Pa, you're not supposed to..."

"Not you too," said Tabor, pulling a wry face. "I'm not going to try to do any work, I just want to see the animals. I've been thinking too, you're going to have to start cutting hay soon. It pains me that I won't be able to help you. You feeling strong enough to do what has to be done?"

He decided it'd be better not to mention his headache because other than that and feeling tired, he was all right. If he was feeling recovered enough to bed Dinah, he could do the chores, including cutting, raking and storing hay. That thunderstorm the other day hadn't lodged the hayfield too badly, and since the weather had dried up again, it was the ideal time to harvest it.

The two walked to the barn together, like old times.

* * *

Julia could hear Maggie was in hard labour, when she let herself into the house. She said a silent prayer that her sister-in-law's delivery would be much easier this time around, remembering what she'd gone through to birth Jake. To begin with, she hoped this baby would be in the correct head-down position in the birth canal and not be quite so large.

Luke met her at the bottom of the stairs. "Ma's in some pain," he explained. "Pa asked me to wait here until you came, then I'm to take Jake outside with me. He said we could go fishing back at the pond." Luke hesitated. "Is Ma going to be all right, Aunt Julia?"

"Your Ma is having a baby, Luke, as I'm sure you know. It's painful to give birth, so she's not feeling her best at the moment. I'm here now, so you and Jake can go to the pond. Have you got your worms all dug?"

Luke shook his head. "What we could find. The ground's so dry all the worms have gone deep. We're going to dig over by the manure pile and see if there's any there. I want to get some nice, big, fat, juicy ones. I promised Pa we'd bring home enough fish for supper. Ma loves fresh trout. That'll make her feel better."

Julia ruffled his thick dark hair. "Good idea, Luke, and take your time. Your Ma is going to be feeling poorly for some time yet. You don't have to hurry. And remember, if you hear your Ma crying out when you come back, it's just a birthing. Nothing to be afraid of. Remember that."

Julia was mopping Maggie's forehead with a cool cloth when she heard the doctor and Brogan come in an hour or so later. Brogan directed the doctor up the stairs to the bedroom, then retired to the barn where he'd keep himself busy out of earshot.

As before, the birth proved to be a difficult one. Poor Maggie didn't seem to be able to avoid it. Fortunately, the baby wasn't breech this time, so she didn't have that to contend with. The newest member of the brood turned out to be a healthy girl, smaller than her brothers at birth, and with a light complexion. They called her Maisie. The baby gave a lusty howl once she was safely ushered into the world.

But it became immediately apparent there were complications, as Maggie began to haemorrhage heavily. The doctor massaged the uterus to stem the flow, but it refused to slow. As the minutes passed, Maggie grew increasingly more pale, the lifeblood draining out of her. The doctor's brow was beaded with perspiration as he worked tirelessly on the young mother, but the haemorrhaging continued. Julia could plainly see that if something didn't change right away, Maggie could bleed to death.

When Julia had finished cleaning and swaddling the infant, she placed her in Maggie's arms, keeping an eye on the doctor. His grim expression was a clear indication that he was still struggling to stop the bleeding. Maggie moaned weakly.

"Start that baby to suckling right away," the doctor instructed Julia urgently. "It should help her uterus contract."

Julia set about accomplishing that task, nestling Maisie into position. It took long minutes before the baby began to successfully latch on, but once started, Julia stepped around to the end of the bed.

"Is it slowing up yet, doctor?" she whispered.

"Not yet," he replied tightly, continuing his palpitations.

"She's not doing very well, is she?"

The doctor shook his head briskly. "I'm afraid to say the situation is becoming critical," he told Julia in undertones, noting Maggie's deathly pallor. "If I can't get this bleeding stopped..."

"Should I go and speak to her husband?" asked Julia as she watched Maggie. "He should be told so he can come to her."

The doctor continued to work in a seemingly vain attempt to constrict the blood vessels. She'd already lost so much blood.

Maggie now appeared to be too weak to open her eyes, her face as white as the bed sheet.

"Yes," he said finally, "he has a right to know that he may lose his wife. Go and talk to him."

Julia flew down the stairs and ran for the barn, where she found Brogan putting hay in the mow. He looked up, then, reading Julia's tearful expression, his curiosity was replaced with alarm. "Oh dear God, no! I've lost her, haven't I?"

Julia shook her head. "She's still with us, but the doctor can't get the bleeding stopped. He's doing everything he can, Brogan, but you should go to her, now, if you want to see her before... She's very low."

Throwing the pitchfork, he sprinted for the house and took the stairs two at a time. Kneeling by the bed, he took Maggie's hands in his.

"Maggie, please don't leave me. I love you so. Oh, Maggie," he implored when she didn't respond. "Oh my God, Maggie! Do something, doctor! Save her, please! I can't lose my wife! I can't!"

The doctor kept at his work, massaging and applying pressure until his arms trembled from the relentless effort. "I'm doing what I can to save your wife, Mr. Kavenagh, but I can't get that bleeding stopped. I'm afraid her body may start to shut down from loss of blood."

The infant, oblivious to the tension in the room, continued to suckle her mother, Julia adjusting the baby slightly to keep her in place at Maggie's breast.

"Maggie," Brogan pleaded, "stay with us. You can't go."

"All right!" the doctor declared triumphantly. "It appears I've finally managed to stop the bleeding, and hopefully it's not too late." Looking closely to examine her again, he breathed an audible sigh of relief. "The haemorrhaging has ceased."

Grabbing his stethoscope, he rushed to the head of the bed and began to listen to Maggie's heart. "She has a heartbeat, but she's lost a good deal of her blood volume, and quite frankly, I'm not sure if she can recover from it. The next twenty-four hours will be critical, possibly longer and if, pray God, she does survive, she will be several weeks in bed. She's young and otherwise healthy, but it will take her a long while to recuperate from this, barring any complications."

The doctor checked Maggie again. "I'm happy to tell you I'm not seeing any more bleeding. It looks as though the blood vessels have properly constricted." He returned his full attention to Brogan. "But under no circumstances is this woman to have another child. She will risk her life to do so. She's not out of the woods yet."

Brogan dried his eyes with the backs of his hands as he continued to hold Maggie's hand. "Thank you, doctor," he managed brokenly, before continuing to encourage his wife to help her make it through the ordeal.

The doctor stayed for several hours to keep an eye on Maggie, and Julia brought the baby in to feed one more time before tucking her back into the handmade cradle.

Unaware of how close they had come to losing their mother, Luke and Jake returned from their fishing expedition with a dozen good-sized trout, and Luke cleaned them while Julia fried them up for supper. The doctor ate a hearty meal before he left for Sackville, where he had another delivery waiting. Brogan would not leave Maggie's side.

Two days later, Maggie was strong enough to give a weak smile. There was rejoicing in the entire Kavenagh clan, and they were able to joke that they should hire their very own doctor to keep everyone healthy, given the events of the past few days.

Julia stayed on for a few more days at Brogan's to tend the baby and see to the other children, and then she felt she needed to come back home for a day or so to attend to her husband.

For his part, Pate was alive with anticipation. He would see Dinah the following morning. It had been three whole days. He knew he was besotted with the young woman, but didn't every young man fall in love sooner or later?

* * *

Dinah slipped into the saddle for her ride to the meadow, and what a spectacular morning it was. As she made her way to the barn, she could already see crews out on the marshes preparing to harvest the endless waves of marsh grass cavorting recklessly in the stiff salt breeze. She didn't especially care for Sackville, accustomed she supposed to the faster pace of Boston, but it was a nice enough place to pass the summer.

"Hold on there a moment," came a familiar voice behind her.

She jumped as she turned around to see Uncle Horace.

"Where are you off to?" he asked.

The chestnut was dancing under her, anxious to be off. He was the most spirited horse in the stable. She loved that the gelding took her on an exciting ride every time she climbed up onto his back.

"You know how I look forward to my early-morning rides, Uncle Horace. Would you rather I take another horse?"

"If you recall, I already spoke to you about it some time ago. I fear that animal may be too much for you at some point, girl. He'd be a handful for most men."

She leaned down and patted the chestnut's neck. "We've become good friends, Docker and I. Haven't we, boy?" she asked the horse. "We understand one another."

"Still, I'd rather you choose a quieter animal. I wouldn't want to have to be the one to tell your father you'd been thrown and broken your neck. Riding is a risky business at best, and you're far too young to be off on your own anyway."

She threw back her head and laughed. "Uncle, I've been off on my own for most of my life. You do recall that I spent many years at a boarding school, and I've basically travelled the world. Being on my own doesn't frighten me."

"Dinah, you're barely of age, and while you're staying in my home, I must insist you follow my rules. I put them in place to protect you, my dear. I'm sure you can see that. I don't need you worrying your Aunt Emmaline. She suffers from nervous prostration, as you know."

"Oh, Uncle! She seems fine. I thought a person was incapacitated with nervous prostration, but she seems jolly enough to me. Why, we had a delightful time at the church bazaar. We made pies together, then spent the day selling them. We had ever so many laughs. I think I'm good for her."

He smiled, but it did little to relieve the austerity of his face, a long, narrow affair with a bulbous nose stuck fully in the middle of it. He may have thought his oversize moustache camouflaged its size, but sadly, it made it seem more prominent, as though it was trying to escape. Add to that a set of beady, bright blue eyes, but no matter, she thought the world of him. None of the Gladstones was particularly good-looking. She'd heard her father described as handsome, but she clearly got her good looks from her mother. She'd been a true beauty.

"You are good for her, Dinah. You're good for both of us. You're more like a daughter to us than a niece, and you know we'd indulge you in anything, but this horse I will not. Please dismount and take another."

"But, Uncle! He's already saddled, and you can see for yourself he's raring to go. You wouldn't deny him a nice outing, would you? I doubt he'd forgive you."

He pulled his mouth into a tight bow, which meant she was going to get her way. She could read him like a book. It didn't take much cajoling to get him to give in.

"Fine, my dear. You have bested me yet again. You go ahead and take Docker here out for some exercise since I can see you both have your heart set on it, but no running, young lady. Now promise me that much!"

She laughed, and that made his smile all the broader. "I promise not to run," although she knew she'd do exactly that once she was far enough away so he wouldn't see. "And I also promise I'll take another horse tomorrow. Which one would you like me to ride for the rest of my time here?"

He hooked his thumbs in his vest pocket. "How about Cocoa? She's a sturdy little mare."

She shook her head. "I want something with life in it, something with a lot more fire than Cocoa."

"You drive a hard bargain. All right, Arthur is a very well-behaved gelding. Take him next time."

She nodded. "Arthur, it is. Now I must be off if I'm to get back at a decent hour."

Off she went at a fast walk, although she doubted her uncle was fooled. What did it matter anyway? This was the last day she would ride Docker. After all, she told herself with a grin, weren't promises made to be broken?

So away she went, first at a trot, then a lope and eventually she let the horse have its head in a full-out run. What fun it was as the wind whipped her hair and the sun warmed her cheeks.

Spending time with Pate in the meadow was as pleasurable this morning as it always was. How many girls had a tall, dark, handsome man waiting for them for a romantic tryst? Not many that looked like him, she assumed. It was like one of the adventures she read about in those naughty dime novels, except this was real life and she was the one living it.

She and Pate wasted no time getting down to what they'd come for, and all too soon it was time to go. Pate was reluctant to let her leave, but she eventually managed to extract herself. With one last kiss, she climbed up onto the chestnut again and rode off without a backward glance. If he waved, she didn't see it. No matter, she'd make up for it next time. He'd suggested tomorrow at daybreak, as usual, but she'd begged off because of prior commitments. There never seemed to be enough time.

Back through the woods she went under the luxuriant canopy of towering hardwood trees. It felt as though she was riding within the continuously altered mosaic of a kaleidoscope, the magical comingling of colour, light and motion provided by sun, shadow and wind. Such an enchanting morning! She wisely slowed to a walk, given the exposed tree roots that snaked across the narrow path. They could easily trip a horse, so caution was key.

Back at her uncle and aunt's stable, she turned her mount over to the groom, then made her way into the house in time for a late breakfast.

Aunt Emmaline met her in the doorway with a broad smile. "There you are, child. You have company waiting for you in the parlour. Your fiancé has arrived all the way from Boston, and he's most anxious to see you."

Chapter 13

Dinah stopped up short. Leander was here? In Sackville?

She swiftly recovered, running her fingers through her disheveled hair. "My goodness, Aunt Emmaline. The way you spring things on me. I'll go to my room and freshen up, straighten my hair before I receive any visitors. Tell him I'll be right along, if you don't mind."

Fifteen minutes later, she opened the parlour doors to find Leander Banks standing by the window overlooking the vast expanse of the Tantramar Marsh. He wheeled around when he heard her come in.

"My darling!" he declared, starting forward. "If you aren't a sight for sore eyes."

Taking her in his arms, he kissed her chastely on the forehead. "Aren't you happy to see me?"

"Of course I am," she answered with a sweetly dimpled smile. "It's just that I wasn't expecting you. I'm sorry to have kept you waiting."

"Where were you off to so early in the morning?"

"I like to go for an early-morning ride as often as I can. You know how much I enjoy riding. The air is clean and fresh here, so invigourating."

He held her back at arm's length. "It certainly suits you. I swear, if you aren't the most beautiful woman I have ever seen."

"Then you haven't seen many women," she teased him, luxuriating in the compliment.

"I've seen my share," he teased, winking cheekily at her. "Boston is full of lovely women, but none so ravishing as you."

She laughed, and she knew he loved the cheerful sound of it if his ever-widening smile was any indication of his pleasure.

"I tell you, Leander, it's the air here. It's good for the body, and the soul."

"Then we must go riding together."

She toyed with an errant lock of his hair. "You know me, I'm one of those people who enjoys my own company. I'm afraid I must insist on going alone, that's the good for the soul part. It allows me the liberty of introspection. Not everything is meant to be shared."

He pulled a look of mock offence. "Not even with me, the man who treasures you more than life?"

"Oh, Leander, your flattery knows no bounds. Come, let's sit down. You must be tired from travelling all the way from Boston. I must say I'm surprised to see you. Didn't you say in your last letter that you wouldn't be able to get away for a visit to Sackville this summer? If I knew you were coming so soon, I might have waited and travelled here with you. I found it very boring on that ship with no one to talk to."

They sat down on a settee arranged along the far wall, a fine piece of furniture upholstered in ivory silk with scrolled armrests and mahogany veneer. She had forgotten how attractive Leander was, tall, light-haired, blue-eyed and blessed with rakish good looks. It was his smile she'd found most appealing when she'd first met him, and she had positively swooned when he'd mischievously kissed her at the ball when he thought no one was looking. She'd just turned eighteen, and they'd become betrothed within a fortnight. But her father had insisted on a courtship of no less than two years.

They were more than a year into that betrothal now, and work was underway in earnest on her wedding dress. It would be white, in salute to Queen Victoria's choice of colour for her *own* bridal gown. Hence the fashion trend, and so Dinah had chosen rich satin, overlaid with matching handmade lace, and a plethora of ribbon, lace edging and chiffon ruching. There were also generous sprays of orange blossoms, both on the dress itself as well as on the elaborate head wreath and the ten-foot cathedral veil. She promised to be the most breathtaking bride during Boston's wedding season.

"Darling," he said adoringly, "I was not trying to deceive you, although I must admit I did like surprising you. I thought you'd be bored by now up here in this tiny village, especially after the social life you're accustomed to in Boston."

"So how did you come to be here?" she asked.

"It was most fortuitous. I had to make an unexpected business trip to St. John, so I made my way there by boat, then took the train on down to Sackville last evening. Imagine my surprise that you were not home when I arrived early this morning." He took hold of her hands again. "I've missed you, Dinah. I cannot possibly explain how much."

"And I've missed you. How long do you plan to stay?"

He frowned. "Not nearly long enough, I'm afraid. We'll have to be satisfied with a quick hello, and then I'm off again first thing tomorrow morning. I need to be back in Boston for a very important meeting. This was a brief aside, but it was worth the extra effort to see your face again."

She smiled, her thumbs caressing the tops of his hands that still held hers. "But I left you a picture of myself."

He groaned. "A poor substitute, my dear, when the real thing is but a few days away. And may I ask why you are not wearing your diamond engagement ring?"

"Because it would break my heart to lose it, so I take it off before I go riding." Pulling her hands away she tenderly cupped his face. "I love you, Leander. The time has seemed so long since I got here, even though it hasn't been, not really. I've tried to keep busy, but you know how it is."

She looked around conspiratorially, then lowered her voice. "I would imagine Aunt Emmaline has put you in the guest room at the end of the hall."

He confirmed that was the case, his eyes never leaving hers, anticipation dawning.

"You could sneak away after Aunt and Uncle have gone to sleep and pay me a visit," she whispered. "Wouldn't that be deliciously naughty?"

His smile was flirtatious. "I thought you wanted to wait for our wedding night."

She lowered her gaze. "What would be the point of that now?"

He became pensive. "I'm so sorry you had to endure that beastly attack three years ago, Dinah. How dreadful it must have been. To have your virginity stolen away by that good-for-nothing scoundrel."

"Hmmm," she responded, trying to remember the sordid details of the story she'd concocted when they'd first met. "But that was such a long time ago, and I have fully recovered from that ordeal. If anything, I believe it awakened me. I yearn for you."

Of course there'd been no attack, but she thought perhaps her intended might be hoping for a chaste bride, and so she'd fabricated the story to manage his expectations. Accordingly, Leander had heretofore been the perfect gentleman, but it was about time he made some ungentlemanly advances now that all of the cards were on the table.

Many women had set their cap for Leander Banks, and he'd had his share of fair maidens to choose from. She had decided she would be the one to steal his heart, and she'd succeeded, with minimal effort.

His eyes were bright with desire. "Are you sure you want me to come to your room, darling?" he asked her seriously. "I don't want you to compromise your virtue just to satisfy me."

"I fear you'll turn elsewhere," she answered him honestly, "and I am ready to be yours in every way. Our only impediment is my aunt and uncle, but I don't think they would say anything even if they did hear us. They know I'll soon be your wife."

He grinned. "Yes, but it's impossible to know how they'll react, and that would be most embarrassing if your uncle took me to task. I would rather not have to answer to your father in that regard."

"Leave it all to me," she said.

Leandre didn't miss the secretive look in her eyes as her glance darted toward the parlour doors, and he chuckled. "What do you have up your sleeve, you little witch?"

"I'm going to come to *you*. I can be as quiet as a church mouse during Sunday service. Sometimes I sneak out at night, you know, to go for a walk, or sit on the veranda, and they never hear a thing. If they did, Uncle Horace would be chastising me for what he'd consider an unwise practice."

"He's right, Dinah. Do you think it's safe for you to go out alone after dark? Sackville has its share of taverns, and lord knows who'd be about at that hour."

"Nobody would bother me here," she assured him before changing the subject. "Have you eaten yet today? I haven't and I'm perfectly starved. Let me go see if Aunt Emmaline has my breakfast ready. She makes enough for an army, so I will invite you to join me, or have you already eaten?"

"Not a bite since last night," he admitted with chagrin. "I took tea on the train, but I wasn't impressed with their selection of pastries, so I kept to the beverage."

Aunt Emmaline did indeed have a late breakfast ready for her niece, the kind-hearted woman preparing enough for both her and her fiancé. Dinah and Leander sat down to a meal of soufflés, pastries and pancakes, and even a side dish of oysters. Emmaline was a superb cook who, despite the fact that her husband had offered on many occasions to hire kitchen help, insisted on taking care of the meals herself.

Both Dinah and Leander ate heartily, then everyone made ready for Sunday service, arriving in a nick of time. Later, they relaxed in the cool shade of the wrap-around veranda.

Uncle Horace joined them minutes later, settling his bulk into another of the wooden leisure chairs. "Is business good in Boston?" he asked the young man. "Industrial textile mills are your line of work, are they not?"

"Absolutely, Mr. Gladstone," Leander answered him politely, "and lately I've begun to invest in railroads. It's all doing very nicely, I'm pleased to tell you."

Uncle Horace smiled, his oversized moustache all but concealing a small mouth. "So, you'll be able to keep our Dinah here in the lifestyle to which she has become accustomed."

Leander smiled that dashing smile of his, the one that made people sit up and take notice. The one that made Dinah's heart skip a beat. "You can be sure of that. I'm a wealthy man, Mr. Gladstone. The Banks are one of the first families of Boston, you know."

Uncle Horace nodded slowly. "I had forgotten that, but I do seem to recall my brother mentioning it. I for one couldn't be happier with this match," he said, glancing cheerily at Dinah and Leander in turn. "I couldn't have handpicked a better future husband for my niece. I'm sure the two of you will be very happy together. And, of course, we expect a lot of little ones."

"Uncle!" Dinah scolded him playfully. "Don't put the cart before the horse."

Uncle Horace chuckled good-naturedly. "All in good time, Dinah. All in good time."

* * *

Dinah lay in bed that night and thought about her life with Leander. What a golden married couple they would make. They'd be the toast of Beantown. She would want for nothing, but then she never had. She couldn't imagine life any other way. Would she have children? Perhaps, one day, but she had a lot of living to do before she became tied down. Leander had countered her nicely on that one, promising to hire a governess for whatever children they had, even a wet nurse if it didn't appeal to her to care for their child in that way. So it might not be too terrible after all. But she'd heard that delivery could be awful. Anyway, she wouldn't concern herself with that at the moment.

She kept an ear tuned to Aunt Emmaline and Uncle Horace's bedroom next door. Uncle Horace snored like a locomotive, so it wouldn't be too hard to know when he'd fallen asleep, and not surprisingly, Emmaline's hearing wasn't what it used to be. She'd wait a few minutes after the snoring got underway to be sure he was well and truly in dreamland. She didn't want to have him come sputtering awake at the worst possible moment and catch her in the hall. If that were to happen, she'd simply use her charm to wiggle her way out of it. She'd been relying on it her entire life. It was her most effective weapon, and it had grown stronger with use.

And there it was! The loud snoring told her the train had left the station. She watched the clock to give Uncle a good, healthy start to oblivion, and then she'd tiptoe down the hall into Leander's room. Given his previous reputation with the ladies, she was sure that premarital bliss awaited her there.

"Are you awake?" she whispered once she was inside his bedroom door.

"Awake and waiting for you. Come to me, Dinah."

"You are so very special," she whispered against his ear once she was in his arms. "I love you, Leander."

* * *

A week later, a horse and buggy pulled into the yard of the Kavenagh farm, driven by a smartly dressed man, sitting tall in the seat and wearing a black bowler hat. He wore long, neatly-kept side-whiskers that framed a no-nonsense expression. Beside him sat a boy of about nineteen, slim but with keen, intelligent eyes.

Pate was coming up from the barn when he spotted the callers and ambled casually over to the buggy to speak to the driver.

The man extended his hand. "I'm Howard Monahan from Sackville, and I hear you have a very fast horse you might be interested in selling."

Pate had reluctantly put out a few feelers in a half-hearted attempt to sell Jacko, but had not received a response. He hadn't ridden the horse again, as he'd promised his father and others he wouldn't, but he'd cast a longing eye in Jacko's direction from time to time.

"I do," said Pate, "but you may find I want too much for him."

Again, another attempt to forestall the sale, but the man persisted.

"That may be so, but I'd like to take a look at him. Where is he?"

Pate invited the pair to go with him to the pasture, and he called the horse over for their inspection. He could see right away they knew they were looking at prime horseflesh, as Monahan ran an appreciative hand down the horse's neck and out along his back.

"He's a beaut, all right. What do you call him?" he asked Pate.

"His name is Jacko, and I should tell you he can be spooky. Jumps at stuff."

The man waved away that concern. "I'm looking at him for the track, and there's nothing out there to scare him, just other horses running beside him. But first, I want Iggy here to try him. Can he take him for a run on the road?"

Pate eyed Iggy. "You know how to ride, do you?"

Iggy glared at Pate. "Since I was three. Your horse'll be safe with me."

"If anyone can get any speed out of him, it's Iggy here," Monahan explained. "Okay if he stretches him out? I want to see what he's got."

"I guess," Pate shrugged. "Let me saddle him up..."

"I'll ride him bareback," said Iggy, patting Jacko. "I don't want him weighed down with tack."

Pate shrugged again. "As you like. We can walk up to the road and watch," he said to Monahan.

Iggy led Jacko out of the pasture, and once they were in the yard, jumped onto his back as nimble as a squirrel. Grabbing two handfuls of mane, he directed the horse to the road and waited until Howard and Pate were watching before he trotted a short distance away, then turned and let loose. Jacko and Iggy swept past them in a flash, the big horse running with ease.

Monahan whistled. "He's the fastest thing I've seen on four legs. You sure he doesn't have wings?" he joked as he and Pate walked back down into the farmyard.

Iggy followed, the horse barely winded.

Monahan went over and ran his hand along the horse's neck again, and down over his powerful shoulders. "He didn't even break a sweat. That animal has some heart in him." He turned to Pate. "Name your price."

This was a crossroads for Pate. He knew Jacko had to go, but the moment of parting, now at hand, seemed to be one of the most difficult he'd ever had to face. He shared a powerful connection with that horse.

Pate stuck out his chin. "I'll sell him to you on one condition."

Monahan looked at him curiously. "What's that?"

Pate held the man's gaze while Iggy waited, obviously very much at home on the horse's back. "I won't sell him if I don't think he's going to be treated well. I'll put him to pasture for the rest of his life rather than sell him to someone who'd abuse him, treat him cruelly. And I have ways of finding that out."

Monahan regarded Pate kindly, "I have a lot of horses, son, and I've always treated each and every one of them kindly. I don't know any other way, but I want him for racing, and unless I miss my guess, this big black lives to run. He knows that's what he was bred for. He has speed he hasn't even used yet, and I can get the most out of him."

Iggy spoke from his perch atop the horse. "I work for Mr. Monahan here, and I can tell you he's good to his horses. None of us would have a job very long if we mistreated any of his animals. That's a rule we all know to follow, not that I'd want to hurt a horse myself, no matter how stubborn some of them can get."

Pate studied Jacko, then looked at Monahan, not saying anything, but the wheels were turning. Could he do it? People bought and sold horses all the time. He was being too softhearted. He knew that. But the truth was, he needed the money to fix up Julia's old homestead. He needed to make a home for himself and Dinah. He couldn't ride Jacko anymore anyway. It wasn't worth the risk after what he'd been through.

Monahan wisely read the indecision. "I said name your price."

Pate squared his shoulders. He'd paid fifty dollars for Jacko, and that was considered a good price. He knew a good, solid horse was worth about a hundred and fifty dollars, even two hundred. He'd gotten the big black cheaper because of his spookiness.

Monahan shifted on his feet. "Time is money, young man. Either name your price, or I walk away and wait for the next one. It's all the same to me."

Pate knew Monahan was bluffing. If he were ready to walk away, he wouldn't have told him to name his price. He was afraid of having Pate slip off his hook, is all, and then he'd have to go fishing all over again somewhere else. He also knew that horses like Jacko didn't grow on trees. Some horses were fast, but Jacko was faster.

Pate looked Monahan in the eye. "I want five hundred dollars for this horse, and not a penny less."

Monahan's eyes widened. "You're crazy! No horse is worth five hundred dollars."

Pate stood his ground. "This one is. There are plenty of horses worth five hundred dollars, and more, and you know it. Do you want him or not? If you do, pay my price or I put him back in the pasture and change my mind altogether about selling him."

Monahan hesitated. "It's highway robbery, but I'll give you four hundred dollars, and that's it. Final offer."

Pate was unblinking. "You told me to name my price. Five hundred dollars is my price."

Monahan set his hands on his hips. "I said name your price, not try to rob me. I should have said name a price that's within reason."

Pate looked up at Iggy. "Get down off him so I can put him back in the pasture. Jacko isn't going anywhere today. I'm not going to give him away."

Iggy didn't budge, but he was smiling.

Monahan shook his head. "All right! five hundred it is." He pulled a brown leather wallet out of the inside pocket of his jacket and counted out the money.

"Iggy can ride him back for me."

"No!" said Pate. "I'll ride him down to Sackville myself. I want that one last ride with my old friend. You can pay me when I get there. Deal?"

Monahan was smiling now. He looked like a man who took pleasure in a good round of dickering. "All right, Iggy, ride him on down to the pasture," he said as he put his wallet away. "Pate here can bring him down this afternoon, if that's all right with you," he said, turning to look at Pate.

Pate nodded. "I'll have him down there by three o'clock, and we'll settle up then."

Tabor came down to the barn after the men left and found Pate standing at the fence rail watching Jacko. "I was sitting on the veranda and heard the whole thing, Pate. If you're not one of the best hagglers I've ever heard, I don't know who is. Five hundred dollars! That's a ransom, but he paid it. I'm glad for you, son, now you've got the money to get started up the road, with plenty to spare. But I'm not in favour of you riding that horse all the way to Sackville."

"I know, but I couldn't help myself. I won't run him, though. I won't go more than a fast walk. I want to take him there, say good-bye on my own terms."

* * *

It wasn't a long ride into the village, ten miles or so, and he was glad he was taking it slow because there were lots of memories to sift through. He knew the horse understood they were going to part company. In fact, he'd already said his goodbye in the barn with no one watching. He knew it had to be, and so did the horse.

249

As he rode along, he thought about Dinah and their meeting this morning. It had been particularly sweet, them talking about their future together. He knew their families would meet sooner or later, and he couldn't imagine the Gladstones accepting the Kavenaghs, but they'd work it out somehow. As long as they had one another.

It was another hot day, and he should by rights be in the hayfield as he'd been yesterday, but this had to be taken care of. Things were moving ahead as per his plan, but none of it was easy.

All too soon, they were entering Sackville, and he followed the directions to the Monahan farm. When he found it, he saw a number of fine animals grazing in several pastures. Monahan said he was into racing, so he was probably looking at some expensive hay burners. Jacko neighed to the other horses, and they answered, trotting over to the whiteboard fence to check out the newcomer.

Dismounting, he tied Jacko to the rail and went into the dim interior of the barn to see if anyone was around. He heard two men talking down at the far end, so he started in that direction. He stopped short when he heard one of them speak Dinah's name. Stepping off to the side in the shadowy interior, he listened.

"You've been with Dinah, too?" one man asked the other.

"Sure, who hasn't?" the other man laughed. "Word gets around fast in Sackville. It's not that big a place. We call it Dinah's meadow. That's where she takes us. How long have you been going there?"

"Since she got here. Sometimes it's at daybreak, which she says is her favourite time of the day, and other times it's in the afternoon."

"So that's where you've been sneaking off to."

Pate froze as he recognized Iggy's voice. He felt as though he was going to be sick.

"She's worth it. She's a real beauty. I want to marry her if she'll have me. She says she's thinking about it."

The first man laughed. "She won't marry you, you knucklehead. You ain't good enough."

"She said she would."

"That's to keep you coming."

"Well, *you* can't marry her for fair, Glen, because you're already married. You get one woman, and that's all."

"My wife don't look like that. I never saw a woman who likes to take her clothes off like Dinah. Not that I mind."

Lewd comments followed, and Pate tried to shut his ears to them, but he knew he couldn't forget what they'd called her. The vulgar things they said about her, and what she did with them. He had treated her with respect, but from what he was hearing now, she was game for just about anything. But could they be making it up? Two randy teenagers trying to outdo the other? It certainly didn't seem so. It didn't feel like it.

He heard one of them say he was meeting her at daybreak tomorrow, and the other one telling him to enjoy himself, followed by more raucous laughter.

Pate backed up into the shadows as quietly as he'd come in and retraced his steps to the entrance again, then started forward. "Hey, anybody here?" he called out.

The low rumble of conversation stopped. "We're down back. Come on down."

Pate walked the length of the barn to where Iggy was standing with another young man, Pate guessed to be in his thirties. At least. A terrible image arose in his mind, but he shoved it away.

Iggy smiled, "You looking for Mr. Monahan?"

Pate nodded. "He said I could find him in the barn. I've got the black with me."

Iggy turned, cupped his mouth with both hands, and shouted to a figure standing at the fence rail of the far pasture. "Mr. Monahan! The man is here with the black!"

Monahan raised his hand in acknowledgement and headed for the barn, where the transaction was completed.

"Now I'll drive you home in the buggy," Monahan told him, and within the hour, Pate was walking up the front steps to the farmhouse, his world lying in pieces around him.

* * *

Pate was out of bed before daylight the next morning, even though it was not his turn in the meadow as he now thought of it. Knew it to be so. Making his way downstairs, he found the Winchester rifle on the wall in the kitchen and made sure it was loaded, then started for the door, his jaw set.

"Where are you going with that so early, Pate?" asked Tabor from the shadows on the veranda where he was sitting.

Pate stopped dead in his tracks, but recovered without comment. "I'm going hunting, Pa."

"For what? We're still eating that beef we killed in the spring. We don't need anything more for the larder at the moment. We'll go hunting in the fall, you and I."

Pate gripped the gun as he turned to go.

"Pate!" Tabor spoke sharply. "Whatever you have in your mind, son, don't do it!"

"Some things need doin', Pa," and with that, he walked away carrying the gun, his father calling after him.

He would go by foot to the meadow and lie in wait for Dinah, and whichever lover she was meeting. He knew she wouldn't be long as he slipped into the underbrush and ducked down out of sight, already hearing the hoof beats of Dinah's horse coming up the path. Dismounting, she tied the horse to the old tree, as was her habit with him.

Carefree and smiling, she straightened her hair from the ride and went to sit on the fallen log. Minutes later, he heard a second horse. Sure enough, it was the man from the barn, the married one. He hurriedly dismounted and went to join her. Not surprisingly, Dinah wasted no time stripping her clothes off, tossing them aside with cheerful abandon, laughing that tinkling laugh of hers. She posed lewdly for the man who was already tearing at his own clothes in his haste to get at her.

Pate watched the sickening scene playing out before him. Hot tears of bitter disappointment temporarily blinded him, but he brushed them away angrily. He carefully raised the rifle and took aim, Dinah's head squarely in his crosshairs. He willed the tremble from his finger as he slid it onto the trigger and began to squeeze.

Chapter 14

He squeezed harder. If the gun had been cocked, she would be dead now. Instead, he forced himself to watch the spectacle being played out before him in case he would ever again be tempted to believe he still loved her. The guttural ooohs and ahhs, her declarations of love. Blessedly, the coupling was brief, and the man, obviously needing to return to Sackville right away, probably to work, got to his feet. That's when Pate cocked the gun. The man recognized the sound in an instant, even though Pate was concealed. With a look of terror, he grabbed his clothes and, clutching them in one hand, ran for his life, just as he was, leapt onto his horse and sped away.

Dinah, thrown completely off guard, rose from the ground in open-mouthed surprise as she watched her lover disappear without so much as a fare-thee-well. And then Pate stepped out of the bushes, the rifle trained on her, and she froze, her look of astonishment instantly turning to shock. Horror.

Sweat trickled down the middle of his back, ran down his forehead and into his eyes, but he blinked it away. A rage he didn't know he was capable of bubbled inside him like a witch's cauldron. He nearly quaked with it, his handsome face a terrifying mask.

"Oh, Pate, I'm so glad you came," she whimpered, "that man forced me…"

"Shut up!" he barked. "I saw the whole thing, you strutting around naked for him, showing every part of yourself. Don't bother with your lies."

Her eyes were impossibly wide, and the handsome emerald green had vanished completely. They reminded him now of the pit viper he'd seen in a book about reptiles.

"I d-d-don't know what came over me. I missed you so much… I love you, Pate, honestly."

"Honestly? You don't know what the word means. How could I have thought you were beautiful? You're ugly. You're nothing but a whore, except you're worse than that because they're just trying to support themselves. You're the worst kind of woman there is. You're a slut, a bangtail straight out of the gutter. You're filth."

"How dare you say such things to me, an uneducated, coarse, no-good son of a dirt farmer! A *Kavenagh*!"

He steadied the gun, taking more careful aim.

She began to cry, holding her hands out to him in supplication for her life. "I'm sorry. I shouldn't have said those things. I didn't mean them, honest. Please don't shoot me,

Pate. I'm begging you. I don't know what came over me, but please give me another chance. We can start over."

He couldn't believe his ears, momentarily lowering the gun. "Start over? With me? You're out of your mind! I think now what I gave up for the likes of you."

He raised the rifle again.

She cried harder. "Are you going to kill me?"

"Yes," he stated flatly as he held the rifle steady, "I am. That's what I came here to do."

Her face wavered before his eyes as she fell to her knees, begging him piteously.

And then he remembered his uncle Brogan behind those bars. The smell of the place. The word Freedom. No, he would not give up his life for hers. It would be a poor bargain.

He lowered the gun and uncocked it. "You're not worth the bullet."

She actually had the nerve to smile at him. "Please tell me you'll forgive me, Pate."

He took a menacing step closer. "You get those fancy clothes of yours, and you get on that horse and take for Sackville," he said. "I never want to see your face again. If you ever come near me, or I hear you're talking about me, about this, I'll finish what I started here this morning. If you're as smart as you think you are, you'll be heading back to Boston on the next boat. I know about the men you bring up here, all of them. You're all done in Sackville."

White-faced, she snatched up her clothes, hauled them on unceremoniously and made a speedy exit. Her horse's hoof beats on the forest path echoed in a farewell tattoo, and he listened until they were far in the distance. Suddenly exhausted, he stood in the meadow and looked around, then turned and headed back via the shortcut to the farm.

His steps were slow and heavy when he got to the yard, and he could see the glow of a cigarette on the other end of the veranda. His father was waiting. Pate unloaded the rifle and slipped the cartridges into his pocket. Leaning the gun by its barrel against the building, he walked up the steps to his father.

"Are you all right?" Tabor asked in a low voice. "That was the longest hour and a half of my life."

"I loved her, Pa, and I thought she loved me."

"I know, son. Love can be a bad business sometimes, but you can't know how thankful I am you didn't pull that trigger."

"I came as close as I ever will to killing someone."

"But thank God you didn't. Someone else likely will one day if what I'm thinking is true."

"It's true."

"Some women don't just break your heart, they beat it right into the ground. You didn't lay a hand on her, did you? Hurt her in any way?"

"I didn't touch either one of them. It was all I could do to hold back, but I did. I kept remembering Brogan in that jail cell three years ago. I didn't want to end up like him. If I did kill her, I could have used the rifle on myself, too, I suppose, but I wouldn't do that to you, Pa."

Pate broke down then, his pent-up hurt and anger pouring out with each raspy sob. He was unashamed to have his father see him cry, but it felt oddly comforting somehow, and then he dried his eyes. The ache in his heart would be a long time healing, if ever.

They sat there, side-by-side in silence for another hour, save for the rooster's persistent crowing in the barn. Another day was well underway, the sun high above the horizon now, its warmth fully upon them.

"Feel like going in and getting some breakfast, Pate?"

Pate sighed as he shifted forward in the chair. "Might as well. I'll go get the porridge started. Sure do miss Julia, and not just for the cooking."

"From what Brogan said last night, Maggie is coming along fine, getting her strength back. She's eating plenty of red meat to help build her back up, and it's working, but it'll be a while yet before she can tend that baby on her own. They're grateful to have Julia there, but she said she's coming back on Sunday for the day. I guess that baby is a real howler. Julia said it's hard for any of them to sleep."

Pate found himself chuckling. "What was I like as a baby, Pa? Was I a howler, too?"

Tabor chuckled. "You never shut up."

Both men laughed, easing the tension as they got up to go into the house.

* * *

The weeks passed as July mellowed into August, the countryside ripening in the relentless summer heat. Maggie had improved to the point where she was able to be up and around, which meant that Julia could return home. Baby Maisie had thrived under Julia's care, as well as that of her doting parents and brothers.

Pate assumed that Dinah had returned to Boston after her comeuppance in the meadow, but he would have no way of knowing. One thing he did understand for certain was that what he had believed to be love had been infatuation or just pure lust, but he wasn't ashamed that he'd been intimate with her. He had not treated her disrespectfully. He'd wanted to take her for his wife and knew he had providence to thank that his eyes had been opened in time. It would have been disastrous to marry her if it had gotten that far, which he doubted now, it would have. Thankfully, too, if she brought a child into this world as a result of her

260

sojourns in the meadow, it wouldn't be his. Whatever had led her to behave the way she did, he couldn't imagine. He didn't care to know, and his only memory of her now was a bad one. She was no better than a bitch in heat. He had been spared.

He often thought about Colleen and what a fool he'd been. Sweet Colleen, beautiful inside and out, the perfect choice to be the mother of his children if he hadn't been so stupidly blinded by false charms. He thought about going to see her, hat in hand, but he hadn't worked up the courage to do so yet. He would, someday, like in a few weeks, as he slowly talked himself around. In the meantime, he was busy.

His pa was fully mended now and feeling better than he had in years, in every way. He said so himself. He'd never known his father to be cheerful, so it was like getting to know him all over again. Pate knew life was good, except for his badly bruised heart. He now understood how hard it must have been for Colleen when he'd broken off with her so abruptly that day. He'd thought he was doing the honourable thing, which in a way it was, he supposed, rather than seeing Dinah behind her back, but he'd still hurt her.

And he missed Jacko. He'd considered, at one point, driving down to visit him, but he didn't want to see Sackville again for a good long while.

"You look like you're deep in thought," Tabor said as he walked out onto the veranda. "You're looking serious. What are you thinking about, son?"

Pate shrugged. "This and that. I think we can get most of that second cut of hay this afternoon if the weather holds. It isn't much of a cut, but we'll get what we can."

Tabor looked out at the sky from under the veranda roof. "It looks as though it might. The crop's not going to be too good this year, not with the small amount of rain we've had this summer. It's stunted."

Julia walked out onto the veranda, picking up the thread of conversation. "And the garden's dry. One good thing, there hasn't been an overgrowth of weeds, and we're lucky to have a spring nearby to keep it watered. I wouldn't be surprised if the potatoes are small, and I can't keep the peas from burning up right on the vine. I think I'll give them more shelter next year in case we have another summer like this."

All three were now taking the shade on the veranda before the men headed back to the fields.

From where he was sitting, Pate could watch Freedom grazing in the pasture, and Tabor followed his gaze.

"What are you planning to do with that young stallion, Pate? Sell him? You decided not to geld him, and that was a wise choice, but this farm isn't big enough for two stallions."

Pate nodded. "Freedom is over three years old, and I think he's going to be the best horse I've raised yet. That horse means everything to me, and he's ready to stand at stud now, but I don't like to lose Silver Billy. He's a good animal, and I paid a decent price for him."

Tabor studied the young horse a little longer before he spoke. "Silver Billy *has* been a good stud. He's sired some nice babies, but he's what, fifteen now, and I'd be thinking about the future. Of course, it's your decision, but I'd sell Billy or retire him along with that older bay mare. Your chestnut mare is in estrus again, so I'd start introducing her to Freedom."

Pate nodded. "I've been thinking about that."

Julia smoothed her apron. "You've got quite a few horses now, Pate, including the babies. Do you plan to take all of them up the road with you?"

Pate took another drink of tea. "Nah, I'll be selling the bay mare for starters once her baby's weaned, and the stud, Silver Billy, I mean. Arnold Wilson's got some good stock over there. He's interested in the babies once they're off the teat, so I might make him a trade."

Julia smiled. "You're quite the businessman, Pate. I don't think anyone could get anything past you."

That stung a bit, although he didn't say anything. Julia had no idea what he'd been through in terms of dealing with deception of the worst kind. It had been a bitter lesson, but it was one he would not repeat.

Tabor sensed the awkward moment. "I'll say he's a top-notch haggler. You should have heard him dickering with that fellah from Sackville when he sold the black. I was impressed."

Julia smiled. "You're in the right business, Pate. You're a natural-born horse trader. How are you making out up the road? I don't imagine you've had much of a chance to do a lot because you've been so busy here."

Pate set his empty cup on the floor beside his chair. "I'm starting to make some headway. Brogan came up last week and gave me a hand with the fencing, and next week I'm hiring Luke so we can finish the rest of it. I've also got the barn roof patched, and now I've got to get some hay in. Great fields up there."

Julia smiled wistfully. "My father said they were some of the finest hayfields around, save for the marsh. They're all timothy, no real scrub to speak of. There's even alfalfa in places. I think you'll be very pleased with the crop you take off them."

Pate leaned back in his chair, balancing on the hind legs. "I know I will be. And now that you have what you're taking out of the house, I can start thinking about moving in. I won't be doing anything about it, though, until the end of this month or the first of September. That's when I'll start taking the horses up. Thank you, too, for cleaning the house. I swear I don't know where you get all of your energy."

Tabor chuckled. "I think she takes a secret pill or something. She doesn't stop from morning 'til night. She's a wonder all right."

Pate caught the side-eyed smile between them, and it pleased him to see them exchanging a look of affection.

They heard a horse and wagon approaching and old Peterson Gault drove into the yard, shoved the brake into place and climbed down.

He already had his pipe out as Tabor gestured to the empty chair on the veranda. Peterson slowly made his way to it, seemingly grateful for the shade. "I come to bring you some news about one of your neighbours up the road a ways," he began. "Johnny Sullivan died last night. Got kicked in the head by one of his draft horses. One of the horse's hind feet got tangled in his lines, and when he went to free it, the foot came back a bit too hard, and Johnny was in the way of it. That team of his was very good-natured. It was an accident, pure and simple, but Johnny's dead. They say it killed him right on the spot. Thought you folks might want to know about it. They're going to bury him tomorrow."

Pate was stunned. Johnny Sullivan was a good man. He thought about Colleen. She'd been close to her pa, and this would be a terrible blow.

Tabor leaned forward. "I can't hardly believe what I'm hearing, and him not yet fifty years old. What will his wife, Callie, do now? Who'll run the farm?"

Gault got his corncob pipe going with gentle puffing, then settled it comfortably into the corner of his mouth. "The two boys are going to take it over, they say. Callie's fit to be tied, right in a proper state of shock. Goes to show. One minute you have someone, and the next minute you don't. Folks are gathering at the house tonight."

Julia stood up. "I'll get a stew started right away to take up with us," she said, "and some biscuits. I already have a cake in the cupboard, so I'll take that too. Callie will have a lot of mouths to feed tonight, and she might not feel much like cooking in the days ahead."

Pate thought about seeing Colleen again. He might not be welcome in the house, not after the way things had gone. Not that he'd done anything so terrible, but he'd broken Colleen's heart and family members didn't take kindly to such things. But of course, he'd go up with Tabor and Julia tonight. He'd also offer his help with the haying if they needed it. As tragic as it was to lose someone, there was a lot of work to be done on a farm this time of year. The animals had to be tended, crops gotten in and preserved, and the winter's hay harvested. It'd be a mighty long winter with nothing for the stock to eat.

Gault took a steady draw on his pipe. "It's been a hard summer around here," he said. "Folks sick and all, or getting themselves hurt. Having babies. I saw that Dr. Mains going the other day, looked like he was in a hurry. I expect someone was having a baby, although I'm not sure who it would be. I haven't heard of such in my travels."

Julia stopped on her way to the kitchen to see to the new round of cooking. "Can I get you a cup of tea, Mr. Gault?"

Gault politely refused. "No, but I'll take a finger or two of something stronger if you have it."

Tabor laughed. "I keep a bottle under the cupboard in case of frostbite. You can have a drink of that."

Pate chuckled. "It's cooler this afternoon."

"You never know," said Tabor with the ghost of a grin. "Always better to be on the safe side."

Gault turned his attention to Pate. "You goin' to go up to the Sullivan's too?"

Pate looked at the old man, surprised. "Why, sure, I'm going to go. Why wouldn't I?"

"Not sure you'd be welcome is all. Didn't mean to ruffle your feathers, young fellah."

Pate didn't pay Gault much mind. He was a harmless old man who took his job of news carrying seriously. No one needed a newspaper as long as Peterson Gault was on the move.

Pate chuckled. "You'll know it if my feathers get ruffled, Gault. I'll be going to pay my respects, same as everybody else."

Smoke encircled Gault's head in a pungent cloud. "Goin' to the funeral too? I won't be. I don't hold much with funerals. Can't seem to take to them at all, not since I lost my wife and young 'uns."

Pate nodded. "I'll be going to the funeral too. It's the least I can do. Johnny Sullivan was a fine man. He was good to me."

The truth was, he'd been thinking about Colleen a lot lately, especially this last week or so. He missed her. He'd doubted before as to whether he actually loved the girl, and he'd come to the mistaken conclusion that it must not be the real thing if his head could be turned by another. But the more he thought about it, the more he realized his true feelings. What he wouldn't give to turn back the clock a few weeks. He would do things much differently, but then again, wouldn't everybody who'd made a big mistake?

He remembered how Colleen's hair smelled like spring sunshine, and the way her eyes danced when she laughed. They were a lovely shade of soft blue, like a summer sky. And how had he forgotten how much he liked her little turned-up nose, and the smattering of freckles he used to tease her about? She'd pretend to get mad, but it didn't go very far. Colleen had been a lot of fun. Most importantly, she had loved him, and what had he done? Dropped her like a sack of spoiled potatoes.

* * *

That night, his father, Julia and he drove up to the Sullivan place in the old farm wagon. The yard would be full once they got there, so it would be prudent to take one vehicle that would hold them all, along with the raft of food Julia had prepared.

There were a lot of people at the Sullivan farm when they arrived. The house was full, and most of the men were lingering in the yard, talking quietly among themselves. Children raced around, oblivious to the gravity of the situation. Brogan, Luke and Jake had made the trip down the road, but it was much too soon for Maggie to travel.

Pate found Colleen inside, talking to Rev. Williams. She looked pretty, despite her tear-swollen eyes, and his heart gave a lift when he saw her. If he could have a moment alone with her, to talk, apologize again, he wouldn't waste the opportunity, but he couldn't very well pull her away from those who had come to offer condolences. As the immediate family of the deceased, they were obligated to receive mourners, and being the only girl, she would step in and take over for her grief-stricken mother.

He caught her eye and nodded, and she nodded back, although somewhat coolly, he noted with disappointment although he

269

knew he deserved no less. He waited for his turn to speak to her, ignoring the unfriendly side-glances of some. Tabor and Julia would of course experience the same thing, but the Kavenaghs were used to it. Finally the long-winded reverend let Colleen go, and he stepped up.

"I'm very sorry for your loss, Colleen. I understand your father was taken instantly."

She dabbed at her eyes with a lace-edged handkerchief. "It happened so fast. I didn't see it, but they were over by the barn and big Toby got backed up too far or something, and his foot got hung up. Both of those horses were so gentle. I know he wouldn't mean for it to happen, but as Papa bent down the horse's foot came free and struck him."

She bent her head and her shoulders shook. "I can't believe Papa is gone. We will all miss him terribly."

He wanted with everything that was in him to put his arms around her shoulders, but wondered if he had the right to do so anymore. He didn't want to overstep, so he took hold of her hand instead and gave it a sympathetic squeeze. She pulled it away. That was not a good sign.

"I'm sorry about your pa, Colleen. I liked him and he *is* going to be missed," he said.

He felt awkward, like a fish out of water. Where had the ease gone that had once existed between them? What he wouldn't give to have it back.

"Thank you," she said simply, already looking past him to the next person in line.

He'd come here tonight with the idea of speaking to her, personally, about them. He knew the timing wasn't the best, but he had a gnawing suspicion there were things that needed to get said, tonight, if they were going to get said at all.

Leaning in closer he spoke against her ear. "I'd like to talk to you, Colleen, alone, before we leave. Do you think that will be possible?"

She looked at him, surprised, but there was no warmth in her eyes. She was obviously put out with him, likely assumed he was still keeping company with Dinah. He was here to tell her differently. Perhaps see if she had any feelings left for him, or if they had been successfully extinguished. His grandmother had told him once that it was possible to kill love, and perhaps that's what he'd done.

It took her so long to respond, he thought she was going to ignore him, then she said simply, "Go down by the barn and I'll be out in a few minutes. There's something I want to say to you, too."

His heart gave a leap. Was there a chance for them after all? He would beg her to forgive him. He would promise to love her for the rest of his life. He would tell her about his new homestead. He would ask her to be his wife, right here and now, tonight. It was how he felt, and now given hope, he intended to act on it without delay.

As promised, Colleen came to the barn a few minutes later, but kept her distance. Fine, he deserved that.

He took a step nearer, and she backed up an equal distance. Not good.

"Colleen," he began anyway, "I was a complete fool when I broke up with you. I know that now, but..."

She cut him off. "She dropped you, didn't she?"

"No, I walked away from her, but I don't want to talk about her ever again. I made the biggest mistake of my life going with her, and believe me, I've paid for it. And now I'm asking you to forgive me, to please give me another chance. I want us to get married, Colleen. I want you to be my wife. My horse business is coming along fine, and I bought a new property. I want us to make our home there. I love you, Colleen Sullivan. Will you marry me? I'll even get down on one knee if you want me to," he added with a grin to help break the ice, but she had not even begun to thaw.

"I wish you the very best, Pate. I really do, but that's all. I laid everything I had on the line for you and made a fool of myself in the process, but you turned me away. You had no time for me once that hussy from Sackville caught your eye. I would never be sure you wouldn't do the same thing again when another pretty face came along. No, you had your chance. It's over between us."

"But we had two years together."

"That didn't seem to count for much when I didn't want to lose you, did it? You were gone without a backward glance. Anyway, things have changed in the past few weeks. I have a new beau. His name is Elmer Carruthers, and we've been seeing each other quite a lot, actually. I like him and he likes me, and I think there might be a future for us."

Pate could see out of the corner of his eye that someone was striding toward them, and a stocky young man quickly came into view.

"Is this man bothering you, Colleen?"

She gave Pate a long look, ice in her eyes. "No, Elmer, everything's all right. He was just leaving, weren't you, Pate?"

Chapter 15

Pate was rocked back on his heels. If she wanted to hurt him, she'd done so, and it did hurt, a lot. But he didn't believe she would deliberately do so. The simple truth was she'd moved on with her life, as he'd suggested she do. Colleen was a prize, he saw that now, and so did Elmer Carruthers. He'd certainly been ready to defend it.

"Yeah, I was just leaving," he said, looking straight at Colleen and ignoring Elmer. "I expect Pa and Julia and I will be getting on home now. Again, sorry about your father, Colleen. If there's anything any of us can do to help, make sure to tell either of your brothers to drop on by and we'll come right away."

Elmer had the good grace to stay quiet, and Pate took his leave in a leisurely fashion. If Carruthers thought he was going to run him off, he had another think coming. Well, he *had* run him off, but he wasn't going to take to his heels like a scared rabbit. So Colleen and Elmer Carruthers were an item. Hmmm.

The truth was, he felt numb as reality continued to sink in. He'd lost Colleen.

Somehow, he'd thought she'd always be there waiting in the wings, but he'd found out differently. While he was busy going around with the likes of Dinah Gladstone, other people were noticing Colleen. And hadn't she tried more than once to get him to change his mind about breaking up with her? Indeed, she had, but she'd been shut down every step of the way. He knew he had no one to blame but himself, but that didn't help ease the ache in his gut from the huge boulder he'd just swallowed.

Tabor and Julia were waiting for him in the wagon when he walked up from the barn, and he took his place in the wagon bed behind them. It was pleasantly warm with crickets serenading the countryside, and fireflies blinking in the gathering darkness.

"I hear Colleen has a new beau," said Julia, probably in an effort to break the silence as they made their way along the road.

"*Julia*," Tabor cautioned her under his breath.

"Oops. I'm sorry, Pate. I thought you knew."

Pate realized that others had already known and hadn't bothered to mention it to him. After all, hadn't he told anyone who asked that he and Colleen were no longer a couple? "That's all right, Julia. I hope they'll be very happy together."

But when they arrived home and the wagon was unhitched, Pate saw to the horse, then went up to bed without offering further conversation. As he lay in the darkness, he couldn't help but realise how badly he'd bungled things with Colleen. He'd ruined the summer and possibly the rest of his life because that's what it felt like. He should never have woken up from that injury. He'd been happy, or so he thought, before the fall.

Now he'd move into his new homestead and become a lonely old man because everything looked dismal at this point. He doubted anyone else would turn his head. How could he trust another woman? He could trust Colleen, but he'd gambled with her and lost. And then another terrible thought came to mind, and that was Elmer kissing on Colleen and perchance doing more. He balled his fists at the notion. She'd been saving herself for him, and he'd foolishly walked away. Would she now give herself to another man? What if Elmer were rough with her? What if he wasn't worthy of her? What, like you? The taunting reply reared up to slap him in the face. Why was he worrying about another man? He'd hurt her plenty himself.

He slept fitfully, dreaming about the meadow and a gun, Dinah laughing at him. A casket with Colleen standing beside it, him pleading with her, and her turning him away, Laughing. "You had your chance," she threw at him in the dream. "You didn't want me, and now I want someone else."

He woke up, drenched, the air hot and sticky in the upstairs bedrooms. He guessed it to be around four-thirty, and for a fleeting second, it occurred to him he was late for something. No, he wasn't, not anymore. Getting up, he found his pocket watch in his trousers. It was four forty-five, so he *was* a bit late. He grabbed his clothes, wishing it were a bit cooler as it usually was in the early morning. They needed another good thundershower to clear the air, but not before they got the last of that second cut of hay in. It was already down and raked into neat windrows, it just had to be loaded on the wagon and put into the loft.

Julia was at the stove stirring the bubbling oatmeal, the coffee already made, its inviting, deep, rich aroma flooding the kitchen.

"Pa out on the veranda?" Pate asked her.

"Yes, dear. He's out there having his coffee. Breakfast won't be ready for another few minutes. I'll call you both when it is."

Tabor was taking the last puff off one of his hand-rolled cigarettes.

Pate settled into the empty chair beside him. "You know, Pa, I've been thinking."

Tabor chuckled quietly. "I don't think I have to ask about what, or should I say who."

Pate took a long draw on his coffee before he spoke again. "No, I suppose you don't. But what I was going to say is I think I'll take me a train ride. I think I'll go on up to that place where Garrett lives now. Akerly

I think he called it. I might go there and see what that place is like."

Tabor turned sharply. "You mean leave Westmorland County? Move up there?"

"I wasn't thinking of doing that, but I do feel a powerful need to start over."

"You've had a couple of rough months, Pate. It passes."

Pate swallowed a mouthful of coffee. "I asked Colleen to marry me last night. I apologized for everything, all of it."

Tabor began to roll another cigarette, not a heavy smoker by any means, but he did favour two or three for veranda sitting. "I figured that was coming, but something tells me she said no. Is that about right?"

"Yeah, that's about right."

Tabor struck a match. "She's got that other beau now. She couldn't very well accept your proposal if she's betrothed to another man."

"Betrothed!"

"She didn't tell you that?"

"No, I didn't hear anything about them being betrothed."

Cigarette smoke filled the air. "She told Gault that from what I understand, but then it's hard to tell with Peterson. He gets stuff mixed up sometimes when he's pulling on the jug."

Pate puffed a sigh. "It makes sense, though. A pretty girl like Colleen isn't going to stay single very long."

"You left the henhouse unguarded, Pate, and a fox got in. You can't blame the fox, or the hen."

"I'm not blaming anybody, except myself. Anyway, we'll get the rest of the hay in today, and I think you can spare me around here for a few days or a week or so. I kind of want to travel on one of those trains. I haven't been on one before. It might be interesting."

"It would do you a world of good to have a change of scenery for a while. I'll see to what's going on here, Julia and I. Everything's in good shape, and I'm back up to full steam, so there'll be no problem. You're going to be moving away soon anyway. Write Garrett and tell him you're coming through, so he'll know not to be away or something."

And so the decision was made, the letter written that very day telling Garrett of his planned arrival in a week's time. Pate would travel by rail to St. John, in a roundabout fashion, then catch a riverboat up the St. John River to Washademoak Lake. Garrett could pick him up at the landing that Abby said was but a few miles from where they lived.

He had long wanted to take a trip on one of those side wheelers that Abby had told them all about when she and Garrett had paid them a visit after they got married. It had held his fancy all these many years. He'd imagined he and Colleen could take that trip for their honeymoon. Well, he'd be taking the same trip ... without a bride.

* * *

When the time came to depart for the train station, a week later, Pate was impatient to be off on his adventure. Julia packed him a substantial lunch, and his father had actually sent his best wishes to Garrett and Abby, as did Julia.

He took one long last look at the farm before climbing into the buggy, his father driving him into Sackville to catch the train. He would miss this place, but then again, he wasn't going to be gone for long, he reminded himself. It was time to step away from what was familiar, even for a while.

The sky was promising to send some much-needed rain as Tabor turned the buggy to make the return trip to the farm, so up went the canopy, and he was off, Pointer stepping lively in the traces. Pate watched him until he was out of sight. He went inside to buy his ticket, only to be shocked by the exorbitant price of $1.50, then found a seat in the passenger car. He had intended to lie his head back for a rest once on board, only to discover the spartan construction of the seats was not suited to his tall frame.

Presently, the train began to move, chugging away slowly from the station, then gradually picking up momentum until it felt as though they were hurtling along at

280

breakneck speed. Now this was the way to go! He hadn't experienced anything quite like it before, and he felt like a king sitting up in that polished wooden seat, watching the countryside fly past. About forty miles per hour, the conductor had told him to expect when he punched his ticket. He couldn't believe it, although he dared say that Jacko could match it. He thought about his old friend and wondered how he was faring in his new home.

"I hope you're doing better than me," he mumbled aloud.

"Talking to yourself is a troubling sign," said a woman who'd come to stand next to the empty spot beside him. "Do you mind, sir, if I join you? I realize there are plenty of other seats, and if you prefer not to have my company, I will completely understand. I encourage you to decide the matter before I'm upended onto the floor."

Pate looked up into the face of a smartly dressed lady of perhaps sixty years. "Sure, you can sit beside me," he told her with a smile, appreciating her humour.

She settled in rather than simply sitting down, and he was immediately assailed with the fragrance of rosewater. It disgorged memories of Dinah that he was trying his best to forget. Used sparingly, it could be rather pleasant, but being doused in it produced the opposite effect. It then became cloying as he found it now, so he lowered the window slightly.

"I am a woman travelling alone," she set about explaining once she'd sorted herself out and seemed ready for conversation. "I'm not naïve enough to think I'll have to beat off the men," she said with a twinkle in her eye, "but I do feel so much safer with a man by my side. Where are you travelling to, young man? If you say St. John, I shall be ever so grateful."

"I am going through to St. John."

"Saints be praised," she said, her neck folds jiggling with her enthusiasm. "Don't these things streak along at a frightful speed? We can only pray to the dear Lord up above that the wheels remain where they were designed to stay. There wouldn't be enough left of us to mail home to loved ones if we were to go off the rails."

Now that was a gruesome thought, but he nodded, extending his hand politely. "I'm Pate Kavenagh."

She took his hand in her gloved fingers. "Mrs. Harriet Trecartin."

Pate shook her hand, or rather her fingers. "Nice to meet you, Mrs. Trecartin."

She released him. "Pate. I don't believe I've heard that name before. What is its origin may I ask?"

"Scottish, in my case anyway."

"It's a very nice name. Very friendly sounding, and you're a handsome young fellow too, I must tell you. It's not often you see hair so black paired up with eyes quite the colour of grey that yours are. Very fetching indeed. If I had a granddaughter your age, I'd be wanting to introduce you, but I don't. I expect you're of marrying age, are you?"

Pate shrugged. "I suppose so. I turned twenty-four the end of June."

"You're ripe for the picking," she said with cheerful candour. "Why, my husband and I had been married four years by the time he was twenty-four. But I expect you've got a little dove waiting in the wings somewhere. Are you going to her now?"

He cringed. If he'd thought he was going to be grilled like this, he might have suggested she keep going. He was trying to get away from his troubles, not be reminded of them. Nevertheless, he couldn't politely send her away now, and she was likeable.

"I'm single and I believe destined to remain that way."

"Nonsense! A bachelor who looks like you? But I do believe I'm beginning to understand the situation. There's a sadness about your eyes, Pate Kavenagh. You've had your heart broken, haven't you?"

He sighed. He wasn't the type to lay everything out for inspection. But she seemed to be a kindly soul, so he'd let her have her way. What could it hurt to acknowledge the truth?

"Something like that," he acknowledged, "not that I think it will do any good to talk about it. Those things happen."

Her gloved fingers tapped him lightly on the arm, meant to be a comforting gesture. "They do indeed happen. You see, I was left more or less at the altar by the boy I believed I was in love with. I was mad for him, but he found happiness with another, and so I was left holding the lilies, as they say. I was devastated, and how was I to know at the tender age of seventeen that there was any hope at all for a bright future after such a disastrous experience? I truly believed my life was over because I had been thusly deceived. And to think that the young lady I was thrown over for was my own sister. That was undiluted acid poured into the wound. Some mountains do seem insurmountable, but you can, and do, recover from such things. The sun will continue to rise in the morning, no matter how wronged you've been. I didn't feel as though I wanted to go on at all, but I did find love again in the person of my husband, Penrose. I was even more smitten than I thought I'd been with the young man I had originally agreed to marry."

Pate stared. Now that would have been a terrible thing to have happened. It made his circumstances pale by comparison.

"How did you meet the man you married? I'm sorry, I shouldn't be so forward as to ask such a personal question."

She waved away his concerns. "I'm a wise old bird. You'll not throw me by asking a few questions. I met him the very next year while visiting relatives in St. John. I'd heard of love at first sight, and while I strenuously disagreed that such a thing was possible, I found it to be true. We met and married within a remarkably short time, but we didn't have a family. I lost him a little more than two years ago. It's a wrenching subject for me, but it helps to talk about it at times."

Harriet Trecartin had a hypnotic quality to her storytelling, and he found himself pulled in, now thoroughly enjoying her company. She reminded him in a way of his dearly departed grandmother, whom he missed terribly after nine years gone. Harriet, too, was a plain-spoken woman, and he'd come to the conclusion a long time ago that it was his preference for any female.

"I'm sorry you lost your husband. Was he sick for a long time, Mrs. Trecartin?"

"Not at all, the whole thing was quite by accident, I'm afraid. Rather sudden for us all. I'm sure you've heard of what's called the Great St. John Fire."

His mouth flew open. "I have! It happened a couple of years ago, in the summer, didn't it? That's all everyone was talking about at the time."

"Indeed. June 20, 1877 was a day that will live in infamy. It was a Wednesday, hot and dry, and the blaze was rumoured to have begun in hay stored down on the waterfront at York Point. It was also very windy, and the fire spread rapidly."

"They must have fire brigades in St. John."

"They do, but the fire rapidly gained strength and was too much for them. My husband and I lived in a marvelous home on Queen's Square. Since the fire was so far away, we in that part of the city thought we'd be spared. However, the smoke was choking, billowing, people in a frightful state because of it, and we were wondering how we could help those poor unfortunates. Within the hour, we were included in that number. The flames were at *our* doorstep, and our home was destroyed. Penrose was a downtown merchant working in the heart of the mercantile area, and he was tragically lost in the blaze, as were many other doomed souls at work that day. I took refuge in the Square and was saved, along with a great number of others who were huddling there. The air was full of burning firebrands being carried by the wind, and we were terrified they'd be rained down upon us. The hours seemed endless, but thankfully, it wasn't winter, and we were spared. They say the flames consumed two-thirds of the city centre, and the fire didn't burn itself out for nine long, agonizing hours."

"Was nothing saved?"

"Very little in the path of that inferno survived. Churches, public buildings and countless businesses were razed to the ground. Every profession, from bookbinders and sailmakers to confectioners and iron merchants, and everything in between, was wiped out in a few short hours. Many hundreds of homes were reduced to ashes. Ships at anchor at Market Slip were burned where they sat. It was a catastrophe of monumental proportions, Pate. The landscape was nothing but charred ruins with blackened brick chimneys sticking up all over the place. And the heat! I heard that fully two hundred acres were burned, everything lost."

Pate thought he'd had a decent understanding of what had taken place from reading newspaper accounts, but hearing about it first-hand, he couldn't imagine the horror of it all. And in the middle of it was this brave lady. What courage it took to get through something like that, to selflessly help others and then realize she'd lost her husband.

He laid his hand on her arm, and she broke from her monologue to look fully into his face. "I am so very sorry for your loss, Ma'am. I can't imagine what a nightmare that whole thing was for you. And you came to Sackville."

She smiled sadly. "It was my sister who'd stolen my beau who came to my rescue. You see, her marriage didn't last. She fell on bended knee to ask my forgiveness two years after the divorce, and I gave it. Now we're closer than ever before. She has been a godsend to me in my time of need. Things have a way of working out."

He thought about the train rushing to its eventual destination of St. John, but what would be left when they got there? He'd heard about the 1877 devastation, but hadn't given it much thought when he'd decided to go there to catch the riverboat. The truth of it was, those who hadn't experienced a calamity tended to forget about it.

"What's the city like now?"

Mrs. Trecartin smiled. "Bigger and better. You know, they said within a few weeks of the fire, all of the rubble had been cleared and carted away, and rebuilding began on a grand scale. I was one of the fortunate ones who received insurance benefits. Many did not. Because of the sheer scale of loss, many insurance companies fell into bankruptcy. So I was blessed in that regard. But I'm not sure whether I'll ever live there again. I *would* consider doing so if I could convince my sister, Esther, to come with me. I do believe she would like it there, as I did."

Pate thought about his own small world. Everything in his life revolved around his family, the farm, his horses and now his new homestead. He didn't even care much to go to Sackville, making the short trip when he absolutely had to. His world was very small compared to most people's. He simply did not have a yen to travel, his present adventure notwithstanding.

In fact, he was already homesick, thinking about the farm and his father, Julia, and the horses. He returned his attention to the woman sitting beside him. She'd produced a fan and was busy fluttering it in front of her face. It *was* warm in this car.

"Would you like me to lower the window a bit more, Mrs. Trecartin?"

She chuckled. "Mercy no, my boy. I won't have a hat if the wind gets at it. I just bought this contraption, and I'm not happy at all with the way it sits on my head. I have a notion it's going to fly away of its own accord at any moment anyway, without the help of the wind. I barely made it onto the train in one piece."

Pate laughed, despite himself. Mrs. Trecartin was jolly good fun. "It is quite windy out there. Look at those trees!"

She harrumphed. "It's from the wind kicked up by these wheels. I'd forgotten how these things whiz along. I say again, I dare not think what would happen to us if we had to halt in a hurry. Anyway, my trusty fan here will do the trick in terms of relief. I hope you're also getting some benefit from it."

All it succeeded in doing was stirring up the rosewater fumes, but if that were his greatest hardship to bear, he'd be all right.

"Do you like horses?" he asked her on impulse. "I mean good ones."

She regarded him with a wide grin. "Do I like horses? Why, I should say so. I'm originally from up Dorchester way, the shiretown, and I grew up around horses. My father raised them. Fine horses suited for both pleasure and carriage driving. I was quite a horsewoman in my day. My husband and I owned a dashing pair of bay geldings, and we took carriage rides out into the country on Sunday afternoons. What intelligent animals they were. I knew they were sound when we set out to purchase them, but my father made the trip to St. John by stagecoach to make sure we were getting good horseflesh. He wasn't long giving his blessing."

Pate tried to push the unimaginable away. "And they were lost in the fire?"

"No, Albert and Tom had long since been retired to the country by that time, but we had another fine pair, and they were lost. Countless horses perished, many first-rate stables went down. Why do you ask me about horses? Is that an area of interest for you?"

Now he was in his element. Horses, and the next hour or so, was spent in a lively discussion about their finer points. Harriet Trecartin was very knowledgeable on the subject. She was knowledgeable about a lot of things, and as it turned out, thoroughly entertaining company. She was most interested to hear all about Freedom, and let him go on at length about the promising young stallion. Freedom was his future.

* * *

When they arrived in St. John, he was pleasantly surprised to behold a vibrant city well on the way to reclaiming its former greatness. There was an air of contagious exhilaration about the place. Mrs. Trecartin had explained that following the fire, notable architects had flocked to the city from Halifax, Toronto, Montreal and as far away as New England to compete for rebuilding opportunities. And judging from the impressive stone and brick buildings that populated the downtown core, both in size and intricate detail, they had indeed helped St. John rise from the ashes in grand style. And this splendid cityscape was set against the backdrop of a sapphire-blue harbour sparkling under the summer sun. He'd never seen anything quite like it.

At Harriet's insistence, they took their evening meal in the handsome dining room of the new and stately McCoskery's Hotel that fronted on Prince William Street. She also, despite his protests, secured a room for him at her expense, before she summoned the services of a horse-drawn hansom cab to take her to her destination to visit friends. However, despite the opulence of the room, Pate spent a restless night, eager to reach the busy Indiantown Wharf the next day. He arrived in plenty of time to board the side wheeler preparing to steam up the St. John River on this golden August morning. He was within hours of seeing Garrett and Abby again and looking forward to it.

The voyage aboard the steamboat The Aristotle was every bit as magical as Abby had described her experience on The Bluebird in 1870. And now he was one of one hundred and forty passengers headed up that same river, riveted to the side rails, watching some of the prettiest countryside he'd ever been blessed to lay eyes on. From farmlands to miles of uninterrupted forests, the rural landscape was awash in a kaleidoscope of greens beneath a cornflower blue sky. He held his hat in his hands, lest he lose it, luxuriating in the stiff breeze that ruffled his hair as they cut through the waves at a modest five and a half miles per hour. It was not as fast as the train, but thoroughly exciting in a different way.

He didn't care to go into the dining room to partake of the elaborate menu. Instead, he chose one of the several seats on the upper deck and tucked into the lunch Julia had packed for him. He doubted any of the dining room fare could compare with her light-as-air biscuits, generously spread with fresh-churned butter and slathered with this year's strawberry jam. And then there were the molasses cookies, all washed down with spring water. It wasn't as cool as it had been when he first started out, but he doubted he'd find better-tasting drinking water anywhere.

When he'd satisfied his hunger, he repacked what was left and reclined lazily in his seat, satisfied. Stretching out his long legs, he thought he'd take a short nap, like he and Pa did on the veranda after they ate. He missed the homeplace with a keen longing. If he were there right about now, they'd be finishing their noon meal and drinking their tea before they headed back to the fields. No matter where he went or what he saw, nothing could be as good as that. And soon he'd be making those memories at his new place, although he couldn't help but feel it might be a tad lonely sitting on *that* veranda all by himself.

Lost in thought, he didn't notice when a woman with long red curly hair sat down in the vacant seat next to him.

Chapter 16

Minutes later, he opened his eyes, his vision briefly distorted by the bright sunshine. It took him a few seconds to focus. Dinah? Here on the boat? But a closer look revealed it was not the redheaded vixen from Sackville, but rather another woman who'd sat down nearby in hopes of catching his attention. She seemed pleased to have gotten it.

"I'm sorry, I was staring," he apologized. "I thought you were someone else."

'And if it was the person I thought it was, I'd be over the side of the boat by now,' he would like to have added.

"My name is Bernadette," she said, extending a slim hand. "Berna, for short. Are you travelling alone too?"

He wasn't in the mood for company. He much preferred to be alone with his thoughts. If the woman beside him looked like anyone else in the world except Dinah Gladstone, he might have been happy to pass some time talking to her, but the sight of that long red hair brought back too many unpleasant memories.

"I am," he said. "I'm to meet my family when I get to The Narrows. Until then, I think I'll sit back and..."

"And be lonely?" she teased, with the same tilt to her chin as Dinah.

It was uncanny, although where Dinah had been strikingly beautiful, Bernadette was just passably pretty, her eyes a penetrating shade of blue. Off-putting in a sense. But it didn't matter. Red hair or not, pretty or otherwise, he was still smarting about Colleen, and in no mood to move on. The idea was to get away from such things for a while, not jump back in with both feet.

"I'm not lonely," he assured her politely. "I'm simply enjoying the day."

She was miffed, although she continued to smile brightly, the artifice as obvious as long ears on a donkey. "You don't want to talk to me?"

He shook his head slowly. "I know you're trying to be friendly. I don't mean to be rude, but I'm not in the mood for conversation. No offence meant at all."

Her face flooded with colour as she rose to her feet and took her leave in short, choppy strides. Yes, it was much too soon to jump back into the dangerous waters of romance, he told himself with a smile. Much too soon.

He went back to the rails, leaning heavily against them, loving the sun and wind on his face. He should be there in another couple of hours, and he was almost reluctant to have this riverboat trip come to an end. If there was a more pleasant means of travel, he wasn't sure what it would be. The train ride had been exciting, the sheer speed of it, while this was a calmer, unrushed way to go. It was all part of the same adventure. He wished again that Colleen was here to share it with him. How perfect that would have been, but he had to close that off now. He had messed things up in a big way, and now he was forced to live with the consequences.

He was in no hurry to go ashore when the riverboat finally docked at The Narrows wharf, allowing all of the other passengers to disembark ahead of him. When he finally stepped off, he could see a grand hotel nearby with guests strolling leisurely about the spacious, immaculately kept grounds. That establishment would be too rich for his purse. Besides, Garrett would insist that he stay with him and Abby during his visit.

Pate spotted Garrett standing beside a handsome horse-drawn carriage a short distance from the landing, and lifted his hand in greeting. Garrett did the same. His uncle was in his early thirties now, and he looked different from the last time he'd seen him, more filled out. All of the Kavenagh men were tall and strong of build, even Garrett whose real father, Nathanial Henry, had been a big man. But where Bart Kavenagh's sons were dark-haired and green-eyed like himself, Garrett was blonde and blue-eyed, although Pate always thought of him as a true Kavenagh.

"Pate! Good to see you!" exclaimed Garrett after Pate hurried to his uncle's side. "I swear you've gotten taller, sturdier. You're as tall as your pa now."

Pate grinned. "Taller by an inch, I think."

"And you're looking hale and hardy," he said, giving his nephew a robust hug. "Let's head on down to Akerly. You can catch me up on the news from home over the past few months as we ride along."

And Pate did, telling Garrett about his father's illness, and recovery, about Maggie's close call giving birth, and that he had a new niece called Maisie. He also told him about his fall, but didn't lean too hard into that. He'd come out of it all right, so no need to go into unnecessary detail.

Garrett took him to the carriage factory first, and Pate was truly impressed. To think his uncle owned this whole place. It was much larger than what he'd imagined, but then Garrett was not one to overstate things. The showroom had several fine vehicles on display. Pate knew he already had an adequate buggy at home, but what he wouldn't give to own one of these beauties. He didn't know a lot about such things, but he recognized exceptional workmanship when he saw it. These were some of the best-looking horse-drawn conveyances he'd ever laid eyes on. He could tell Garrett was proud as he stood nearby, all smiles.

Pate squatted down for a look at the undercarriage of a shiny black phaeton. "You still doing wheelwrighting, Uncle Garrett?"

"Not so much as I'd like to. The office and such keep me busy enough, but I get into the workshop as much as I can. Wondering if you might be interested in joining me. I've got a man leaving in a couple of months. I'd be proud to start training you if you had a mind to stay. I think you'd like it here, Pate. Akerly is a good place, great people."

Pate straightened. "I can tell you one thing, it's a very tempting offer. I don't think I've ever seen prettier scenery, and right on the water, the way you are, you'd never want for supplies, would you? I imagine they're brought practically right to your doorstep on one of those steamboats. You'd have access most of the year, and an ice highway during the winter."

"That's right, it's ideal. We have a high quality of life here. So can I tempt you to stay? It would be mighty fine to have you with me, Pate. Carriage making is a good trade."

Pate shook his head, with an attitude of apology. "As tempting as it is, I'd have to say no. I've got my own place now, and I'm doing real well with my horses. I've got one young stallion I call Freedom. It was Uncle Brogan who named him, that very night when they'd jailed him in the shiretown. He said it was the best word he could think of. I'd say it is for all of us."

"I wasn't surprised to hear about any of that in Julia's letter. Those Burks! I had a run-in with them, too. Actually, that's how I came to leave Sackville. Does the name Kavenagh still give people sleepless nights in those parts?"

"Some, although I try not to pay any attention to it anymore. As long as I can go about what I want to do, I don't care, and there's enough good people around so I can."

"This young stallion of yours, Freedom, he's a good horse, is he?"

"The best! I've already got my stud sold, Silver Billy, and my older brood mare. I accepted an offer just before I left on this trip, and they're coming for them while I'm away. Freedom is a little more than three now, so the timing is right. I've got a great future with that horse. He's going to sire some fine babies. When I get back home, I'm going to start looking for another brood mare."

"It sounds like you've got a great thing going, Pate, and I'm glad for you. You've worked hard at it."

Pate looked around him." "And you've made a big success of things here. Now, enough about business, where's Abby?"

Garrett's smile was wide and telling. "She's home. That's my place right across the road."

Pate's gaze swung to a large, whitewashed farmhouse and outbuildings overlooking the spectacular Washademoak. "That big farm!"

"It went with the factory. Mr. Anderson left everything to me, the whole kit and caboodle. I'm a very fortunate man."

Pate whistled. "Gee! But I also know how hard you work. You earned every bit of it."

Garrett clapped his nephew on the shoulder. "Come on, let's walk down and see Abby. She's been waiting for you to come. I knew my wife wasn't much of a cook when I married her, but she's one of the best there is now. She's even got some baking done for you. I believe she's shelling peas this afternoon. I brought a woman in to help her for a while, during the heavy summer months, with so much to do in the garden and all. You'll see."

Pate was shocked to see Abby, who was obviously pregnant, when he walked in, and he looked at Garrett questioningly. He'd overheard Julia telling his father that Abby was unable to bear children.

Abby crossed the room and gave Pate a welcoming hug, then rested her hands atop her large belly. "Big surprise, right? I know it's not genteel for women to speak about such things, but Garrett and I are expecting our first child. Something of a miracle baby, and I know you'll understand if I don't explain."

Pate reddened. Abby was another forthright woman. Seeing her with child set him to missing Colleen all over again, and the children they'd never have together.

"Let's go sit on the veranda under the trees," Garrett suggested. "It's cooler out there in the shade."

A fiftyish woman with a severe salt and pepper bun atop her head hastened into the kitchen.

Abby smiled at her before returning her attention to their guest. "Pate, I'd like you to meet Mrs. Anita Hanson. She'll be staying with us for the next few months."

Pate acknowledged her with a friendly smile, and it was returned in kind.

"I have some fresh-made lemonade waiting," the woman announced. "I put it in the root cellar to keep it nice and cool. If you'd all like to go out onto the veranda, I'll bring it right along."

* * *

Pate was up early the next morning, as was Garrett, and Mrs. Hanson had breakfast ready for both of them.

"I half expected you to be eating oatmeal," Pate teased his uncle. "We were raised on the stuff."

Garrett was in his usual cheerful mood, obviously a contented man. "I've kind of gotten away from that. I like side bacon and eggs for my breakfast now, although I have a nice big bowl of porridge with fresh cream from time to time, mostly in the winter. It sticks to your ribs in the cold weather. How long are you planning to stay, Pate? A week, hopefully."

Pate stirred cream and sugar into his coffee, his spoon clinking against the inside of the ceramic cup. "I figured a week, but unfortunately, no more. You know how busy the farm is in the summer. There's a lot to be done before fall. Pa and Brogan helped me with making hay at my new place, but we're just getting started. I'm going to need a lot more for the winter."

"I was surprised to see you up here now, summer being the busiest time of year and all. But then again, the weather wouldn't be fit for travel most other times. Just like home, the roads are a sea of mud here in the spring. They don't dry up until long into May, and then you're contending with dust. And when the roads are hardened up in the fall, the snow starts to fly. It comes early hereabouts and keeps piling up. It's very nice in the summer, but very hot. Abby minds it a lot since she's been with child."

"She looks good, though."

Mrs. Hanson, having finished serving breakfast, had gone outside to see to the garden before the heat of the day made outdoor tasks uncomfortable.

"She says she feels all right."

Pate set down his cup. "Aren't you scared?"

"About Abby, you mean?"

"Yeah, since what I told you about Maggie."

Garrett chewed a mouthful of bacon thoughtfully, his gaze trained on the view from the window on the other side of the room. "I'm scared to death if you want the truth. The doctor said there are a lot of things against her, but she's managed to carry the child this long. Now it's just to get it born, getting both Abby and the baby through it. I try not to think about that part too much."

"With what I've seen, I don't think I want to have children when I get married, if I ever do."

"You'll get married someday, Pate, and you'll have children. It's the natural thing to want to do."

Pate fidgeted with his fork lying on his plate. "Sure, but I doubt I'll get married now, and if I did, I'd be scared of losing my wife during childbirth. They say Maggie came about as close to dying as you can get. And my mother died bearing me, although I know a lot of women who don't seem to have any problems. Remember Mrs. Titus from up the road? She had thirteen."

Garrett pushed his plate aside. "I married Abby believing she couldn't have children, and I was fine with that. It's risky for some women to have them for sure, but Abby wants this child. She knows the risks, and so do I, but that didn't stop us, I guess. We honestly didn't think she could have children, so that's why she's calling this a

303

miracle. We'll only have to rely on the good Lord above to see her through it. The Narrows has a doctor again, a middle-aged man with lots of experience, and he'll be here with her for the birthing.

"Mona Allen is a very good midwife from this area, and that's who Abby wanted, but I insisted on a doctor. The midwife will be here too, so between the two of them, we're praying there are no complications. We'll only have the one because of Abby's age."

"You hoping for a son?"

Garrett smiled widely, anticipating the blessed event. "I'll take whatever comes along, and be thankful for it. We had planned to try to come back home for a visit in the fall, and then Abby fell pregnant, and that changed those plans. The doctor said she was to take it easy, stay off her feet as much as possible, so I hired Mrs. Hanson right away. She was very happy to oblige. Abby's well-liked by the people here. She has learned how to cook and quilt, and she gets together with the local ladies as much as possible. Not so much lately, though, and she'll likely be too busy after the baby comes, but she's a big part of the community."

"You'll write and tell us how things go, won't you?"

"You bet I will! Now, I've got to get up to the factory. Why don't you come on up? I can put you to work if you want."

* * *

Before Pate knew it the week was at an end, and it was with a heavy heart he bid his farewells. He didn't know when he'd see either Garrett or Abby again because of the substantial distance between them. He doubted they'd get very far at all after the little one came.

He'd been looking forward to the boat ride back down the river, but it was raining heavily the day he left, and he spent the entire time inside. He didn't see the redheaded lady again, so he assumed she'd either stayed in the area or already returned to St. John, and that was good. He still thought about Colleen, although he'd done his best during the past week to keep her relegated to the back of his mind.

Once back in St. John, he discovered the train back home didn't leave until first thing the next morning, so he was forced to find lodging that wouldn't cost him an arm and a leg. In any case, it had stopped raining, the sun hanging low in the sky on a pleasant late August evening. Storing his satchel in his room, he decided to go for a walk through the uptown streets of the city and try to visualize what Mrs. Trecartin had told him about the fire. There was scant evidence of that horrific situation now. With new buildings everywhere and people bustling about, life seemed to have resumed a normal rhythm

305

despite that appalling interruption just two short years ago.

She'd told him ninety-one people lost their lives, with scores of others injured, and he thought about that as he looked around him. It amazed him that the death count hadn't been much higher. She'd also explained that in the aftermath of the disaster, many had stepped up to lend a helping hand to the beleaguered city in its time of need.

He found his way to King's Square and rested for a few minutes on a wooden bench, watching the pigeons bill and coo at the pedestrians' feet. But now, as darkness began to descend and with his stomach rumbling, he returned to his room and dove into the lunch Mrs. Hanson had packed for his journey. He'd already dipped into it on the boat, but there was plenty left to see him all the way back home.

Early the next morning, he happily embarked on the last leg of his journey, and he sat dozing on the train, having grown tired of watching the countryside, much of it scrub woodland, pass by his window. He was anxious to get back to see his father, from whom he'd never been separated, and Julia, and of course his horses. He felt as though he'd been away for a month, a year. He was a true homebody, and he didn't mind admitting it.

"Pate?"

He slowly opened his eyes to see Marilyn Patterson, a girl he'd gone to school with, standing beside his seat. He'd not known her to be nice to him, but they'd been children then. Perhaps she'd changed.

He blinked away his drowsiness. "Hi, Marilyn. Riding the train too, I see."

She smiled. "May I please sit down?"

"Sure. We don't have much further to go anyway. How did you find me? It's kind of crowded in here today. There was a gentleman sitting beside me, but he got off at the last stop."

"I saw you get on," she explained as she sat down beside him, resting her reticule on her lap, "and I saw the man get off. Can I ask you a question?"

He shrugged. "What do you want to know?"

"Are you invited to the wedding?"

He looked at her, perplexed. "What wedding?"

"Colleen and Elmer's, of course. They've set the date. They're getting married at Thanksgiving. Doesn't that sound absolutely perfect? I think they make such a beautiful couple. He's so good to her, and she simply dotes on him."

Pate felt blindsided. Thanksgiving! That was just over a month away. He felt bile rise in his throat, and he realized at the same time that Marilyn was still as mean as she'd ever been. She and Colleen had always been somewhat friendly. Had Colleen told

Marilyn about their breakup? How he'd come back and proposed, and she'd sent him packing? Had they had a good laugh together about it? He immediately thought better of it, though. Colleen was not like that. Hers was simply a passing friendship with Marilyn. The right of it was that Marilyn had asked Colleen a question or two, then decided to make trouble with what little information she was able to obtain.

He felt sick to his stomach, but he wouldn't give her the satisfaction of letting her know the news had upset him.

Instead, he smiled. "A Thanksgiving wedding does sound nice. Hopefully the leaves stay on so there's lots of colour. Thanks for the news!"

She smiled coyly. "You should drop by and see Colleen marry a real man. Toodle-oo," she said, toggling her fingers at him playfully as she left to go back up the aisle.

* * *

Julia was waiting for him at the station, and he was glad to continue on his way back home. Taking over the reins, he waited until they were on the road before he turned to her. "I heard from an old classmate on the train that Colleen is getting married at Thanksgiving. Is that true, Julia, or was Marilyn Patterson up to her old mischief?"

Julia's face settled into a sad smile. "I'm afraid it's true, Pate. I'm surprised they'd go ahead with it so soon after her father's death, but apparently they'd already begun to plan it. I'm so sorry."

He glanced over. "Don't worry about it, Julia. I was just wondering, is all."

Julia laid her hand on his arm. "I'm afraid I have some very sad news for you, Pate."

His heart leapt in his chest. "Oh no! Something happened to Pa!"

"No!" Julia rushed to assure him. "Your pa is fine. It's Freedom."

"Freedom! What happened to Freedom?"

"He has colic, and it's very bad. Your pa's been doing what he can for him. Brogan has even been down to try to help, but the horse doesn't seem to be improving."

"When did it start?"

"This afternoon. He's in a lot of discomfort, and it doesn't look as though he's going to make it. I'm so sorry. I hate to meet you with such terrible news, but they're doing everything they know how. Even Peterson Gault has been by to see if he could help because everyone knows how much that horse means to you."

Pate slapped the reins onto Pointer's rump, and the gelding picked up his pace, although maintaining a safe speed. It seemed like forever before they pulled into the yard. Julia took over the reins as Pate jumped out and ran to the barn.

"Pate, you're here!" Tabor called out. "I'm afraid there's no improvement. We've given him what we can, how any of us have treated any other horse who's colicked, but this fella doesn't seem to be coming out of it. You know, most times they don't."

Pate watched the beautiful stallion, sweating, swinging his head to look at his flank. Then he got to his feet, pawing, his ears pinned back, then down once again. Freedom was in pain.

Uncaring of his good trousers, Pate knelt on the floor beside the horse's head, talking to him soothingly, and that's where he stayed with his pa for the next hour, in silence. There just wasn't anything to be said. When Pate glanced over, he caught his father holding his side.

"Pa, you're in pain."

"It's the position I'm sitting in, son. It's nothing I can't stand."

"I know you've been down here for hours. Julia told me. You might as well go on up to the house, there doesn't seem to be anything else we can do anyway."

"I'm staying with you, Pate."

Pate had tears in his eyes. "You don't understand, Pa. I'm saying if he's going to go, I need to be here with him, alone, to say goodbye. I thank you for all you've done, but please leave me here with him. I'll be up by and by. I'll let you know when he's gone, or if he comes around."

Tabor laid a hand on his shoulder before leaving the barn and heading on up to the house.

Pate continued to kneel beside the horse, stroking him as long minutes passed.

"When one of *our* horses got colic, Pa used to press on the side of the hock. He said that helped to release the intestinal area where they're bound up. An old settler told him that."

Pate scrambled to his feet, wheeling to face Colleen. He gawked at her.

"There's also another point. Pa would put pressure on the last vertebrae in the tail. That helped too."

Freedom had gotten back to his feet, in obvious distress. "Come on and try it then," he told her urgently. "I'll hold his head while you do that with his tail."

Colleen found the spot she was looking for on the tail, pressing her thumbs on it and holding it tightly.

"How long did he hold it?"

"I can't remember, but I'll keep doing it and see what happens. He won't kick me, will he?"

"No, he's not a kicker. He's a quiet stallion."

Pate moved to the horse's hind leg. "And you say on his hock too? Like this?"

She bent to look as Pate held his thumbs on the front of Freedom's left hock. "Yes, just like that, except rotate it first with your thumb. Okay, now put pressure on it, right in that same spot."

Both continued to hold their positions, Freedom's head twisted, nuzzling his flank, which was the equine equivalent of saying I'm really hurting.

Long minutes later, Freedom began to pass gas, a lot of it, and it was the sweetest sound Pate had ever heard. More flatulence followed, and then Freedom had the king of all bowel movements. Colleen let up the pressure, standing clear.

"I think it was starting to come anyway," she said, relieved, "but this may have helped it along some."

Pate felt weak with relief as he let go of the hock. "You helped it along a lot. Horses can move their bowels and still be colicked, but I think we got lucky and he's going to be all right now. He looks better, not as agitated, but I'm going to stay down here with him for the night just to be sure."

He patted the horse's neck. "That feels much better, doesn't it, boy, eh? Don't you ever do that again," he admonished the horse playfully. "You gave us a terrible scare."

He returned his attention to Colleen. "Thank you for coming by to help, Colleen. You're a good friend. I can't tell you how much I appreciate what you did tonight. I am in your debt. If there's anything I can do to repay..."

She started to cry. "You hurt me, Pate. You broke my heart."

Stepping away from the horse, he opened his arms and she fell into them.

He held her, stroking her hair. "I know I did, sweetheart, and I'm so sorry about that. I was nothing but a damned blind fool. I had the best thing a man could want, and I walked away. I hope someday you can forgive me."

She wept softly against his chest. "When you almost died from that fall was the worst night of my life, well, except for losing my pa. I do love you so, Pate."

"Then why are you marrying Elmer Carruthers?"

"I'm not marrying him. I called the wedding off. It wouldn't have been fair to him at all. I feel just awful about it because Ma and everyone promised to have everything ready by Thanksgiving. She said it would help take her mind off losing Pa. Oh, Pate, this has been such a terrible time. I have missed you so. I cried all night after you left that evening down by the barn. I have not stopped loving you, but how do I know you won't have your head turned again by another pretty face? You know what they say, if they run once, they'll run again."

Pate was overjoyed. Colleen was back in his arms.

"I made a mistake, a terrible one, and I will not make another, not like that. I love you, Colleen Sullivan."

She began to cry harder. "There's more, Pate. I have to tell you the truth. I made a mistake with Elmer. I'm so sorry. I did it to spite you, and then afterwards I felt like the worst person alive. I still do."

"Don't feel like that, please. I made the same mistake, Colleen, only for worse reasons. But it's over now, all of it. We're back together. I mean, if you'll still have me for your husband."

She leaned back to look up at him, and he dried her tears with the pads of his thumbs.

"Yes, I'll have you for my husband. It's what I've always wanted."

He hugged her tightly. "It's going to be so good, us on our homestead together, raising horses and babies. I want you to come up tomorrow and see the place. Tell me how you'd like to arrange things. You can move in whatever stuff you want. You can even start doing that tomorrow if you want to. I'll bring my wagon…"

She laughed. "Aren't we missing something, Pate?"

"What's that?"

"We need to get married first. Why don't we keep the Thanksgiving date?"

He swung her around. "Why not! I can't think of a better way to spend Thanksgiving this year," he laughed, kissing her.

Freedom nickered.

Epilogue

Pate and Colleen were married that very Thanksgiving, as planned, and began their life together on the Maple Crest Horse Farm. A year later, Colleen gave birth to a dark-haired, blue-eyed girl they named Belle. Over the next twelve years, Pate and Colleen would add four boys and two more girls to their family, and their seven children would go on to give them a remarkable fifty-two grandchildren.

Tabor and Julia fell even deeper in love as the years passed, and both lived happily into old age.

Brogan and Maggie went on to live a long, happy, relatively uneventful life together. Luke, Jake and Maisie together provided their parents with seventeen grandchildren.

Luke Kavenagh's desire for higher education was realized when he became the area's first veterinarian.

Garrett and Abby welcomed a son, Rory Garrett, in November of 1879. Abby surprised everyone by easily delivering the healthy, full-term baby boy. Rory would be their only child. He married in 1902, and fathered thirteen children.

Dinah Gladstone never returned to Sackville after her comeuppance in the meadow. In the spring of 1880, she married her long-time fiancé, Leander Banks, in what was described as the most lavish event of the Boston social season. The couple remained childless.

Peterson Gault, despite his advanced age, was able to get up and down the road, happily continuing to carry news to his neighbours. When his health began to fail, Tabor and Julia took him in.

Freedom became an outstanding sire, widely celebrated for his incredible progeny performance. At the grand age of twenty, he retired in the lush pastures of the Maple Crest Horse Farm.

The End

Eden Monroe loves giving voice to the endless parade of interesting characters who introduce themselves in her imagination. She writes about real life, real issues and struggles, and triumphing against all odds. A proud east coast Canadian, she enjoys a variety of outdoor activities and a good book.

She is at: https://www.bookswelove.com/shop?tag=Eden%20Monroe

Please visit her webpage: https://edenmonroeauthor.com

You can find here on Facebook at: facebook.com/AuthorEdenMonroe/

Eden Monroe books also published by BWL Publishing
Dare To Inherit
Gold Digger Among Us
When Fate Comes Calling (Book One Emerald Valley Ranch series)
Storms in the Valley (Book Two Emerald Valley Ranch series)
Back in the Valley (Book Three Emerald Valley Ranch series)

Incomplete Truths (Book Four Emerald
Valley Ranch series)
Unforeseen Shadows (Book Five Emerald
Valley Ranch series)
Just Before Sunset
Almost Broken
Sidelined
Looking for Snowflakes
Dangerous Getaway
Sudden Turn (Book One The Martel Sisters
trilogy)
Barlowe Pride (Book Two The Martel
Sisters trilogy)
Sunrise Interrupted (Book Three The
Martel Sisters trilogy)
Who Buried Sarah (Canadian Historical
Mysteries – New Brunswick)
Bound for Somewhere (Book One The
Kavenaghs trilogy)
When Shadows Stir (Book Two The
Kavenaghs trilogy)
Playtime (The Paranormal Canadiana
Collection)